OUT of GRACE

A   N O V E L

TONI WILBARGER

PRESS

ACW Press
Phoenix, Arizona 85013

Cover design by WalljasperDesign
Interior design by Pine Hill Graphics

Packaged by ACW Press
5501 N. 7th Ave., #502,
Phoenix, Arizona 85013
www.acwpress.com
The views expressed or implied in this work do not necessarily reflect those of ACW Press.
Ultimate design, content, and editorial accuracy of this work is the responsibility of the
author(s).

Printed in the United States of America by Bethany Press International, Bloomington,
Minnesota 55438.

ISBN 1-892525-24-0

Dedication

To my parents, Richard and Lola Crouse, for never discouraging my dreams; to my husband, David, for giving me encouragement and time to write; to my sister, Laurie Witt, who never doubted I would write a book; to my good friends Deb Helton and Glenda Sumerel for all their encouragement, to Fred Schmidt, Joseph McBrayer, Mary B. Lee, Emma Szollosi, and all the teachers who saw some measure of talent in me, and to Pastor Robert W. Blohm, Jr. for listening to the idea and deeming it worthy.

Foreword

For the longest time, I had a picture in my mind of someone reviewing her life, and the wrongs she had done, while staring at goldenrod waving in the breeze. I thought I was just weird. Sometimes, I'd try to imagine what she would have done to make her search her soul in this way. Then the image would drift away and life would return to its everyday activities.

I studied journalism in college, and most of my jobs after that involved technical writing. I wondered if I would ever write a novel like I had wanted to from the time I was a little girl. It seemed as if my creativity well was running dry. Then, one day, I realized that God had given me this talent for a reason, and that reason was to glorify Him. That was why I couldn't think of an idea good enough to write about. When I shifted my focus, things fell into place.

I had just finished writing biographies for my maternal grandparents, complete with pictures. I always liked to listen to family stories. Both of my paternal grandparents had died years before, so my dad told me a few more stories about them. It sounded to me as if life was very hard for them.

I started thinking about life back then, and something in my grandparents' lives made me think of the picture of the soul-searching woman. What could she have done that would have been so terrible that she felt God could not forgive her for it? I wondered what she would say to God. Then I realized that the story would have to be about God's grace. God forgives her—and you and me—no matter what we've done. Out of Grace comes God's love and forgiveness. He will never run Out of Grace for us.

Madelene Quaid had a secret. She had kept it for fifty years, but she could keep it no longer. Today, she would tell her daughters the truth. Madelene inhaled deeply, smelling the neighbor's newly mown grass. She sighed and heard the wicker chair beneath her crackle softly. As she gazed at the goldenrod shining in the sun and bending in the summer breeze, she wondered whether she could pinpoint the moment when her life had begun to tarnish. Was it the day she met him? The day she married him? Or that other day? She would never forget that day, for it had hung on her soul like heavy chains for the last fifty years.

"If only I could go back and start over," Madelene said to no one as she fingered the hem of her cotton, flower-print dress. She should have listened to her father, but she had not been in the habit of listening to him in those days. Still, she should have known better. Now it was nearly too late.

The doctors had pronounced her condition: Alzheimer's. She didn't mind taking that journey herself. It would be a great blessing to forget. But she didn't want to torment her daughters with her increasing inability to do anything for herself.

And then there was the secret. She always thought it would die with her, but she must reveal it. Now, before it erupted from the mindless ramblings of a crazy old woman.

For the moment, she could still recall Garvin's features in perfect clarity: his electric blue eyes, that shock of black hair jutting defiantly across his forehead, and the tan face she couldn't resist. If she could go back, would she have done it all exactly the same? Or could she have found the strength to forge a better life?

"How can I tell them?" She cried into the waves of heat enveloping her. Caroline and Helen had grown into fine adults, wonderful parents. Madelene had always thought they were better off not knowing. She had never wanted to destroy their faith in her or the security of a loving family.

She struggled to her feet from the high-backed, white wicker chair, and she paced the long porch. Her daughters needed to know the truth, no matter how late it arrived. Telling them now would give them enough time to forgive her before she was too far gone to understand.

Madelene paused and rested her slender, age-spotted hand on the white porch rail. As she absently ran her hand across its smooth surface, she looked out across the goldenrod to the end of the driveway where an unfamiliar car whooshed past. She closed her eyes, turned her face to the sun, and prayed.

Oh, Lord, I feel you near. I've wronged so many people in my life, but no one more than my daughters. Lord, your Word pounds in my head: 'If you bring your gift to the altar and there remember that your brother has something against you, leave your gift before the altar and go; first be reconciled to your brother, and then come back and offer your gift to God.' Lord, I know you want me to reconcile myself to them. And when they forgive me—if they forgive me—then maybe you can forgive me too. Please forgive me, Lord.

The raw wound on her soul forced hot tears to her eyes. She did not feel forgiven. Before he died, her father had pleaded with her to forgive herself because God had already forgiven her. She had only squeezed his hand and said nothing.

She opened her eyes and reached down to slip a dainty yellowed handkerchief from her dress pocket. She dabbed at the tears before they had a chance to roll down her small, pale face. Over the years, her tears had carved fine wrinkles into her cheeks. She never did see what Garvin saw in her. She had once had translucent skin, and her chocolate brown hair had hung to her shoulders and curled around her chin. She supposed she had been okay-looking, though her fingernails were always broken.

She ambled back to the wicker chair and eased into it. She picked up the worn Bible from the small wicker table that flanked the chair, but she couldn't concentrate.

Looking up the driveway that wound through the goldenrod to Main Street, she thought about how she had lived here in Trennen, Pennsylvania her entire life and had raised her daughters here. The paved roads had been only dirt when she was a child.

Caroline and Helen moved away soon after they got married. Now they would be here in a few hours. Where should she begin? All the faces of her past flashed into her mind at once: Garvin and her father, friends like Ruth, Alice and Ida. She sighed as she remembered the day she and Garvin first spoke. Then, scenes from their first date and their first kiss flickered in her mind.

Madelene remembered the sweltering air shimmering on the dusty road behind the school during that summer of 1940. She was seventeen, and Garvin was eighteen. She saw him for the first time when he and his family sat in the pew across the aisle in her father's church. After that, she saw Garvin fighting other boys in the gritty street outside the neighborhood bar. The sweat and the muscles mesmerized her young mind. She did not pick up on the clues.

Garvin was everything a preacher's daughter shouldn't want— rebellious, and never without a bottle in his hand. But, they dated anyway. Madelene shook her head in shame as she remembered the two of them sneaking around, trying not to get caught. "Don't leave me," he'd said to her as he stroked her chin with his rough fingers. After that, her actions would lead to the secret that had haunted her ever since.

～ One ～

"Wanna hear a secret?" Madelene asked her best friend, Ruth Baldwyn, as they dangled their legs from the swings at the deserted school playground. The leaves rustled in the trees above them, and the sun flickered among their lacy patterns.

"Sure," Ruth said. She twisted the metal chains supporting the wooden swing seat so she could face Madelene.

"Garvin and I are in love." Madelene couldn't stop her grin from opening into a wide smile.

"I know that." Ruth rolled her eyes and brushed a lock of curly red hair from her forehead.

"No, you don't understand. We're really in love. We're going to get married!" Madelene squealed.

"Has he kissed you?"

"Better than that."

"Huh?"

"More than that." Madelene grinned and burst into giggles.

Ruth's blue eyes widened. Her full mouth formed an 'O,' but no sound came out. Finally she croaked, "You mean...."

Madelene hugged her arms to her body and nodded, her shiny dark hair reflecting the sunlight. She laughed out loud, grabbed the swing chains, and pumped her legs. She closed her eyes and felt the warm sunlight on her face and the wind sweeping through her hair. When she had swept back once, then forward again, she heard Ruth yell.

"Stop!"

Madelene laughed and kept swinging.

"Stop!"

Madelene slowed, then stopped beside Ruth. "Are you crazy?" Ruth asked. "Don't you know about getting a—a reputation? What's the matter with you?"

Madelene giggled again. "But it was so wonderful! Oh, Ruth, I hope you feel this way someday."

"Madelene, you're not thinking straight. What will your father say?" Ruth jumped out of her swing and paced the playground.

"He won't know because I'm not telling him and you're not telling him, right?" Madelene's father, the Reverend Daniel Goddard, had been watching Madelene ever since her mother died seven years ago. Always watching. She felt as if she were taking a test that she could never pass. She had been dreaming of her escape for years. Now it was almost at hand. She smiled. "Besides, once we're married, Father won't have a thing to say about it."

"Listen to me, Madelene. You're going too fast."

"I'm nearly eighteen. No one can stop us. Ruth, what's the matter with you? I thought you'd be happy for me. I thought you were my friend." Madelene's face dropped, and she bit her bottom lip. Suddenly, she didn't feel well.

"I am your friend. That's why I'm trying to tell you to slow down a little. Look, after you turn eighteen you can do what you want. I won't say a word, but you've got to promise me you'll slow down. I know how it is when—"

"No, you don't know how it is! You don't know how I feel. You don't know Garvin. You don't understand. We'll get married, we'll…." Madelene felt tears welling up and her face growing cold. Yet, she was sweaty, her stomach churned, and she could feel the acid bubbling.

"What's the matter? You look sick," Ruth said as she looked Madelene in the eye. Ruth's red hair fell forward around her face, highlighting her freckles.

"Must have been swinging too fast," Madelene muttered, swallowing back sour saliva. She clapped her hand over her mouth.

"You're not swinging anymore. Come on, let's get you home."

Madelene stayed in bed for the next couple of days. Her father said it looked like the flu, but he couldn't figure out how she could have gotten it, especially in the middle of the summer when no one in town was sick. At first, she agreed with his diagnosis. But when she couldn't stop vomiting, she suspected the worst. She was going to have a baby.

～ *Two* ～

Madelene stared out of her bedroom window at the apples hanging from their branches in the back yard and counted back the days in her cycle. She had been so caught up in the excitement that she hadn't even noticed her monthly cycle was disrupted.

She turned from the window and sighed. She looked around the room and realized it no longer belonged to her. Its pink-flowered wallpaper, teddy bears, and doll collection belonged to the young innocent girl she had been just one month ago.

Maybe, she could run away. But the next town was across the corn fields, almost 20 miles away, and she couldn't drive. Yet, she couldn't hide forever. Soon everyone in town would know. She realized too late that she did care about her reputation.

"Madelene?" Her father tapped on her door and poked his head through the opening. "Ruth is here. I told her you were still too sick, but she insists on seeing you. Do you feel like having company?"

Madelene looked into his big brown eyes. Since she had gotten "sick," her father's stern face had softened, and his eyes searched hers. How could she tell him? He did not even allow her to date. How could this have happened? She might have laughed if the question hadn't been so serious. She nodded to him, eager to see Ruth.

She heard Ruth climbing the stairs with a quieter-than-usual step. Her father ushered Ruth into the room, then disappeared down the hall. Madelene motioned to her to close the door.

Ruth sat on the yellow, crocheted afghan at the edge of the bed. "Are you...you know."

Madelene grimaced and nodded, and her eyes began to fill with tears. Ruth scooted next to Madelene and hugged her. "It's okay, it'll be all right," Ruth whispered over and over again into Madelene's ear. They sat that way for a few minutes listening to the birds outside and feeling the breeze from the open window. When Ruth finally let go, she asked, "Did you tell your dad?"

"No, I can't. Do you think he'd be this nice to me if he knew? I'd be getting the 'you're going to hell' speech for sure."

"I don't know. Maybe he'd understand. Maybe he'd try to help you."

"Maybe your dad would," Madelene sniffed back her tears. "Your dad is different. He'd try to help. He wouldn't tell you you're going to hell and make you go away somewhere to have the baby. Oh Ruth, I'm so scared!"

Ruth grabbed Madelene's hand and squeezed. "It'll be all right. It will." She paused. "You'll have to tell Garvin, you know. He's been asking about you."

Madelene nodded. Garvin was the least of her worries. Of course he'd be surprised, but then he would ask her to marry him. Marry him! Despite her fears, she felt a shiver of excitement. Maybe this would work out after all. Maybe if she told her father that she and Garvin wanted to get married, then maybe.... She related this to Ruth.

Ruth's blue eyes danced. "And then, after you got married you could tell him about the baby, like it just happened. Of course, then you'd have the baby 'early,' but it could work. I think it's a great plan. When will you do it?"

"As soon as possible. If we're going to pretend this baby is legitimate, we're going to have to get married real soon. Garvin hasn't really wanted to meet Father before now. But after I tell him about the baby, I'm sure he will. Ruth, will you ask Garvin to meet me at the school? Tell him I'll see him there tonight a little after seven, okay?"

Ruth nodded, her red hair bobbing. She giggled for the first time since she walked into Madelene's bedroom. A record time without giggles. "I'm so happy for you," she said as she swept from the room.

Later, Madelene convinced her father she felt better and that Ruth had invited her to supper at seven o'clock.

As the hickory clock on the white-painted mantel struck seven, Madelene stepped out onto the wooden porch and breathed deeply. She hadn't been outside in four days. She walked down the driveway past her father's '32 Ford. Her feet crunched on the gravel drive and locusts buzzed in the huge oak tree shading the front yard. She felt her father's eyes on her, but she didn't turn around. At the road, she turned right toward Ruth's house, even though the school was in the opposite direction.

When she was sure she was out of her father's sight, she crossed the street, visible then to the eyes of Trennen's gossips. She walked behind the hardware and drug stores that faced White street. When she passed the drugstore, she cut left to cross White street and head for the school playground. As she approached the school, she felt as if she were floating. Soon all her dreams would come true. She would be married. She would escape her father at last.

She passed the swings and saw Garvin waiting for her. He looked ten times more handsome than the last time she had seen him. He stood up as she approached, and her heart beat faster.

"Oh my God!" Garvin said when he saw her. That was as religious as he got. "I was afraid you were never going to get well." He wrapped his arms around her and kissed her.

Madelene melted in his arms and kissed him back. Then she broke from him and said, "I've got something to tell you. It's a surprise."

He tilted his head as he looked at her.

Madelene couldn't breathe. Her heart felt like it stopped. She opened her mouth, but no sound came. She swallowed and tried again. "We're going to have a baby."

Garvin's mouth dropped. His bright blue eyes flashed, and he blinked several times. "A what? How—I don't understand." He turned, stumbled away from her, and leaned against the metal supports of the swing set. She saw his knuckles turn white where his hands gripped the metal. He turned back to her and asked, "How could you? How could you do this to me?"

Madelene froze. What did he mean: 'do this to him?' Sure, it was a little early, but they would have had children eventually, wouldn't they? He was staring at her, shaking, his fists clenching and unclenching at his sides like waves slapping against rocks.

"What do you mean? I didn't do anything to you." The evening sun fell behind the trees, and the playground darkened as if storm clouds had blown in. "We did something together. We made something together! I thought you loved me, I thought we'd get married…." Tears brimmed in her eyes. She stood there with her arms out and her hands open. Why wouldn't he come to her now? Why wouldn't he tell her it was okay?

"Where did you get an idea like that?" He stared at her with darkened eyes. "How could you do this?"

"Garvin, please!" Two tears rolled down her face. "Listen to me. We'll go to my father and tell him we're getting married. It will be okay. I love you, Garvin. And I know you love me."

When he replied, his voice was still, quiet, like the eye of a hurricane: "I never said I loved you." Then he ran around the corner of the school, leaving her alone.

She watched the space where he had been, willing him to reappear. But the emptiness of that space and the silence all around her seemed to squeeze her breath into short gasps. Her hands dropped to her sides, and she hung her head. Then she sank to the ground, sobbing, her tears rolling into the grass. How could she have been such a fool? How could she have just given herself to him like that?

What would she do now?

Thirty minutes passed before she rose and drifted back home. She thought about going to Ruth's house, but by then they were probably in their bright living room, laughing and playing cards, as a family. She wanted that kind of life, but she hadn't had it in a long time. Now her baby wouldn't have it either.

She was not ready to face her father. She was hoping to sneak back into the house, but when she opened the screen door, it creaked like the deck of a ship. Her father was sitting at his desk, circling stories in the newspaper that would become fodder for his sermons. At the sound of the door he looked up, and when he saw her crying, his eyes softened into a look of compassion she hadn't seen in years. "What happened? Did you and Ruth have a fight? Why are you back so early?" He stood up, his tall, wide frame filling her sight. His big hands hung at his sides, and the pencil was laced through his large, well-manicured fingers. Somehow, he had never looked so forbidding to her.

"Father, I—I've got—I...." She sighed. "I don't know what to say, I...."

"For heaven's sake, child, what is it? I knew I shouldn't have let you go out so soon. Are you hurt?" His voice grew louder. His thick eyebrows drew downward, and his dark brown eyes narrowed.

"Yes, that's it. I'm hurt." Madelene grasped at the excuse like a life rope. "Someone has hurt me." She made no effort to wipe the fresh tears that appeared in the corners of her eyes.

"Where? What happened? Are you bleeding?" He strode across the room, his steps thudding across the worn, woven rug covering the wooden floor.

"No, Father. It's not a physical injury."

"So it was an argument."

"No, not really. You see, I met—"

"What did Ruth say to you? All this time I thought she was a good friend, that she could help you come out of your shell. I can't believe—"

"Father, listen. It wasn't like that. I'm trying to tell you—"

"Did she call you a name? Did she turn on you?"

"Father! It wasn't like that. You're not listening to me. It's not Ruth. I met someone—"

"Another girl? What has she done? Tell me. I'll speak to her parents."

"Father, it's not a girl! It's—"

"What do you mean?" His voice rebounded off the walls. "You've met a boy? What's going on here? What are you telling me?"

"Father, I've been dating a boy and—"

"You've been what? Dating?" His face grew red and distorted.

"Father, I'm trying to tell you—"

"You went behind my back and deliberately dated a boy, a boy I didn't get a chance to meet—"

"Father, please listen to me—"

"What is the matter with you? Didn't I teach you—"

"Father, I'm pregnant!" Madelene shouted at his red face, unable to bear the pelting questions any longer.

The red in his face disappeared like water down a drain. He stumbled backward, grabbing for the worn velour chair at the edge of the rug and crumpled into it. His long legs bent diagonally, folding in different directions like a broken table. He hung his head and closed his eyes. He said nothing.

Madelene stood looking at his bowed head, her feet feeling like they were sinking into the floor. Her knees trembled, and she bit her lip. She clasped and unclasped her hands, feeling sticky, cold sweat coating them. Her hair hung like seaweed in uncombed clumps, but she didn't care. Garvin had left her to her shame and to face her father alone. God only knew what would happen next, but it would not be the compassionate scene that Ruth had predicted. She was going to hell and she knew it.

"Who is it?" Daniel spoke as he lifted his head.

"Father, let me tell you how it happened. Let me tell you about him first."

"Who is it?"

"Father, listen! We fell in love. It wasn't like that at all. He was kind and understanding. We didn't even kiss at first. He was very respectful. We—"

"Don't. Don't tell me about love and respect. This boy did not respect you! And without respect, there is no love. What you did was just plain lust. You read the word of God every Sunday. Have you learned nothing? What was going through your mind? Obviously nothing. You didn't think! You never stopped to think about what the word of God says, about honoring your body and not sharing it with every boy who looks your way. What is wrong with you?"

Small sprays of saliva shot through his yellowed teeth each time he finished a sentence. Bright red splotches broke out on his face.

His eyes blazed, and he pointed his big index finger at her nose.

Madelene's shoulders rose like a shield around her bowed head. "Father, please. I thought we were going to be married. I thought it would be all right. I thought he loved me." She choked on the last few words as tears dripped off her chin and dotted the rug.

"Know ye not that your bodies are the members of Christ?" Her father fell back on Scripture. "Shall I then take the members of Christ and make them the members of an harlot? God forbid. Flee fornication. Every sin that a man doeth is without the body; but he that committeth fornication sinneth against his own body." He shifted his gaze to the screen door. "What is his name?" he asked.

"It doesn't matter now."

"WHAT IS HIS NAME?"

Madelene's head snapped up, her eyes wide. "Garvin Quaid. His name is Garvin Quaid."

Daniel stormed out the front door. The door slammed shut behind him, almost splintering the wood.

She sank to the chair, her shoulders heaving with quiet sobs. She reached over and dragged her mother's picture from the end table. Caroline Goddard's kind eyes stared back at her, still smiling despite what her daughter had done. Momma! She cried to the picture as she hadn't since her mother had died. What's going to happen now? Momma, please, help me!

But no spirit appeared. As her mother's face swam amid her tears, she heard the mantle clock toll as if it were announcing a ship in trouble at sea. Then silence washed over the room. No spirits, no answers.

— Three —

It was 11:30 when she heard her father's heavy foot-steps shuffling on the front porch. She didn't turn around until she heard the screen door slap shut. He hung his head, so she couldn't see his face. He kept it down and began speaking before she had a chance.

"I went to the Quaid residence. Apparently, your 'friend' hasn't been home this evening. His father wasn't around. His mother didn't know what he had done; she cried when I told her. I impressed upon her the importance of at least making the child legitimate, and she agreed. You're to be married the day after tomorrow."

Married? Madelene couldn't believe it. She jumped from the chair. "Oh, Father, thank you! It's what I wanted from the beginning! I'm sure it's what Garvin wants too, deep down." He had made every-thing all right. She smiled at him.

"Don't—" He held his hand up to her. "Don't think I did this for you. I'm only making sure you do the right thing by that child. If you say you love each other, then you'll do fine. If you find he doesn't love you, then I guess you'll have to make the best of it." Daniel finally raised his head, but he looked beyond her into the kitchen. "At any rate, I want to make this clear. You have dirtied the Goddard name.

You have humiliated me and yourself. I don't want you in this house after your marriage."

Madelene's smile faded from her face. "Of course not, Father. I wouldn't expect you to house us." He didn't need to know that marriage had been part of her escape plan all along.

"I don't think you understand," he said, turning away. He stared at the bare corner of the room. "I don't want you in this house again. Ever. I can't bear to look at you." His voice cracked.

"Father, I don't understand. How can you—"

"I also saw Mrs. Frederichson this evening. She runs a boarding-house on Pine Street. I told her my daughter was getting married and needed a place to stay. You and that boy will live there."

"Father! I can't believe you went ahead and—"

"You can move your things tomorrow. Get Ruth to help you. Or that boy, if you can find him." He turned and walked past her. He stopped for a moment, and with his back to her he said, "God help you."

Madelene stood rooted to the floor. That she didn't want to live here anymore was true, but never again? What about his grandchild? Didn't he want to see it? She placed her hands on her flat stomach. She imagined a warmth there, a tiny cocoon where a new life had begun. A new life! A child that would not know its grandfather. She sighed.

But she was to be married. Now her plans and dreams were coming true. She couldn't figure out how they were going to make Garvin marry her, but it didn't matter. She'd be so good to him that he'd change his mind about her. Things would get better after all.

She shut the front door, then switched off the lamp. She made her way to bed and she even smiled. Yes, things would be better. She'd see to it.

The wedding day dawned hazy. The humid air clung to her skin as she prepared for the ceremony. Ruth arrived at noon. Together, they decided on a cream-colored cotton dress dotted with tiny pink roses. The dress hung just below Madelene's knees. She wore her mother's gold, heart-shaped locket around her damp neck. Ruth tied Madelene's hair back with a pink ribbon, and tried to get her to wear a little lipstick. But Madelene never wore makeup.

The two of them had moved most of Madelene's clothes the day before, along with her toiletries, her knitting, and a photo album they had sneaked out among her blouses. The album had pictures of her mother and her grandma Helen. Madelene wanted to take the picture from the end table in the living room, but her father would question its absence.

Madelene looked at herself in the cheval mirror and sighed. "It's not exactly the fairy-tale wedding dress I dreamed about."

"Well, things being what they are, it's not bad," Ruth said. She handed Madelene's shoes to her. "It's only an hour now."

"I don't even know if Garvin will come. He said he didn't love me." Madelene stared at her left hand, the ragged edges of her nails filed straight for once. "We don't even have a ring."

"He'll be there; his mother will see to that." Ruth sat on the bed and tried to smooth out her red curls that had grown even curlier in the heat.

"Thanks for standing up for me." Madelene grabbed Ruth's hands. "Oh, Ruth, promise me you'll never do anything as stupid as I did. Promise me you'll love a man who loves you back, and you'll have a dream wedding with lots of guests and a big buffet. And music too. Promise?"

Ruth promised with tears glistening in her eyes. Together, they left Madelene's room and descended the stairs.

In the Goddard living room the chairs had been pushed back to make way for the bride and groom, the witnesses, and Garvin's mother. His father could not be found. His mother introduced Madelene to Garvin's brother, Felan, a gangly redhead who had been pressed into service as best man.

Garvin did not speak. He did not look at Madelene. He didn't even look at Daniel, who presided over the service. Instead, he looked at the clock on the mantle. Madelene knew he was willing time to stop before he had to promise something he didn't feel. His mother must have bribed him somehow to get him to go through with this.

Standing with his feet shoulder-width apart, his fists clenching and unclenching at his sides, Garvin's lips curled into a smirk at the words "love" and "honor." When Daniel asked the dreaded question,

Garvin cleared his throat. Just then, thunder rumbled and shook the floor. A gust of wind blew the curtains farther into the room.

Daniel repeated the question. Lightning flashed nearby and made the hair on the back of Madelene's neck stand up. Garvin's mother gasped. Garvin croaked, "I do."

Thunder cracked the sky and shook the walls. Daniel asked Madelene the same questions and she replied, "I do." The wind shot through the windows, blowing the curtains sideways and tipping over Caroline's picture.

Her father pronounced them man and wife as rain pelted the house. Everyone except Madelene, Garvin, and Felan raced to close the windows and the front door. Garvin did not move, but stared at the floor instead. Felan stepped toward her. "A kiss for my new sister-in-law?" He stared lewdly at her, and she jerked away, her brown eyes flashing with the lightning.

She turned to complain to Garvin, but he had escaped the house and disappeared into the storm.

~ *Four* ~

Later that evening, Madelene sat in her boardinghouse room alone. Garvin had not returned. His mother assured her he always took off like that.

Alice Frederichson, the landlady, had shown her the room the day before. "A little bare, I'm afraid, but I'm sure a nice young girl like yourself will create a cozy home," Alice had said as she swept through the room, her legs swishing against each other.

From the windows, Madelene could see the boardinghouse next door and the clothesline, shed, and outhouse in the back yard. Lace curtains hung at the open windows, stirring in the breeze.

Alice patted wisps of her salt-and-pepper hair back into the bun on her head as she fingered the curtains. "As you can see, this little nook set back from the rest of the room gives you more privacy, so I made it into a small bedroom. I made that blue patchwork quilt myself, you know." A walnut veneer wardrobe closet sat on thick feet across from the bed, the pattern on its doors etched in a lazy swirl.

Alice's dark blue eyes sparkled in her wide face as she studied Madelene. But Madelene was sure her father had told Mrs. Frederichson about the "situation," so she dropped her head and waited for the rest of the tour.

Their shoes clunked on the wooden stairs as they descended into the common sitting room. Madelene ran her hand over the forest green velour chairs and noted the knicked pine coffee table in front of the tweed-like sofa. The entrance to the kitchen opened up from the right side of the sitting room.

"Here's where I spend most of my time," Alice said as she waved her fleshy arm from left to right in front of the kitchen. Madelene smiled at the gesture and nodded at the bank of white-painted cupboards and the sink on the right side of the room. A window over the sink showed a big oak tree and the house next door. A coal oil cookstove sat in the far corner of the room. Across from it was a small pantry with five shelves and a light blue curtain covering the opening.

"Have a seat, Madelene." Alice pointed to the large pine table that sat in the open space to the left of the doorway. As Madelene lowered herself into the solid chair, she noticed several pegs on the wall to the right of the door with two aprons and a set of keys hanging there.

"Don't talk much, do you?" Alice's eyes twinkled over her round nose. "That's okay by me. I'll talk enough for both of us, I expect. Anyway, Madelene, the $5-a-month rent covers your room and laundry. Your father paid for it this month, and I understand your new mother-in-law will be paying it after that. I must say it's mighty nice of your folks to help you young marrieds get a head start on your life, don't you think?"

Madelene pressed her lips together and looked away. Nice? She guessed her father hadn't told Alice the complete truth after all. She sighed.

"Well, enough of my rambling. Oh, I almost forgot. You will be sharing the food bill with the other boarders. I hope that's all right?"

Madelene nodded. Alice patted her shoulder and said, "Well then, you go ahead and make yourself at home. Tell your husband that dinner is at five o'clock sharp, okay?"

Tell your husband. Madelene would if she could find him. She wished Garvin could see this room; it was certainly better than the shack that Garvin's family called home. Garvin hadn't wanted her to know anything about his life, but Madelene had crossed the creek to his house anyway. She shuddered as she remembered the broken windows and crumbling cement stoop.

She gazed at her new room again. A hickory wood rocking chair sat on the corner of the rug. A worn, deep blue sofa sat across from the rocking chair with a white embroidered cloth covering its high back and arms. Rounded oak trim outlined the top and front edges of the sofa. A walnut end table with three drawers stood next to it, adorned with a doily and a table lamp. A walnut coat rack stood by the door.

While the intent was for the happy occupants to hang their own touches of home on the walls and to position their own furniture in the bare corners, this was all Madelene and Garvin would have. This is where her baby would be born, with or without its father. Where was Garvin? Why wouldn't he come to her?

Ever since she found out she was pregnant, she had tried to pray. 'Dearest Lord Jesus,' was as far as she had gotten. She wasn't sure she had a right to ask God for anything anymore. Nevertheless, she felt she had talk to someone. She knelt down on the braided, cotton rug and closed her eyes.

God? Oh, Lord, maybe you don't want to hear from someone as evil as I am. But you know I didn't have evil in my heart when I conceived this child. I still love its father, even though it seems he doesn't love me. We did the right thing, getting married and all, so please don't put my punishment on this baby. It's not his fault. Help him... or her be born healthy and have a good life. And God, please help Garvin to accept this marriage. Watch over him as he wanders about town. Help him to love me again.

Madelene sighed. *And if I have no right to ask that, God, then at least help him to love his baby when it comes. I'll manage on my own, I guess.* She sat in the rocking chair while she waited for Garvin to come home. Eventually, she gave up and went to bed.

— Five —

Two days later Madelene sat in the rocking chair knitting yellow yarn into something she hoped would turn into a baby sweater. Garvin had not been home since the wedding. As she pulled the yarn from the skein, the door to their room suddenly slammed against the wall. She looked up and gasped.

Garvin swayed in front of her, his hair hanging to his nose. His wedding shirt hung out of his torn pants. His red eyes and bloody hands stood out against his dirt-covered skin.

"Well, wife, I'm home. Happy to see the old man? Where's the booze?" He looked around the room. "Where's the kitchen? Never mind. Where's the outhouse?" He stumbled from the room, leaving the door wide open. She stared at the space where he had been and shook her head.

When Garvin returned, he slumped onto the sofa and closed his eyes. Madelene stared at him for a moment, then she called to him. He tilted his head toward her and opened his eyes.

"Garvin, I…I guess I know how you feel about this marriage. I'm sorry my father got you into it." The Garvin she knew just had to come back, if not for her, then for the sake of their baby. Her voice broke as she continued, "But I hope we can make something of our lives, something good…for the baby. You know, it won't be good for the baby if you're never home. A baby needs both parents."

He rolled his eyes toward the ceiling, so she decided to try something else. "Besides, what will people think when they see you drinking at the bars? We've got a reputation to uphold now." She stared at him and bit her lip.

Garvin laughed. "A reputation? We've got a reputation all right, and it's not too good. You should hear what they say about you: 'Look at the preacher's daughter and the mess she's gotten herself into.' And as for being seen at the bar, well, didn't you know? When I wasn't with you, or the other women in town, I was already at the bar!" Garvin laughed again, drawing his knees toward his face and shaking his feet in the air. "What a joke on you, huh?"

Madelene's bottom lip dropped down as far as it would go. "The other what? Are you saying there were other women?" Her voice grew louder.

Garvin sat up and laughed again. "You should see your face. You didn't know, did you?"

"You're drunk! You don't mean any of this. You'll be sorry in the morning."

"I'm already sorry!" Garvin shot off the sofa and shoved his dirty, stubbled face in front of hers. He gripped the arms of the rocking chair and leaned in. She smelled the whiskey on his breath, and his unwashed body reeked. She tilted her head away from his face, as much as she could, but he kept leaning in until his nose was even with hers.

"Get this straight. I never loved you. Did you think our 'secret' meeting place was ours alone? I brought lots of girls there. So don't ask me for anything. Don't try to make me love you. We're only married because my mother volunteered to pay for this place so she could get me out of her house. No more whiny little brothers and sisters, grimy kitchen, screaming mother. So I guess we both escaped."

"Escaped? Into what?"

"Why do you question everything I say?" Garvin roared into her face, pushing the arms of the chair and swooping it back almost to its rocker tips. Her knitting needles clattered to the floor and Madelene gasped. She jutted forward, thrashing her legs in front of her to bring the chair under control. By then, he was across the room and staring out the window. She rose and walked halfway to him.

"Garvin, please. Let's start over. Let's...." Tears stung her eyes. Why must she be so weak? Why was she begging him?

"You are so pathetic. You've done nothing but cry, first about your father, now about me. What do you want from me? Do you want me to act like a devoted husband? Father?" He stumbled back and stood in front of her. "It won't happen." He plopped down onto the sofa. In seconds, he was snoring.

She stared at him. She had been so sure he loved her. How could she have been so wrong? How could she be sure of anything now? There was no one to talk to about being a parent—Momma and Grandma Helen were dead. Father had disowned her. And Ruth didn't know any more than she did. She sighed. That left her with Garvin. His snoring rattled the walls. Garvin was nothing more than a selfish drunkard; she knew that now.

She crossed the room and lay down on the feather-tic bed. She curled up as if she could ward off all the bad things around her, but the softness of the quilt could not shield her from despair. She felt the tears come, dissolving into the soft pillow until she fell asleep.

~ Six ~

She woke at dawn after tossing for most of the night. She was relieved to see that Garvin had left. She gathered a change of clothes and headed for the bathroom at the end of the hall.

In the light of day, more practical matters appeared. She needed maternity clothes and she had to pay her portion of the food bill to Mrs. Frederichson. She had no idea how to accomplish either of these things. She had no money, neither did Garvin. How in the world was she going to pay for anything? The only thing she could do was to be honest with Mrs. Frederichson.

Madelene found her in the kitchen. The smell of bacon and fresh coffee wafted through the air. "Good morning to you, Miss Madelene!" Alice Frederichson called. "Come for some breakfast, did you?"

"Mrs. Frederichson, I came to tell you—"

"It's Alice, dear, and please sit down to eat. I've got scrambled eggs and bacon today. Sound good?"

"Alice, I have to tell you something."

"If it's about your, uh, situation," Alice said over her shoulder as she made a plate for Madelene, "then your father already explained. All the more reason for you to eat." She set the plate of eggs onto the big table. "You're the first one down, so these ought to be pretty good." She wiped her face with the corner of her apron. "I'll get you some coffee."

"Alice, I can't pay the food bill right now."

"Ah, so that's what's got your chin dragging on the ground? Don't worry, dear, we'll work something out. Do you know how to cook?"

Madelene nodded.

"Well then, I could use a hand in the kitchen. Your kitchen skills in payment for the food, how does that sound?"

"It sounds great, Alice. Thank you so much. I had no other way."

Alice poured a cup of coffee and set it next to the eggs. "Now eat."

Madelene sat on the wobbly chair and sipped the coffee. She studied Alice's face and read only kindness there. She sighed. "Uh, actually, Alice, paying the bill is not the only thing that's bothering me. I don't know…that is, I'm not sure…." She set her fork on the table and twirled it on one of its outside tines.

Alice lowered herself into the chair next to Madelene's. "Out with it, dear. It's better to get it out in the open rather than letting it fester like a boil."

Madelene dropped the fork and looked up into Alice's eyes. "Oh, Alice. What am I going to do? My husband doesn't want to be married to me. And he doesn't want this baby, at all!"

"Oh, it's okay, dear. He'll turn around."

"How can you be so sure?"

"Well, I don't tell this to many people, but Mr. Frederichson, God-rest-his-soul, and I had a hasty marriage and, shall we say, 'early' baby ourselves. Believe me, Mr. Frederichson was not happy about any of it, to say the least. But once our dearest little Odette was born, well, he came around, he did. He became the most wonderful father. He took Odette out in her stroller, bought her toys, and bragged about her to all his friends. He loved being a father so much that we had three others: Minna, Edwin, and Richard. And 'til the day he died, he said he'd been such a fool about resisting marriage and fatherhood." Alice's eyes were far off in the past, and she sighed.

"But Garvin drinks, Alice. He drinks terribly. And he gets so angry. He stayed away drinking for the first two days of our marriage. This is the third day and he's gone again. I'm afraid."

"Well, Mr. Frederichson and I were a bit older than yourselves, I'll grant you that. I think your Garvin is just trying to stuff a year or two of bachelorhood into a few short months. When he's done that, I'm sure he'll come home to you and your little one." She rose and patted Madelene's shoulder. "I'm glad you could confide in me, dear. It's always good to be honest about things." She swished to the stove, grabbed a cup from the counter, and poured some coffee for herself.

Madelene sighed. "In that case, Alice, I can't eat these eggs on my queasy stomach. Could I just have some toast instead?"

～ *Seven* ～

Madelene made sure she woke before dawn so she could help Alice prepare breakfast for the other boarders. The boardinghouse had three other rooms, mostly occupied by mill workers. Trennen's main industry was the lumber mill, a mile outside of town. After the boarders had worked in the mill for a while and saved enough money, they usually moved into rental houses up the street.

Fred and Ida Roth were the first to arrive for breakfast. They lived in the first room on the left at the top of the stairs. Mr. Roth smiled at Madelene and his deep gray eyes danced. He wished her good morning as he held out a chair for his wife. "Ah, another fine day in the lumber business," Fred boomed to all the women. Mr. Roth was born in an Amish community in nearby Lancaster, but he left after some sort of disagreement. When he traveled south to Trennen, he met Ida.

"Did you fix the delivery truck?" Ida asked as she perched on the edge of the chair that Fred held out for her. Ida's black hair was pinned into a bun that she patted into place.

Her husband cupped her delicate chin in his big hands and smiled. "Purrs like a kitten, now, my love. No need to worry."

Ida smiled at him, then lowered her eyes. Fred scooted her chair in toward the table then swung his long legs into the chair next to hers.

Alice was placing two plates of food in front of the Roths when Karl Rosemonde coughed his way into the kitchen. Everyone looked up as he shuffled in, his red and black plaid bathrobe hanging around him. Mr. Rosemonde lived across the hall from the Roths. He mumbled something that could have been a hello, then thumped into a chair next to Fred Roth. Mr. Rosemonde scratched his beer belly under the bathrobe and asked in a raspy voice, "Any coffee?"

Madelene inched away from Mr. Rosemonde. She never knew what he would say next. No one knew where he came from, but Trennen's gossips said he was once a very rich man who had lost his wife and his entire savings when the stock market crashed in 1929.

"Here's your coffee, Karl, nice and strong just how you like it." Alice bustled in front of Madelene and placed the cup on the table. "We've got pancakes today." Mr. Rosemonde started to growl, but Alice continued as if she hadn't heard him. "Now I know they're not your favorite, but we've got to let everyone else have their favorites once in awhile. Go ahead and eat; it's good for you." Mr. Rosemonde harumphed from behind his coffee cup.

"Good morning, everyone! A rather excellent day, isn't it?" Marshall Alden called from the kitchen entryway. Mr. Alden lived in the room next door to Madelene's. He sniffed the air and grinned. "Ah, pancakes. My favorite!"

"Would you like a ride into work today, Marshall," Fred asked.

"Got the old thing working again?"

"Good as new," Fred said.

"Then I accept. I've got a couple of new men starting for me, and it would be nice to get a head start on the day." Mr. Alden settled into the chair to the left of Mr. Rosemonde and helped himself to the plate of pancakes Alice had placed in front of him. "Thank you, Alice, these look very good." He winked at her.

"You're welcome, indeed," Alice said. Madelene caught her glancing at Mr. Alden's dark blond hair now streaked with white.

Madelene grinned as she fetched the coffee pot. She knew Mr. Alden had never married, and she noticed how he looked out for

Alice. He always wandered around the boardinghouse asking Alice if he could do anything to help. When he did take time to relax, he usually read a book while smoking his pipe—always in full view of Alice.

By October, Madelene had told Alice about her mother and grandmother and most of the story about Garvin. Whenever Madelene spoke of the strained relationship with her father, she recognized Alice's look of pity. Soon Alice convinced Mr. Alden that he needed to watch over Madelene too.

As Madelene's pregnancy progressed, she felt her clothes grow tighter. Mr. Alden surprised her one day when he brought Alice's sewing machine to her room. Not only did Alice lend her sewing machine to Madelene, she also bought a few bolts of cloth at the market. Alice called it a gift. So Madelene sewed maternity clothes by day and paced her rooms at night as she waited for Garvin to come home.

"When he does come home," Madelene said to Alice as they prepared lunch, "he never stays for an entire day. He says he's looking for work, but I know he's not."

"How do you know?"

"Because, Alice, his eyes are bleary, his clothes are rumpled, and his entire body smells of whiskey."

"Maybe he just needs to unwind a little after walking around town. Finding a job can be hard work too."

"So can his birthday, I guess. He spent his nineteenth birthday at the Woodside bar. Some men I didn't even know put him in a wheelbarrow and rolled him home. Rolled him. Can you imagine? He was so drunk he couldn't walk."

"It happens, dear."

"Oh, Alice. You should have heard them laughing when they dumped Garvin onto the lawn. I tried to move him into the boardinghouse, but I couldn't budge him." She wrinkled her nose. "Then he drooled on himself and tried to grab me. I just pushed him away and left him sprawled there on the lawn. How can he be so, so…disgusting?"

Alice patted her shoulder. "He'll grow out of it, once the baby is born."

Besides Alice, there didn't seem to be anyone else in whom she could confide. Ruth was finishing her senior year like Madelene should have been doing. If only she hadn't let things get out of control with Garvin. She could have finished school, maybe have gone to college or gotten a secretarial job somewhere. Her life would be different now.

She thought of her father often. She had not seen him at all in the three months since she'd been married. She hadn't gone to his church, either. She was sure she no longer belonged there.

She called him once and begged his forgiveness. His voice crackled in the receiver: "You've made your decision; now you must live with it. You've shamed yourself and you've shamed me. Please, don't call again." Then he quoted more Bible verses about the evils of fornication before he hung up on her.

And as if her personal problems weren't bad enough, it seemed the world itself had gone mad. As she and Alice worked in the kitchen they listened to "Ma Perkins" on the radio, but news bulletins frequently interrupted the show. Hitler and the Nazis along with their Italian friends, could not be appeased. They took over France! Madelene found it difficult to understand how an army could just march in and take over an entire country.

Alice wiped her eyes with the corner of her apron as she listened to the news bulletins. "Why does Germany need more countries?" she asked. It didn't make sense.

⌒ Eight ⌒

Soon, Christmastime approached. Madelene usually danced through the holidays. She loved seeing the decorated trees in the shop windows, caroling, drinking hot chocolate, and attending the church services. But this year, everything seemed cloudy and gray.

She helped to decorate the tree in the sitting room using Alice's glass ornaments which gleamed silver in the candlelight. While they strung popcorn, Alice chatted about her children, Christmas dinner, and the lack of snow. Madelene listened with only half her brain. The other half was busy comparing this Christmas to previous ones.

Even though Madelene and her father had never decorated their house, she still missed the familiarity of having a home. As things were now, she might have been an orphan. Tears rose to her eyelids and she dropped the popcorn string into her lap.

"What's the matter, dear?" Alice hoisted herself out of the sofa. She stroked Madelene's hair. "It's all right. Let it out. Despite being a time of joy, Christmas can be sad for a lot of people. I'm so sorry you're one of them."

Madelene wiped the tears that brimmed over the rims of her eyes. "I'm okay, Alice. I'm just feeling sorry for myself. It's supposed to

38

be the season of good will, but my father doesn't understand that. Why won't he forgive me?"

"I don't know, dear. I guess some folks have a hard time thinking in any colors but black and white. But, things change."

"I know, but I don't like it."

Alice sighed. "Even when you have a good life, things change. I miss Mr. Frederichson a lot this time of year. And my Edwin joined the service, so he and his family won't be home for Christmas. I miss them already. But the rest of my family will be here. You'll like them."

Madelene smiled through stiff lips. "I'm sure I will. And you're right, of course. I can't expect things to stay the same. When I first married Garvin, I thought we would have a little family Christmas together. But, I have no illusions now." The baby kicked her then, and a true smile spread across her face. "Next year will be different, though. I'll have my baby to brighten the holidays." She rubbed her growing abdomen.

"I've got an idea," Alice said. "Since you're feeling left out of the Christmas spirit, why don't you go to the Christmas services at your father's church? Maybe you could patch things up with him."

"Oh, I don't know. I don't want to embarrass him. I don't even belong there anymore."

"Nonsense, child. Everyone belongs in God's house, no matter what they've done."

Alice's children and grandchildren arrived on Christmas Eve morning in their shiny black Chevrolets and Fords. They tumbled out of these cars, laughing, their arms piled high with gifts wrapped in bright reds and greens. Odette was a younger version of Alice, but thinner with shiny black hair that framed her creamy, heart-shaped face. Richard and Minna were tall with blond-white hair. Odette had four children ranging from ages two to nine. Richard had two children under five, and Minna had one daughter who was four. The children romped around the boardinghouse playing "tag" until their parents made them play outside before they broke something.

Alice introduced Madelene as her "young friend." Odette and Minna asked about the baby and her preparations. As she began telling them about the blankets and booties she was knitting, she realized how much she wanted a family with loving adults and happy children. Maybe mending her relationship with her father was the best way to achieve it.

That night, she walked to Main street and headed for St. Paul's church.

Her winter coat didn't button around her anymore, so she walked with her arms wrapped around her to hold the coat closed. She started out late on purpose because she wanted to slide unnoticed into a back pew after the service had begun. As she approached the white church candles glowed in all the windows and she could hear the congregation singing "Joy to the World." The sound enveloped her as she opened the door.

The only open pew was in the front of the church, facing the pulpit where her father was preparing to preach, so she stood in the back and leaned on the hard wooden doorjamb. When the last "heaven and nature sing" echoed into the rafters and her father stepped to the pulpit, Madelene stepped back into the shadows to listen.

Dark circles rimmed her father's eyes, and he gripped the rim of the pulpit with both hands. "We're here tonight, friends, to celebrate the birth of our Lord Jesus. It's different than a regular birthday party. There are no hats, no cake. There are presents, but we give them to each other since He has no use for them. But, with each gift you give, try to remember that Jesus was God's gift to us. Don't get caught up in how much you receive or how much you spent, for that is not God's way. Remember Jesus in your celebrations.

"For, this birth is what we're about. Without the Father giving Jesus to us, we would never find our own way into heaven. Jesus is out there for you to find, for you to repent to, so you might escape this world and its reward.

"And once you have found this Jesus, you must strive to live a pure and decent life so you can be like these candles, lighting others' way to Jesus by your example. Once you find this Jesus, you can no longer live like those who don't know him: in drunkenness and violence, fornicating, lying to those who love you—" He tilted his head up to the rafters and closed his eyes for a moment. "For if you behave this way, then where is your example to others? Where is your belief? How are others supposed to know God when they see you acting in these ways and walking in the shadow of sin? It would be better to be an unbeliever than to lead others astray through your sins...."

There he goes again, Madelene said to herself. Even on the holiday celebrating God's gift to His people, her father still found a way to lash out. Couldn't he ever give a gentle sermon? Must he always dwell on sin? On her sin? It must have been her that he meant when he talked about behaving in an ungodly manner. She knew she was unworthy.

The baby kicked again, and she placed both hands on her abdomen. But this, this was joy! Regardless of how this child was conceived, it was a new life. A joy for her, perhaps to console her for Garvin. Perhaps this child would do something wonderful with his life. Perhaps God would make something wonderful in spite of her sin. Wasn't there a chance? How could everything about this situation be wrong?

But she never thought about her actions leading others astray. If her sin caused someone else to think about doing what she had done, then maybe she didn't belong at the church after all.

Daniel finished his sermon and the strains of "Oh Come All Ye Faithful" floated from the organ pipes. She decided to wait outside until everyone had left. The congregation sang to the faithful to come, but she felt forced to leave. Madelene did not miss the irony. She walked down the steps and waited in the shadows around the corner.

Soon, Daniel was standing at the door shaking hands with the parishioners and wishing a merry Christmas to them. As the last family headed home, Daniel turned to walk back into the church. Madelene stepped out from the shadows and called to him.

He stopped, but he did not turn to face her. She hurried to the front of the church and called again as she climbed the steps.

"Father, please." Now that they were alone, her eyes began to mist.

"How long were you here?"

"I came late and stood in the back. I didn't want to embarrass you." Madelene searched his eyes for some sign of softening. His eyes

41

glanced at her abdomen, then sought out something over her shoulder and across the street.

"Well. Thank you for that. What do you want?"

"I think we should try to put this behind us. I—I miss you. Especially at Christmas." She hung her head and bit her lip.

"I'm sorry about that, but you did it to yourself. I know your husband drinks his meals and spends time in that house of ill repute on Oak street. Obviously, this man doesn't love you. What made you give yourself to him? How could you have been so short-sighted, so…so—"

"Stupid? Father, please. Must we go over this again? I know what my husband does. I'm not proud of it. I'm not proud of me, either. But there's another life to think about now and I don't want this baby to grow up without his grandfather. He already doesn't have a grandmother or a father. Listen to me. Mrs. Frederichson's family is visiting. There are children and grandchildren who laugh and joke and care about each other. It's called family and I want my child to have one. Please, Father, don't let this child suffer for what I did. It's not fair."

"I'm sorry. You of all people should have known how to live a godly life. But you gave in to sin. The Bible says: 'For I the Lord thy God am a jealous God, visiting the iniquity of the fathers upon the children unto the third and fourth generation of them that hate me.' I can do nothing about your child." He sighed and rubbed his eyes.

The cold wind whipped his robes then, and they both shivered. The wind brought with it the sound of people laughing in the distance.

"I made a mistake." Madelene grabbed his robes. "Don't people make mistakes? Aren't you supposed to forgive your congregation when they make mistakes? Aren't I a part of your congregation?"

Daniel tore his robes out of her hand. "Not anymore. How am I supposed to tell others how to live when my own daughter never heard me? Go back to the boardinghouse. Go back to the life you foolishly made for yourself and that child." He turned away from her and walked back into the church, slamming the thick wooden doors behind him.

Madelene stood looking at the closed doors, her father's words echoing in her ears. She couldn't believe it. She crumpled onto the steps as tears rolled down her cheeks. She heard her father leave the church by the back door, but still she sat alone and cried in the dark. Minutes passed and the chill penetrated her coat. She shivered. No more, she told herself. If she got sick, then she wouldn't be helping her baby. She trudged back to the boardinghouse.

When she got to her room, she could still feel tears stinging her eyes. Merry Christmas, indeed. Her father didn't want her anymore. Her husband didn't want her, either.

She sank onto the sofa and rubbed her abdomen. This was all wrong. "Somehow," she whispered to the life inside her, "Somehow, I will make a good life for you, free of closed-minded grandfathers and drunken fathers. If you're a girl, I will protect you from them. If you are a boy, I will teach you how not to be like them. I swear to you, little one, your life will be different."

~ Nine ~

On Christmas morning she woke, still lying on the couch. She had heard snoring, but she thought it was odd that she could hear herself snoring. Then realization came to her. She was not alone. She sat up and saw Garvin sprawled on the feather tic bed with his cheek scrunched up on the quilt and his mouth hanging open.

She rose, tiptoed to the bed, and stared down at him. He had slept in his clothes, and his hair stuck straight up on one side. He had come home for Christmas after all. If only she could have been sure he meant to stay, to change his ways. If only she had done things differently, maybe he would have been happy to be her husband. "Oh, Garvin, what have I done to us?"

His next snore caught in his throat, and he coughed. He opened his eyes and saw her standing above him. "What...."

"I didn't hear you come in." She smiled in spite of herself.

He rolled over onto his back and rubbed his eyes. What time is it," he rasped.

"I have no idea. But it's Christmas. Thanks for coming home."

He yawned. "The bars are closed on Christmas."

Madelene shook her head and felt her heart sink. She walked to

44

the window. "At least you've got your priorities straight," she said as she fingered the lace curtains. She looked up into the dark blue clouds that threatened snow.

"What's that supposed to mean?"

"Oh, Garvin, you know what I mean. Do we have to go through this again? I'm tired of it. I don't feel like fighting with you today."

"I got a job."

She whirled to face him. "Really? Where?"

"My dad got in at the mill. They needed one more, so I applied." He was sitting on the edge of the bed smoothing his hair with his fingers. His bright blue eyes glanced up at her before he looked away. "I start tomorrow."

"Garvin, that's wonderful. Now maybe we can pay our portion of the food bill. Maybe we can buy some things for the baby."

"I haven't even started yet, and you've already got my money spent. Understand this, wife. It's my money, not yours. I'm going to spend it how I please." He stood up, pointing his index finger at her with each sentence.

"Look, Garvin, this child needs to be taken care of. I don't care if I have to keep working in the kitchen to pay the food bill, but this baby will need milk, cereal, clothes, and diapers! Haven't you thought about that?"

"Stop harping at me about my money!"

"Well how do you intend to spend it? On liquor and those—those women?"

"How I spend my time is none of your business," Garvin's fists clenched and unclenched at his sides.

Madelene saw the gesture, but she couldn't stop. She had made a promise to her baby, and she intended to keep it. "Look around you. Does this place look like it's ready for a baby? There isn't even a cradle. Where is the baby supposed to sleep when it gets here? We need money for the baby, don't you understand that? What's the matter with you?"

"No, you look." Garvin crossed the room; his steps thundered on the wooden floor. He stuck his face in front of hers so their noses almost touched. "This is my money. We're married in name only.

None of this 'what's yours is mine' stuff. You need money? Get your own job."

"Why shouldn't that money be put to good use? All you'll use it for is whiskey and women, and we both know it." Heat rose within her like a tidal wave. "Is that all you got a job for—more women and more whiskey? Did your women stop supplying you with liquor? What's the matter, Garvin, don't they want to give it to you for free?"

His hand flashed out of nowhere and slapped her across the face. Her head jerked to the side as the sound of it rang in the room and through her brain. She stumbled sideways and stared up at him. He raised his hand again, and she stepped backward, shielding her face with her hands.

Garvin dropped his hand. He raced out of the room and slammed the door behind him. The walls shook.

Madelene reached behind her to grope the wall. *Oh, my God! He slapped me! He struck me! Help me, Lord! Help!* The phrases raced over and over again in her mind. She reached up, touched her jaw, and winced. Ice. She needed ice.

Tears threatened to flow as she stumbled to the kitchen. Alice was humming Christmas carols to herself when Madelene appeared in the doorway. "Alice? Do you have any ice?" Madelene's voice broke.

Alice looked up from the bowl in front of her and gasped. "Oh my dear! What in the world? Sit down, hurry. Let me check the icebox. I don't think I used it all up yesterday." Alice grabbed a piece of ice and wrapped it in a towel before handing it to Madelene. "What happened?"

Madelene couldn't say it. She sat in one of the pine chairs. The table was set for breakfast.

"Did you fall?" Alice scooted a chair next to Madelene's, the chair creaking under her weight.

"No. It was Garvin, he…."

"What happened? Did you have an accident?"

"No, he meant it." Tears rolled down her face.

"What did he do?"

"Oh, Alice! He hit me!"

"He what? Oh my Lord. That's despicable! That—that's horrible!" Alice jolted out of her chair, jingling the silverware on the table.

"I'll not have any of that here! How dare he! Just because he's married to you, he thinks he has the right to—Oh!"

The ice soaked through the thin towel, stinging Madelene's fingers. She laid the ice on the table. "How could he do that, Alice?"

"I don't know, dear. But rest assured, he won't do it again. I won't have it! If I see him anywhere near here, I'll dispense with him myself." Alice tried to smooth Madelene's ratted hair. "Now don't you worry. Everything will be okay from now on. I'll see to it."

They fell silent for a minute or so, neither one knowing what to say. Then Alice said, "Maybe your father could help. Did you patch things up with him?"

"No. It's even worse now." She had been having nothing but arguments lately. First her father, now Garvin. It was Christmas, and she was alone.

"Never mind then," Alice said. "Join me and my family for breakfast."

Madelene bit her lip and squeezed her eyes shut. How wonderful to pretend to be part of Alice's family, if only for one meal. But she couldn't. "Breakfast sounds lovely, Alice, but I'd better get back to my room. I'm pretty tired."

Alice protested, but Madelene did not want to intrude.

In the following weeks, all Madelene could console herself with was the child growing inside her. Every time she felt the baby kick, a wave of joy surged through her. Soon she would be a mother. She didn't need her husband or her father. She had friends like Ruth and Alice, and she had a baby.

And then the time arrived.

47

~ Ten ~

"Push! Okay, you're doing fine." Mrs. Meinke, the local midwife, had arrived a few hours earlier at Alice's summons. The snow had begun to fall that morning as Madelene's contractions began. It was February 20, nearly two weeks too early for the baby. Mrs. Meinke assured her that even though two weeks was a little early, it was nothing to be alarmed about.

Mrs. Meinke's square face filled Madelene's vision as Madelene lay propped by pillows in the feather bed. Sweat had matted her hair to her face, but she didn't care. Alice stood by the bed with a cool cloth, but Madelene hardly felt it. Instead, nearly endless waves of pain rolled through her.

"A couple more pushes should do it," Mrs. Meinke said.

Madelene felt the pain rise again. She bit her lip to keep from crying out. She grabbed Alice's hand and bore down. The pain was unbearable! She didn't think she could take it any longer.

"One more," Mrs. Meinke urged.

Madelene sank back onto the bed. "No. I can't do it."

"Yes, you can."

Once more she felt it. Madelene squeezed Alice's hand and bore down with her remaining strength.

"It's coming, coming...."

Despite her best efforts, Madelene cried out. "Help me!"

"There he is! Just a moment now, let me get the shoulders through."

Please, God, help me!

"There." The baby's wails filled the room. "It's a boy, Madelene. A healthy baby boy."

Suddenly, waves of relief and joy washed over her. She smiled through her tears. *My baby. Oh dear Lord, thank you. I have a son! Thank you!* "Please, Mrs. Meinke. Please let me hold him. Please? I need to hold my son."

"Just let me cut the cord first."

Alice loosened her hand from Madelene's grip. She shook her hand in the air and said, "Madelene, dear, you almost twisted my hand off, but I'll forgive you this once." She looked down at the baby. "He's beautiful, Madelene. What will you call him?"

Mrs. Meinke cleaned the baby and laid him in Madelene's waiting arms. As Madelene stared down at him, she caressed his tiny face. He was perfect, so perfect. He had black hair, just like his father's. He had her thin lips. His tiny arm flew up in the air, and Madelene placed her finger in his hand. He grabbed it, and she smiled down at him. What perfect fingers.

"What will you call him, dear?" Alice asked again.

"His name is Adam," Madelene said. To her, the name meant beginning, starting over. For, that is what she had decided to do. She had no more room for anguish and sorrow. She would start her family over, just she and her son.

Madelene telephoned her father the next day. "I have a son."

She heard only silence from the other end of the line.

"You have a grandson."

She could hear him clearing his throat, but still he said nothing.

"His name is Adam. He was born yesterday at four o'clock. Don't you care?"

"What do you want me to say? How can I be happy now that my daughter's sin has come to fruition? How can you be happy with that reminder of your shame staring up at you?"

"Adam is not, and never will be, a 'reminder of my shame,' Father. He's a beautiful reminder that despite what I did, God made something good out of it. Why can't you see that? He's my son and I love him. What's the matter with you? Why can't you—"

A click sounded in her ear, and the line went dead. She stared at the receiver in her hand. What was wrong with him? Was he so pious that he couldn't love a tiny baby, just because of how that baby had been conceived? Adam had done nothing wrong. It wasn't fair.

The next day, Garvin burst through the door to their room. She could hear Alice yelling, "You get away from that girl! She doesn't need you making any more misery in her life! Do you hear me?"

Garvin's clothes looked like he'd slept in them for a week. His hair stuck out in several different directions. His eyes darted back and forth and finally settled on the cradle that she had borrowed from Odette. In three giant steps, Garvin stood at the foot of the cradle and stared at his son. Madelene did not smell whiskey on him, and his eyes were clear.

Alice swished into the room behind him, panting. She was about to yell again, but Madelene held up her hand. "It's okay, Alice. Let's not wake the baby."

Alice clamped her mouth together and nodded. She turned to walk out, then turned again to glare at Garvin. Madelene assured her that Garvin would not hurt their child. Alice closed the door behind her.

"His name is Adam," Madelene said to Garvin.

"You named him without me?"

"You weren't around the last two days. Besides, I thought you told everyone you weren't sure the baby was yours. What do you care what I name him?"

"It was just the booze talking, you know that. I came as soon as I heard. He's…he's really something. My son. I have a son." Madelene looked up at Garvin to a tiny smile playing at the corners of his mouth.

What was this? Could she have seen a transformation? Maybe Garvin would settle down now, get a job. Maybe he'd quit drinking. "Would you like to hold him?"

Garvin nodded. She picked Adam up and laid him in his father's arms. She showed Garvin how to hold Adam's head, then she stood back to watch.

Garvin's arms were stiff, and for a few moments he continued to stare. Then he balanced Adam in his left arm and brought his right hand up to stroke Adam's head. "He has my hair."

Madelene nodded, and tears sprang to her eyes.

"You know, I've been thinking," Garvin said while he stroked Adam's hair. "Maybe I could come back here, live here, you know, and help you take care of him. I'll start saving money from my job. My son's got to have clothes."

She nodded, unable to clear the lump in her throat. Her son would have a father after all.

True to his word, Garvin spent the night. He got up when Adam cried. When Madelene told him Adam was hungry, he seemed disappointed because there was nothing he could do to help.

The next morning, Garvin touched her shoulder to wake her. Her eyes widened when she saw him. He had washed and shaved. He had combed his hair. He wore clean clothes. She smiled.

"I'm going to work now," he whispered. "Take care of my son."

～ *Eleven* ～

Early the next week, Madelene was diapering Adam while she prepared to go downstairs to supper. She planned to dress him in a pale blue sweater that Ruth had brought a few days earlier. Madelene sighed as she recalled the visit.

Ruth had announced that she was getting married to George Warren, a boy in their class. They planned to marry right after graduation, but Ruth was afraid to tell anyone because the whole romance would be less "dreamy."

Madelene couldn't believe what she had heard. Life wasn't a dream, she told Ruth. When you lived at home with your parents, you just didn't think about paying bills and feeding yourself and finding a place to live.

But Ruth didn't understand. Madelene decided to tell her about how Garvin had slapped her while she was pregnant. Yet, she was able to convince Ruth that Garvin was getting better now. Plus, Madelene realized it was her own fault. If she hadn't baited him into it, Garvin never would have struck her. She would be more careful from now on.

She sighed. She felt a hundred years older than when she was in school. Now Ruth was getting married too. Things changed.

Madelene glanced at the clock on the nightstand. She had to be down for supper soon, but Garvin was late. Ever since Garvin had gotten a job, he had been home almost every night, and they had eaten supper together with the other boarders.

She remembered that first supper. The other boarders had been surprised to see Garvin. Mr. Alden had said he hadn't known her husband was living.

Garvin didn't speak to anyone. He scowled into his soup, studied his beef, and wiped his mouth with his sleeve. He grunted a good bye and left the table, leaving Madelene alone.

"Charming sort," Mr. Rosemonde commented. Madelene flushed and turned back to her food.

She shook her head at the memory. She decided to wait to go to supper until Garvin returned.

By eight o'clock Garvin still had not returned. Madelene paced the room wondering whether he had needed to work late. But maybe he was drunk again. She hoped not, especially when everything seemed to be turning around. He wouldn't break his promise, would he?

Adam cried, a loud wailing that shattered the silence. She checked his diaper and changed it. Then she picked him up and cooed to him. She rocked him in her arms while she paced.

At 8:30, she heard Garvin shuffling down the hallway. He thudded against the door before finding the handle. Oh no, not again.

He stumbled through the doorway and grinned. She smelled the alcohol in the air.

"Hi, wife. Sorry I didn' make it home fer supper. I had a meet'n with the boys. Lemme see my kid." He shuffled toward her, but she backed away.

"Did you get paid today?"

"Yup. It's great ta have money, isn't it?"

"You were supposed to bring money home for the baby and our expenses. Did you forget?"

"I got some money left. I saved a lil' fer Adam. It's just that Frank and Joe and the boys said 'let's go down to the Woodside,' and I didn' wanna be, you know, not part of the gang...."

"So you drank away most of your paycheck. Is that right?"

"Aw, it was only one time." He stepped toward her again and reached out for Adam. "Lemme hold my kid."

"Not in your present state," Madelene pulled Adam closer.

"Gimme my kid."

"Not until you've sobered up. Now go away!"

Garvin backed her up against the wall and flashed his fist in her face.

Madelene flinched and covered Adam's head. Her heart hammered in her chest. Adam whimpered as if he sensed his father's mood.

Garvin looked down at his son. His eyes widened, and his mouth slackened. He dropped his hand. "I'm gettin' jus like my father." He turned away and shuffled back to the door. He looked back at Madelene where she stood clutching their son. Then he disappeared through the open doorway.

Garvin returned the next morning, sober. He apologized and promised it would never happen again. He gave her the rest of his money, then he fell onto the bed and went to sleep.

~ Twelve ~

A few days later, Madelene was ready to resume her kitchen duties. She finished dressing Adam and was looking for a receiving blanket. She asked Garvin to move the cradle downstairs to the kitchen.

"I don't think it's right for you to work all day. I'm making enough money now," Garvin said while he finished buttoning his shirt.

"If you recall, on Friday you drank away most of the money, Garvin. I need to work in the kitchen to earn our keep around here, at least for this week."

"You don't need to remind me like I was a little schoolboy. I said it wouldn't happen again, and it won't."

Madelene finished wrapping Adam in the blanket and looked up at Garvin. He was staring at her. She wondered what he saw.

"I guess for this week, you'd better continue in the kitchen. But next week…. I just don't think it's healthy for a baby to be in a hot kitchen all day, especially where a bunch of people go in and out and breathe on him. Rosemonde has a cough, you know."

"Mr. Rosemonde smokes, Garvin. Of course he coughs some."

"Well don't let him smoke in front of Adam."

"Afraid Adam will pick up some bad habits?"

Garvin grinned. "Gotta go." He walked toward Madelene, leaned down, and kissed his son's cheek. She thought maybe he would kiss her. She knew now that he hadn't really loved her, at least not the way she had loved him.

Those last few nights while he slept on the sofa and she lay in their bed, she had felt something for him that she hadn't felt in quite some time. She surprised herself. She always assumed that once her baby was born she wouldn't need anyone else in her life. But, she realized she wanted Garvin to be part of this family too.

There was always hope, Alice often said. Madelene stood up and glanced back at the cradle. Garvin left without moving it. She sighed. Sometimes hope seemed pretty scarce.

As April approached, dots of purple and white crocuses splashed up through the dull brown grass outside the kitchen window. Tiny wisps of snow feathered around the tree trunks.

As life began again outside the house, Adam's life began inside. He slept in a cradle in the corner of the kitchen near the coal oil cookstove while Madelene and Alice worked. Madelene decided the warmth was good for him. And besides, whenever he cried, Madelene was there. She would carry him upstairs to her rooms to feed him, then bring him back when she resumed her duties.

Alice took a few extra steps during her day in order to pass by Adam and smile at him. "He's such a joy, your little one. He reminds me of my own grandchildren."

Then Alice seemed to drift to a place where Madelene couldn't reach her. "If only my children lived closer. Minna only lives a day's drive away, but I still wish for more. And my Edwin…Hawaii has to be the farthest any of my children have gone. He's in the Army, did I tell you that?"

Madelene nodded. "Hickam base, right?"

"That's right. Here, look at these snapshots he sent me with his latest letter. Look at those beautiful beaches and flowers, Madelene. With scenery like that, it's no wonder he never comes home."

"Alice, you know he loves you. When is his next leave? I'm sure he'll visit you when he can."

Alice blinked and turned away. Madelene knew at that moment that Alice saw only the brown trees and not the purple flowers.

About a week later the radio reports relayed news about the war in Europe. The Germans had attacked Yugoslavia a week earlier. Belgrade had fallen, and the Yugoslav army had surrendered. At supper each evening, the war was the main conversation topic. One night in mid-April, everyone except Mr. Rosemonde sat around the supper table. He had complained of a nasty cough and had declined to join them.

The smell of roast beef, hot rolls and fresh coffee filled the kitchen as the boarders passed serving dishes around the table. Silverware clinked against porcelain as they talked of the war in Europe.

"Why is everyone just lying down for Germany? Why don't they fight harder," Mr. Roth asked.

"You forget Britain," Mr. Alden said.

"Britain alone then, it seems," Garvin jumped in. "Everyone else is dropping, hardly putting up a fight. Czechoslovakia, France, now Yugoslavia. Now if it were Ireland they were trying to conquer, then we'd have a different story."

"But Germany is not the only aggressor. There are the Italians and the Japanese," Ida said. The men glanced at her for a moment, and she dropped her head.

"If the United States thinks she can stay out of this war, then she's just fooling herself," Mr. Alden said. "Roosevelt ought to realize there's no way for us to stand by and do nothing while Britain gets pounded and France goes down. How does the U.S. think she'll find future allies if she lets down her current ones?"

"This country has no business in this war. It's none of our affair," Mr. Roth's voice grew louder.

"Gentlemen, gentlemen," Alice said. "We can barely keep track of each other, let alone a group of countries on the other side of the world. Let's change the subject and talk of things closer to home."

A few weeks later, Madelene and Alice prepared supper and talked of upcoming events in town. They chatted easily now.

Madelene had come to think of Alice as a friend and surrogate mother. They were discussing what to do for Mr. Alden's birthday when Mr. Rosemonde's raspy voice called from the doorway.

"Hello! What's the conference about? Can anyone join?"

Both women whirled to face him. He coughed and shuffled over to them. His silver hair stood out from his head, his eyes drooped, and his wrinkled plaid bathrobe hung unevenly over his stooped shoulders.

"Mr. Rosemonde! Feeling a bit better today? How about some coffee?" Alice headed for the stove.

"Sounds good. Yes, I'm feeling a little better. This cold has gotten me down." He shuffled to the table and sat down. He coughed again, a deep guttural sound that started in his chest.

Madelene frowned and glanced over at Adam sleeping in his cradle. "I'd better take Adam upstairs for a moment." She picked up Adam and headed for the doorway.

"Let me say hello," Mr. Rosemonde said.

"Well, I don't think—"

"Here's your coffee! Drink it while it's hot." Alice stood in front of Mr. Rosemonde.

"I haven't seen him in a few days," Mr. Rosemonde said as he rose from the chair.

Madelene had started to walk away when Mr. Rosemonde reached out and pulled the blanket away from Adam's face. "Ah, I think he's grown a bit in the last week. Gonna be quite a man, he is." He leaned in for a closer look. "Looks like your mister. I'll bet he's a proud one. There's nothing like a father and son. Why I remember—" Mr. Rosemonde choked for a moment and coughed again. He coughed a few times more, then covered his mouth.

Madelene quickly drew Adam against her and covered his head with the blanket. She scowled at Mr. Rosemonde and walked out of the kitchen.

A few days later, Madelene and Garvin relaxed in their room after supper. Garvin watched Adam sleeping while Madelene rubbed her feet. "Ow! It was like I had never been in that kitchen before,

Garvin. I stubbed my toe on the table legs, bumped my knees on the cookstove, and cut my finger with the paring knife. I don't know what was wrong with me today. Thanks for watching Adam. The way my day has been, I'd probably have dropped him."

"You don't have to thank me for watching my own son. This is much more pleasant than arguing with that Alden character again. He goes on and on about how if the Germans could take France, then they could take the U.S. as well. He's so in awe of the British and their stance against Germany, yet he doesn't think the U.S., which is ten times as big, could possibly stand against the Germans. It doesn't really matter anyway since Hitler wouldn't dare come after us. We should just keep our noses out of it, that's all."

"Garvin, I really get tired of listening to all the arguments. Hitler has to be stopped, yes. But you're right; it's not our war."

"If we did get in it, we could stop them."

Adam coughed and woke up. Garvin lifted him out of the cradle and Adam started to cry. "Here, son, your dad's here."

"Maybe he needs to be changed?"

Garvin sniffed Adam's backside, wrinkled his nose, and said, "And your mom's here, too, Adam my boy."

Madelene smiled and limped to the sofa to take Adam from Garvin's outstretched hands. "Mr. Rosemonde wasn't at supper again, did you notice? I thought he was getting over his cold."

"That old coot? He probably fell asleep in his chair with his booze and his cigarettes. There's nothing wrong with him."

"Alice said she took some chicken soup to him today. He told her he was getting better, but she thought he looked really flushed. She said he had the blanket up to his chin, too. It's a little too warm to be covered up like that, isn't it?"

"Well for April, it's still too cool. I'm going out for a while." Garvin reached for his tattered wool coat lying where he had thrown it onto the sofa.

"I thought you were in for the evening. You said you were going to read a book and go to bed."

"Well, it's Frank's birthday, and a few of us are meeting him at the Woodside. Just one or two beers, that's all. See you later."

Madelene sighed. One or two beers. If it wasn't someone's birthday, it was another celebration, or even a funeral. Two or three times a week Garvin would go to the Woodside bar and stagger home well past midnight.

Adam gurgled and she felt his tiny lips against her skin. She smiled. At least she had her son. Then Adam coughed again, a raspy cough. Madelene frowned and looked at Adam's flushed face as he began to wheeze. If Adam caught Mr. Rosemonde's cold, she'd personally flog that man.

Adam's coughing subsided, although the slight wheezing continued. She decided to take him to the kitchen where she could get some steam going on the cookstove.

She approached the kitchen and was surprised to see the light on. Alice was at the stove. She turned around as Madelene entered.

"More chicken soup for Mr. Rosemonde," Alice said. "I checked in on him after supper, and he doesn't look good. I'm calling the doctor in the morning. What are you doing here with the little dear?"

"He's been coughing a little, and his breathing isn't quite right. I thought maybe some steam would help."

"I sure hope he hasn't caught that awful cold from Mr. Rosemonde. That man is so stubborn! He's complaining of chills, yet he's burning up. And he won't see the doctor. He says his arthritis is keeping him from getting out of bed, but I didn't think his arthritis was that bad, did you?"

"No. Uh, Alice, I don't have anywhere to lay Adam. Would you heat some water for me while I hold him?"

"Sure, dear. I'm sorry to go on about Mr. Rosemonde when you've got your own troubles. I saw Garvin go out. No trouble I hope?" Alice searched in the cupboard for an aluminum saucepan.

Madelene shook her head.

"We'll get this going in a minute. Little Adam will be good as new in no time."

Adam coughed again and started to wail. Madelene tried to comfort him, but he continued to cry. Soon she and Alice were almost yelling over his cries, so their words dwindled to silence. Alice left to take the soup to Mr. Rosemonde.

Eventually, the steam calmed Adam's cough and he fell asleep.

Madelene wiped the perspiration from her forehead and carried him upstairs to bed.

The next morning, Madelene and Alice sipped coffee in the kitchen while Dr. Dallan examined Mr. Rosemonde. Dr. Dallan was in his fifties. He was a thin man with wispy, steel-gray hair combed neatly over his head. He always dressed in navy blue suits with white shirts and he wore round, wire-rimmed glasses on the bridge of his nose. Since the clinic was located only a couple of blocks from the boardinghouse, Dr. Dallan had walked over.

When the doctor returned from examining Mr. Rosemonde, Alice poured a cup of coffee for him.

"Well, it looks like he has influenza," he said. He sat down, took off his glasses, and massaged the bridge of his nose. "I wish he hadn't waited so long to see me. There's not much I can do except to let it run its course. The main thing is to make sure he stays in bed for the next few days and drinks lots of water." He sipped the coffee. "I hope he had sense enough not to walk around and infect everyone else."

"My son," Madelene said. "He coughed on my son a few days ago." She glanced at the cradle. "Would you look at him?" Madelene picked Adam up from the cradle and heard him wheezing again. "He started coughing and wheezing last night. I started some steam to help him breathe."

Dr. Dallan pulled his stethoscope from his medical bag. He held Adam in his lap and removed the baby's shirt. Then he thumped Adam's chest. Adam cried in protest. "That's it, little lad, give me a good cry." Dr. Dallan listened to Adam's breathing. He placed the stethoscope on Adam's heart, chest and back. When he placed his fingers on the baby's neck, Adam coughed and cried.

Madelene bit her lip as she watched. *Adam's so young. He's too young to get sick.*

Dr. Dallan removed the stethoscope from his ears and fastened Adam's shirt. "Well, your boy has a cold. Using steam to help him breathe was a good idea, and you can continue that for the duration. Make sure he gets extra liquids. Give him a bottle of water in addition to his milk. If he gets any worse, call me." He handed Adam back to Madelene. "And now, ladies, I must get back to the clinic. Thank you for the coffee."

Madelene looked down at her son. It was only a cold. She kissed Adam's head as his cries tapered to whimpers. Then she laid him back in the cradle.

~ Thirteen ~

Ten days later Mr. Rosemonde's color had returned and he was dressed and washed. But Adam's cold had grown worse. Madelene and Garvin skipped supper that night to take care of him. Alice called Dr. Dallan.

Upstairs in their room, Garvin paced, clenching and unclenching his fists. Above Adam's cries he asked, "Where is that doctor?"

"I don't know, but your yelling is not going to bring him here any sooner." Madelene clutched Adam to her breast. She whispered to him, soothing him as he wailed and coughed. Suddenly, Adam's little body shuddered in her arms. "What was that?"

"What?" Garvin whirled to face her. His eyes narrowed.

"I—I don't know. He just shook terribly for a moment. But it went away, I guess. I wish Dr. Dallan would hurry." Adam's cough sounded thicker. Between coughs, his cries grew high pitched.

"Where is he?" Garvin shouted.

A knock sounded on the door and Alice brought in Dr. Dallan. She looked from Madelene to Garvin to Adam. Before she closed the door, Alice placed her hands in the prayer position to show she was praying for them.

"I'm sorry I couldn't get here sooner," Dr. Dallan said, "but it seems quite a few families in town have come down with influenza. Let's see what we have here." He took Adam from Madelene's arms.

The doctor repeated the tests he had performed earlier. He also placed his hand on Adam's forehead. He frowned and grabbed a thermometer from his bag. He placed it in Adam's mouth, but Adam thrashed and cried too much to keep it there.

Dr. Dallan shook his head. "I broke the rectal thermometer this morning. I think your son has a very high fever. And his lungs don't sound well at all." He shook his head again as he handed Adam back to Madelene.

"What is it? What does he have?" Garvin asked.

"I think it's pneumonia."

"Pneumonia!" Madelene cried. "A week ago you said he had a cold."

"Well, in some cases a viral infection can turn into a bacterial infection such as whooping cough or pneumonia. I'm afraid that's what happened here. I've got to go back to the clinic. There are some sulfa drugs I can give him. I'll be right back, don't worry." Dr. Dallan packed up his medical bag.

"What are we supposed to do in the meantime?" Garvin asked.

"I'll be right back. It should only take 20 minutes. Just keep him comfortable." Dr. Dallan left the room.

"Twenty minutes? Keep him comfortable? What does he think we've been doing?" Garvin paced the floor and banged his right fist into his left palm.

"Pneumonia? But just a few days ago he said…." Madelene's heart broke as she heard Adam struggle to breathe.

Adam's cough deepened and Madelene stroked his hair. "Hush, sweetie, Mommy's here." He coughed again and pink phlegm sputtered from his mouth. He screamed and thrashed his legs. Madelene's eyes widened at the pink phlegm on Adam's lips.

"Oh, God, help us," Madelene began to cry. She smoothed Adam's black hair and rocked him in her arms. "He's so hot."

"I'll go down to the kitchen and get some ice," Garvin said. He hurried out of the room, his steps thumping in the hall.

"Oh, God. Lord, please," Madelene repeated through her tears.

She started pacing and rocking Adam in her arms, wincing with every cough. "Adam's just a baby, he's just—shh, little one, shh. Oh Adam, Mommy loves you. Hold on, sweetheart, the doctor will be back soon. Shh."

Garvin returned with some ice wrapped in a dish towel. "Alice said to tell you she's praying. I hope that God of yours is listening." He marched to the side windows and peered into the street below. "Where's that doctor?" He banged on the window with his fist. "We can't just sit here and do nothing. What's taking so long?"

Madelene glanced at the clock next to the bed. It had been only ten minutes. It would take the doctor that long just to walk to the clinic and get the medicine. He'd spend another ten minutes getting back here. She had never known a longer ten minutes in her life.

She continued pacing, and rocking Adam, pausing only to wipe the phlegm from his lips. He coughed again: It was a horrible, hacking sound. This time, bloody phlegm spewed from Adam's tiny mouth and spotted his shirt. Madelene shrieked.

Garvin ran to her side and glanced down at Adam's shirt. He gasped and stumbled backward.

"Garvin, help. Help us."

Garvin's eyes brimmed with tears. He blinked them back and said, "I'm leaving. I've got to find that doctor!" He ran from the room.

Where was Dr. Dallan? Madelene glanced at the clock again. Forty minutes.

Garvin burst into the room twenty minutes later. "I couldn't find him anywhere. He wasn't at the clinic. He wasn't on Pine Street or Main Street. I went to his house on Oak. I don't understand it. How can he just leave a baby to die? How can he do that?" Garvin slammed the door behind him.

"Maybe someone else could help us," Madelene pleaded through her tears. "Wait, what about Mrs. Meinke? She's the midwife I had. She has to have some medical training, doesn't she? But I can't remember where she lives. Oh, think. Think! Wait!" Madelene's head snapped up. "Alice would know; Alice called her. Garvin, find Alice. Ask her where Mrs. Meinke lives. Hurry!"

Garvin ran from the room again. A few minutes later, she heard Alice at the door. "May I come in? I brought some more ice." Alice opened the door and exclaimed, "Oh, my Lord. Your precious boy."

The ice was wrapped in another dish towel, and Madelene took it and laid it on Adam's forehead. Adam wailed and choked. Another fit of coughing seized him; bloody phlegm rose to his lips. "Oh please, God, please help my baby. Please." She felt Alice's arm around her back, but she shrugged it off and began pacing again.

Madelene glanced at the clock. It had been almost an hour and a half since the doctor had been there. What had happened? Where was he? Adam screamed, and she winced.

Another twenty minutes passed, then Garvin shot through the room. "Mrs. Meinke has the flu too. She can't come." Garvin glared at Alice.

"I'll leave you two alone," Alice said. "I just wanted to help."

"Well you helped enough, I'd say, letting your sick boarder cough all over my son. You helped enough, allowing an infant to lie in that kitchen all day with people breathing on him and coughing on him. Get out!"

Alice shuffled from the room and shut the door behind her.

"Alice is my friend. You didn't have to shout at her like that. Besides, I was the one who had Adam when Mr. Rosemonde coughed on him. He stuck his face right into Adam's and coughed on it before I knew what was happening."

"What? What's the matter with you? Didn't you know any better? Why did you let him do that?" Garvin's blue eyes were wide in his red face as he yelled over Adam's cries.

"It just happened, it just—"

Adam coughed again and began to choke.

"Adam!" Madelene clutched him to her shoulder and thumped his back. She heard his cries again and she felt her knees wobble. Still patting Adam's back, she sank to the sofa.

Garvin railed at her again: "What kind of a mother are you? Don't you know how to take care of a baby? You let that old man cough all over him—"

"Garvin, please!"

Adam gasped. They could hear him choking. His body shuddered in her arms as he struggled to breathe. Madelene thumped his back a little harder this time, but nothing helped. Adam wasn't breathing.

"Give him to me," Garvin demanded.

"No!" Madelene shrieked. "Adam, please sweetheart, please breathe, breathe for Mommy." She thumped him on the back again, longing to hear his cries. But even the choking sound had ceased, and Adam became limp in her hands. "Adam!"

"Give him to me!" Garvin snatched Adam from her arms. He gently shook Adam and thumped his back. He placed his fingers under Adam's nose. Then he held the baby in his shaking arms and started to cry. "My son, my son."

"No.... No...." Madelene sunk to the floor, sobbing. "He's got to breathe. He's got to! Do something!" But they heard nothing more from their son.

At that moment, she felt a cold hand ripping her heart from her chest. Nausea rose up through her and she screamed again. "Why, God? Why? He's just a baby!"

Garvin looked down at her. "There is no God." He took Adam's body to the cradle and laid him in it. Then Garvin stumbled from the room.

"Adam?" Madelene cried again. She crawled to the cradle and took his small hand. "Please, Adam, Mommy loves you. Please come back. Please? You're all I have. Mommy loves you. Please come back. Breathe for Mommy. Adam? Please, sweetie, you can do it. Mommy loves you, Adam. Mommy loves you. Please don't leave me."

～ *Fourteen* ～

A few days later, Madelene realized she was sitting in a funeral parlor. Amazed, she stared at her black clothes, black gloves, and black pumps. Why was she here? Why was she dressed in black?

Ruth grabbed her hand. "Madelene, I'm so sorry! Oh, I can't believe it," she said as she used a handkerchief to wipe tears from her eyes.

Madelene stared at Ruth. Why was she sorry? What had happened?

"Madelene, honey, you're scaring me. Why are you looking at me like that? Madelene?"

"It's all right," Madelene heard Alice say. Why was everyone here?

"She's had a terrible shock, that's all. I don't think she's ready to face what happened to the little one."

Ruth nodded, still clutching Madelene's hand. The little one? A child had died? Whose child? What did he die from? Oh, this was too sad. There had been so much influenza around lately, and now it had claimed a little child. She glanced toward the front of the room where a tiny wooden casket was perched on a table. Judging from the size of the casket, it must have been a baby that had died. How horrible for its mother.

At least she still had Adam. Where was he? She looked back at Ruth. "Where's Adam?"

"Oh!" Ruth let out a tiny scream and clapped her hands to her mouth. She turned and ran from the room.

Suddenly Alice's round face appeared before her. Alice's eyes were red-rimmed and swollen. "Now listen, dear. Remember what we told you? Remember? That's Adam up there in the casket. Adam was suffering so much that the Lord decided to take him up to heaven with Him. Do you remember? The doctor was on his way back with Adam's medicine, but Mrs. Miller's husband was having a heart attack. That's why the doctor couldn't get back. Do you remember? Adam's all right now. He's with God in heaven." Tears welled in Alice's eyes.

Madelene drew her brows together. How could Adam be in the casket when he was with her? How could Adam be—"No!" She shot up and pushed Alice out of her way. "Adam! Adam! Mommy's here!" She ran to the casket where the Roths and Mr. Alden were standing. "Get out of my way!"

The quiet hum among the mourners stopped. Heads turned toward the tiny casket and the young mother.

Madelene stopped in front of the casket and looked down at her son. Adam lay nestled on a snowy white blanket in the pine box. His eyes were closed in gentle sleep, and the black hair on his head had been combed. He was wearing one of the sweaters she had knitted for him. "Come on, sweetheart, Mommy's here to take you home. Time to wake up now." She reached into the casket.

"No, Madelene. No, you don't understand," Mr. Alden said as he grabbed her arms.

"Why do you people insist on keeping my son in this casket? Haven't you ever seen a sleeping child before? Adam, sweetie, it's time to go home…." She brushed her hand against Adam's cheek. His face was like ice! She jerked her hand away. Why was he so cold? Why, just yesterday, he was burning up. He was so sick and….

No. Oh, no, Lord, no! The reality of the last few days smacked her in the chest. She gasped for air, but nothing entered her lungs. Several people rushed toward her. Someone cupped his hands over her nose and mouth, and her breathing gradually became regular. She couldn't stop trembling. She heard Alice's soothing voice repeating words she didn't hear.

Adam was dead. Her baby was gone. Adam! Sobs ripped through her. Through a mist of grief, she was aware of Alice helping her to lie down in another room, of Ruth's face hanging over hers, of other people sniffing back tears and shaking their heads as they passed.

Thick, smoky blue clouds blocked the sun, and a cold wind blew down on the mourners as they stood by the grave. It was the first week in May. The preacher from St. Andrew's delivered a small sermon. He preached about not questioning God's wisdom and living each day to the fullest.

Alice and Ruth stood on either side of Madelene and gripped her elbows. Garvin stood on the opposite side of the grave with his fists clenching and unclenching. Garvin's mother was at his right. A black scarf was tied over her head, but her dirty-blond hair escaped the scarf and whipped across her face.

Madelene noticed only one other figure standing several yards away, partially hidden by a tall tombstone. She stared at the figure's dark hair and stocky form. It was her father. Alice told her that she had called him first, but he refused to bury Adam since the child had not been baptized. He cited Romans 6:23: the wages of sin is death. He said Madelene was receiving her punishment. Alice hung up on him.

"Earth to earth," the preacher said. He scooped a handful of dirt and poured it onto the casket.

My baby!

"Ashes to ashes…." Garvin turned away, his back heaving.

"Dust to dust. May God grant you His mercy." The preacher stepped back from the grave. The undertaker stuck his shovel into a mound of earth. He threw the dirt into the grave; the sound was like a heavy door slamming: thunk. Madelene clenched her fists as Alice and Ruth tried to make her leave.

"Come on, dear. You don't need to see this," Alice said.

Madelene stood still. The undertaker threw another shovel full of dirt into the grave: Thunk. She saw Adam's happy face in her mind. She heard his gurgling. She could still feel his soft skin and his tiny fingers wrapped around hers.

Thunk.

How could he be in that hole, being covered by dirt? How could she face his empty cradle? How could she wash his clothes and put them away? How?

Thunk.

"Madelene, please," Ruth said. "We've got to go now."

She turned to Ruth and asked, "How?" Tears streamed down Ruth's cheeks as she shook her head. Ruth and Alice led Madelene away from the grave.

— Fifteen —

When Madelene returned to her rooms, the cradle was gone. She looked for Adam's clothes, but they had been taken from the drawers. Even his toys were gone. It was as if she had never had a son. As stumbled toward the bed, her foot hit something soft. She stooped to find a small brown teddy bear. It must have fallen and been kicked under the bed, forgotten. Her eyes filled with tears as she clutched the bear to her chest.

She sat alone in the room and rocked in the rocking chair, all the while holding the bear. Throughout the day she squeezed the bear and cried, talking to it as if it could hear and understand. The clouds turned darker and rain spattered the windows. She rocked and cried, while the light faded and darkness crept in.

She was sitting in the dark when she heard Garvin's footsteps in the hall. She heard his slurred words as he cursed at no one.

The door flew open and slammed against the wall. "Where are the lights? Gimme some lights!"

Madelene unfolded herself from the chair and walked to the end table.

Behind her, Garvin stumbled and crashed into the coat rack, sending it clattering to the floor. "Ow! Come on, Madlin' turn on the light!"

She lit the lamp and turned to see Garvin swaying and rubbing his knee. She smelled the whiskey. His shirt hung out, and his tie hung unknotted from his neck. He stumbled toward her with clenched fists.

"I had to 'splain to all those jerks in the bar about my kid dyin'. D'you know what that's like? 'Sorry,' was all they said. Stared into their glasses, talked about the Joe Louis fight. They didn't understan' 'bout my wife exposin' my kid to pneumonia. They didn't think it was anybody's fault, called it a tragedy. They didn't know. But we know, don't we, wife?"

Garvin stalked her. His knuckles were white, and his eyes were blazing. Madelene's heart raced. She backed away from him, moving to the far corner of the room.

"It was an accident, Garvin. It was. You've got to believe that. If I had known, I certainly wouldn't—"

"You shoulda known! My mother raised ten kids. Ten kids, and not one of them died. Not one. But you can't even take care of one, the only one that mattered to me! What's the matter with you anyway? Huh? You couldn't keep my son away from sick old men, couldn't keep 'em from breathin' and coughin' on him. You couldn't even do that right. What's the matter with you? You're worthless!"

She winced. His eyes bored into hers as he kept walking toward her. She felt the rough plaster on the wall behind her. Garvin stood face to face with her as tears gathered in the corners of his eyes. Her heart thudded in her chest; her knees wavered beneath her. "Garvin, I swear, I—"

His hand slammed into her face, and he screamed.

Tears welled in her eyes. Her cheek throbbed with fire. "Garvin, please—"

"You killed my son!"

"Garvin!"

"You killed him!" He punched her jaw, and she crumpled to the floor. "You killed him! You killed him!" Pain erupted in her stomach, her hips, and her head as he kicked her.

She heard voices at the door and footsteps pounding toward them. Then her view of the floor faded to black.

— Sixteen —

"Dear Lord, please help my friend Madelene. She's been through so much in her young life, and now her husband has beaten her. When you said that wives should be submissive to their husbands, surely you didn't mean this. Please help Madelene, then help her husband. He's not well. He drinks all the time. Being a charitable person and all, I'd like to say that his son's death caused him to drink. But I know that's not true."

Madelene heard the voice praying above her, and she struggled to open her eyes. She saw Alice with her hands clasped, staring at the far wall. "Alice?" The ceiling did not look familiar. The air smelled medicinal. "Where am I?"

"Oh, thank God." Alice looked down at Madelene. She smoothed the hair from Madelene's forehead. "You're at the clinic, dear. Mr. Roth and Mr. Alden rushed in to pry your mister from you. After they sent him to sleep it off, they helped me bring you here. Dr. Dallan said you have a concussion, but nothing is broken. You're just cut and bruised."

"How long have I...."

"Just overnight. The doctor says you can go home if you want, but you need to rest for a few days."

Madelene sighed. She remembered Garvin kicking her and yelling at her. Something about her having killed someone? Oh, yes. Adam. The sound of his name caused tears to well in her eyes. "Alice, what am I going to do?"

"Well, you're going to go home and rest just like the doctor told you. I'll bring you some chicken soup and make sure you're comfortable."

"No, I mean about my life. About losing Adam. Garvin. My marriage."

Alice sighed. "I really don't know, dear, but I've been praying about it. The only thing I can say is that I think you should do the same."

"Praying is not going to keep him from hitting me again."

"No, Mr. Roth, Mr. Alden, and I have decided to take care of that. If he comes to the door, one of us will ask you if you want to see him. That's that. What I meant is that you should ask the Lord to help you through your grief. You never know what the Lord can bring out of a disaster like this. Ask Him to help you decide what to do about your husband and your marriage. Maybe you can help your husband through his grief, too."

"Alice, I don't know if there is a God anymore."

"Hush! Don't ever doubt that, dear. He's there, waiting for you to talk to Him. He wants to help you."

"But what kind of God would let a baby die? He was an innocent baby who never harmed anyone." The tears that had welled in her eyes spilled over onto her cheek.

"That's a tough one, dear. Death is inevitable for everyone, no matter how good they are. It's man's nature to die because it's man's nature to sin. Death is the consequence we face. No man, or woman, or child can escape that. Maybe Adam died a little too early, that's all."

"Are you saying that Adam was not innocent? That somehow he sinned? What did he do, steal milk? When he cried to be fed or changed, was he lying? What's the matter with you, Alice? How can you say that about my Adam?" Madelene turned her head away as her tears rolled down onto the rough sheets.

"I'm not saying that Adam openly sinned. I'm saying that

because he was human, his nature was sinful. We can't escape our nature, no matter how 'good' we are by human standards."

"Go away, Alice."

"But I only—"

"Go away! If that's what you think, then I guess you aren't the friend I thought you were."

The chair creaked as Alice rose. "It doesn't matter what you think of me. What matters is what you think of our Lord. Please read your Bible, dear. The answers are all there for you." She swished to the foot of the bed and turned back. "If you'd rather not see me, Mr. Roth and Mr. Alden will drive you home."

⌐ ◦ ⌐

Mr. Alden brought her home the next day and helped to settle her on the sofa. Madelene sat for hours thinking about the violence bubbling in Garvin. How could she have been so wrong about him? She remembered how he used to kiss her and how he couldn't wait to see her. Then she remembered his red face, his wild eyes and his clenched fists. She touched her tender jaw and winced.

Her thoughts swirled around Garvin, her father, and Adam. In her mind, she saw Adam's blue eyes and heard his happy gurgling. How could God let him die? People like Hitler lived on, trying to destroy an entire race, while defenseless babies like Adam died. What kind of justice was that? If God were really here, watching things, taking control…then why?

According to her father, God was punishing her for her actions. Well, she felt severely punished. She had learned a bitter lesson. Wasn't God satisfied with that? What else did He want her to do? Did He want her to make things right with Garvin? Was it her fault Garvin drank too much? What was she supposed to do? What?

She leaned back against the sofa and closed her eyes. Alice had said: Just read your Bible. Madelene's Bible was still in the nightstand where she had placed it nearly a year ago. All those years of Sundays, wasted! She had sat in her father's living room merely pretending to read. She had turned the pages of her Bible, proud of herself for keeping one step ahead of her father, while she had daydreamed about being a famous actress. She shook her head in disbelief. How could she have been so stupid?

Madelene lowered her legs to the floor. She rose and grabbed her side where Garvin had kicked her. Limping to the nightstand, she pulled out the drawer. The Bible sat there, its black leather cover untouched and its pages sadly compact and like new. She settled herself against the pillows on the sofa, and opened the book.

~ *Seventeen* ~

Madelene started reading the Bible from the beginning. It was very difficult to understand. How did the problems of Cain and Abel, Noah, and Moses fit into her life? She saw herself as Eve, the woman who lost a son, instead of Eve, the woman who had led mankind astray. She was as the Israelites had been, wondering whether God would really take care of them. As she read further, she realized she would never be a woman of great faith like Ruth. The first few books of the Old Testament only proved to her that she was not what God wanted.

Even the laws depressed her. She had always discounted much of what her father had preached. But according to the laws set forth by Moses, she realized her father was right. She could never live up to those standards. How could anyone?

Alone in her rooms, Madelene continued to study the Bible, wrestling with its passages and strange sayings. Mostly, she felt as Job had: abandoned in pain and suffering. God seemed so very far away.

In June of 1941, she had been Ruth's bridesmaid. Soon after, Ruth and George moved to nearby Lancaster. Madelene could not visit since she didn't have a car, or know how to drive. They lost touch.

It wasn't long before Madelene and Alice made up. She knew that Alice was her dearest friend. She also knew the answers she sought were indeed in the Bible. She just hadn't found them yet. Between the three of them: Alice, Mr. Roth, and Mr. Alden, Garvin had been kept away from her. But when her wounds had healed, she realized she couldn't avoid him forever. He was her husband, after all.

～◦～

It was a Sunday in mid-August when Madelene allowed Garvin to see her. Alice was at church, but Mr. Roth announced that Garvin was outside. She walked to the window at the end of the hall and peeked into the front yard. Garvin stood still, his head bowed under the midday sun, his clothes neatly pressed. If she didn't know how much Garvin hated church, she could almost guess that he'd been there.

"It's okay, Mr. Roth. You can let him in."

"Are you sure? I wouldn't trust that man, Madelene. Not after what he did to you."

"He was drunk, Mr. Roth. But he seems sober today. He's not even yelling like the last few times. I think I'll be all right."

"Well, at least see him in the sitting room downstairs. That way I can be in the kitchen in case anything happens."

Madelene shook her head. "It's all right. You can stand in the hallway if you're worried."

Mr. Roth shrugged and headed downstairs.

Madelene walked back to her room and stood by the sofa. She wanted to stand, to face him as he walked through the door. Despite her cold hands, she felt her heart racing and a tingling heat rising up within her. She bit her lip and waited.

Soon, she heard his footsteps in the hallway. The doorknob turned, and Garvin stood before her. His blue eyes glanced up at her, then down toward the floor. His hands hung at his sides; and she could see that his nails were clean. He wore a crisp, white cotton dress shirt tucked into what he called his "Sunday" trousers. He glanced up at her again, and a lock of his black hair fell across his forehead.

She hadn't been sure how she would feel when she saw him again. But here he stood looking almost like he used to, before the liquor. Before Adam. Before the beating. She bit her lip. It was as if his blows, her aching loneliness, and her sense that he, too, was hurting all became part of the same blood that that now rushed through her veins.

Realizing that the silence between them was growing, she cleared her throat. "I…I'm not sure what to say, Garvin. I'm glad you're sober." She shook her head, surprised at her own sarcasm. "What do you want?"

This time, Garvin raised his head. "I just want to say that…that I'm sorry. I was drunk. I was so angry at losing Adam, I just didn't know what I was doing. I can't believe I hurt you like that. I didn't mean it. I was just so confused and…and angry with everyone. Not just you. But you were here, and—"

"Stop it, Garvin."

"I just wanted to tell you that it will never happen again."

"Until the next time you drink with the boys at the Woodside."

"No. I'm not going to drink anymore. I swear."

"Oh, Garvin, I want to believe you. I do. I'm just so afraid. You said this before, just after Adam was born." She brought her hands up in a slight shrug, then she let them drop to her sides. She sighed and sat down on the sofa's armrest. "I'm so tired. I'm nearly 19 years old and I've lost my father because I did something stupid. I lost my son because I did something stupid. I might have had you once, Garvin, but forcing you into marriage was the quickest way to lose you. I'm sorry. I'm sorry I messed up your life. I'm sorry that because of my stupidity our son died—" She choked on the words. Garvin had suffered too, and she knew she was responsible for at least some of it.

Then she saw something in Garvin's eyes that she had never seen before: compassion. He rushed to her and threw his arms around her.

"I never meant to hurt you, Madelene. Never," he whispered into her hair. "Things just got out of hand." He placed his hands along her jaw and kissed her cheekbone as he moved his face in front of hers.

"But Garvin, it all hurts so much." Tears sprang to her eyes.

"I'm sorry." He gently kissed her lips. "I'm sorry," he repeated, and he kissed her again.

She felt a fluttering within her. She didn't believe it was still possible to feel something for this man. His sudden tenderness reminded her of their early days. She looked up and saw him staring at her as if he could see through to her heart. He leaned his face close to hers again and she kissed him back.

They wrapped their arms around each other. Before she realized what was happening, she felt the soft quilt on the bed beneath her.

Then the tiniest voice inside her said: No. She tried to ignore it, but it repeated Garvin's words as he bragged about the other girls he had known while he was dating her and the women he had visited after they were married. No, the voice insisted. This was not right.

His lips caressed her neck. She felt his hands on her shoulders. Then another scene flashed through her brain—those hands becoming fists aimed at her. He'll do it again, the voice warned.

He promised he wouldn't.

Then she remembered: He had promised the same thing before while she was holding Adam.

See, he already broke the same promise once before, the voice said. Stop it now! Tell him no!

"No," she said and pushed his hands away from her.

"It will be all right."

"Garvin, I don't think we should do this."

He tugged at her clothes. "You're just scared, that's all. It'll be all right." She tried to get up, but he pushed her back.

"Garvin, I said no!" His hands caught hers and pinned them to the pillow above her head.

"Just relax." He covered both her wrists with his left hand.

Mr. Roth was still in the house. She thought about screaming. But then he would come in and find them…like this. It was time to fight her own battles.

"No, Garvin. Please. No!" She thrashed her legs, but he was too fast.

"No," she whimpered. Her arms ached where they were stretched above her head. Her wrists were numb. Tears slid from the corners of her eyes to her ears. "No…," she whispered.

Afterward, Garvin said, "See, I told you it would be all right."

Madelene turned on her left side with her back to him. Hot tears rolled down her face and dampened the quilt.

"Well, I've got to go out awhile. I promised my mother I'd find my old man for her. I guess she needs him to fix something."

She couldn't believe he didn't realize she was crying. What was the matter with him? Did he not hear her?

He headed toward the door and called out over his shoulder. "I'll be back for supper." He shut the door behind him.

She curled up into a fetal position. Her insides shook; her hands and feet felt like ice. Tears burned trails down her face.

A firm knock sounded at the door. "Madelene?" Mr. Roth called out.

She wiped her eyes. She had to answer. She cleared her throat and called, "I'm all right. You can go now."

"Well, okay. I'll be down the hall if you need me."

She thanked him, and she heard his footsteps retreating from the door.

Madelene could not uncurl herself. Her hands and feet were cold, and her body ached. Her mind was numb. Minutes seemed like hours while she waited for her limbs to stop shaking. Gradually, warmth spread to her extremities.

She rose and tried to still her trembling fingers as she reached for her clothes. The cold fog in her brain started to dissipate, but she still could not make sense of things. At first, she had felt something for him. He had kissed her sincerely. She was sure of it. Then that voice had intruded, and when she said no….

She bit her lip as she got dressed. She really had no right to refuse. He was her husband. But when she said no, he should have…. Her breath quickened. It wasn't right. He should have listened to her!

He said he would be back for supper. But she knew now that she couldn't face him. She wondered if Mr. Roth and Mr. Alden would still protect her. She glanced at the clock on the nightstand. Alice should be home from church now.

Madelene smoothed her hair and walked with shaking legs. She looked around as she entered the hall to make sure everyone's door was closed. She climbed the steps to the third floor attic where Alice lived. She knocked on the door and waited.

The door creaked open. "Madelene! My dear, I don't get many visitors up here. You've never seen my little nest, have you?" Alice drew her brows together. "Something wrong? This isn't a social call, is it? Come in, sit down." Alice showed her to an overstuffed chair slip-covered in a pattern of green vines and violets.

The heat in the attic room hung around them, making it difficult to breathe. Madelene wiped perspiration from her brow and fanned herself with her hand.

Alice apologized for the heat as she sat down across from Madelene. "Now you know why I spend so much time downstairs. I tried to counter the heat with cool colors: the violets, the blue rug, green curtains. But I guess you can only fool yourself for so long." She glanced at Madelene again. "Tell me what happened, dear. I can see it in your face."

Alice's words about fooling yourself rang in her ears. She took a deep breath; the hot air caught in her throat. She coughed and began. "Alice, I don't know if you heard, but Garvin came to see me again."

Alice nodded.

"I told Mr. Roth to let him come up because I could see that he wasn't drunk or behaving angrily. I thought it would be all right. And it was, for a while. He apologized. He promised it wouldn't happen again...."

"Go on."

Madelene bit her lip. "We apologized for things. We kissed. We...." How could she say it? Madelene took another breath. "We...we started to...you know. But then this voice inside said it wasn't right. I started remembering the last time he promised to quit drinking and hitting me. Somehow I knew that if we got back together, he'd do it again."

She fell silent. She wasn't sure she could say the rest. A clock ticked somewhere.

"Something else happened?"

Madelene nodded, but she couldn't say the words. She glanced around the room, and her gaze fixed on the desk and the photographs of Alice's smiling grandchildren.

"Madelene?"

She sighed. "I said no. I said I changed my mind, that I didn't think it would be a good idea after all. But he…he didn't listen to me. It was as if I didn't matter to him. He pinned my wrists to the bed—" Tears gathered again at the rims of her eyes. "He forced me, he—"

"Oh, no." Alice got up and knelt at Madelene's feet. She wrapped her warm, fleshy hands around Madelene's shaking fingers.

"So, I was wondering," Madelene said while tears streamed down her cheeks, "whether your offer of protection is still stood. He's coming back for supper." She turned her face away from Alice and cried.

Alice hugged her. "I'll do everything I can to protect you. So will Mr. Roth and Mr. Alden."

"Oh, Alice!" Madelene grabbed the sleeve of Alice's blue cotton dress. "Don't tell them what happened. Please?"

"No. No, of course not. We'll just tell them you've decided to stick with the original plan, that's all. They don't have to know. And Madelene, that husband of yours will never come inside this house again, not as long as I run it. That's a promise."

At supper time, Madelene stood at the window in the upstairs hallway that overlooked the street. Garvin sauntered toward the house whistling an unfamiliar tune. Madelene ducked away from the window as he approached.

She heard the front door open and Mr. Roth's voice saying, "I'm sorry, you'll have to leave."

"What the—" Garvin exclaimed. "Let me in! My wife and I are going to have supper."

"I'm afraid she's changed her mind. You'll have to leave now."

Madelene heard footsteps scuffling across the floor in the foyer. "Let go of me," Garvin said. "Madelene!" Garvin's anger rushed at her like a firestorm. "Tell them I'm coming for supper. Tell them it's okay now."

She shrank against the wall, her fingers gripping the cool plaster. Her heart thudded in her chest.

"I'm afraid the lady has changed her mind," Mr. Alden said.

"Madelene! Get these idiots away from me. Tell them it's okay. Tell them!"

She heard Garvin grunting as he tried to shove past Mr. Roth and Mr. Alden. Then Alice said, "You are forbidden from entering this house. I've arranged to have your things sent back to your mother's. You are not welcome. Please leave the premises or I'll call the police."

"Why you big, dumb—"

"That's it!" Mr. Alden roared. "Get out!"

Madelene heard more struggling, then Garvin crumpled onto the porch. "Madelene!" he yelled. The front door slammed. A picture rattled on the wall behind her. She peeked out the window again and saw Garvin standing on the front lawn looking up in her direction. Then he whirled around and kicked the picket fence. He yelled her name again and cursed before storming through the gateway and running down Pine Street.

Madelene stood transfixed at the window with her breath heaving and her hands shaking. She felt someone behind her and she jumped. Mrs. Roth laid her hands on Madelene's shoulders and said, "It's okay now. Let's go down to supper."

⟿ Eighteen ⟿

Several weeks later, Madelene woke up feeling nauseated. That roast pork from last night's dinner had not tasted right.
Now she would be paying for it. She sat up and felt her stomach
churn. "Ugh." She had to get dressed. She glanced at the clock. It was
already 7 a.m.! How could she have overslept? She always made it
down to the kitchen by 6:30 to start the coffee.

Madelene rushed through her morning toiletries and burst
through the entry to the kitchen. Alice was scrambling eggs at the
cookstove, and the smell of fresh coffee wafted through the air.
Madelene apologized as she grabbed her apron from the peg on the
kitchen wall.

Alice looked up from her work and frowned. "My dear, you look
very pale. Are you feeling all right?"

"Just a little nauseated." Madelene reached for the loaf of bread
cooling on the countertop.

"How long have you been feeling like this?"

"Oh, I just seemed to wake up with it. I don't think the pork was
right, do you? Surely you must feel a little queasy yourself."

"No, I feel fine. Do you get sick from food often, or...."

"Or what?" Madelene looked at Alice, who had tilted her head and raised her eyebrows. "Alice, I don't have time for games. No, I don't get sick often, in fact, only when I was—Oh!" She clapped her hand over her mouth. Surely she wasn't…. Her knees began to shake.

Alice took the pan of eggs off the fire and set it on a cool corner of the stove. "Perhaps you should sit down, dear."

Madelene paced in her rooms that night and ran her fingers over the furniture. Garvin had a right to know. But, she had thought she was rid of him. No, she was just putting things off. Now that there was another baby, she should reconcile with Garvin. Or divorce him, another voice said.

Divorce him? How could she do that? She had humiliated herself and her father enough already. Why should she give the town something else to talk about?

But reconcile? How could she reconcile with a man who got drunk and beat her, or worse. Another baby. She was afraid. Would she ever love another child like she loved Adam?

Yet, a tiny part of her was happy. God had given her another chance. Once again, God had turned something wrong and distasteful into something good.

Throughout the following weeks, she wrestled with how to tell Garvin about the baby. One morning in mid-October, she and Alice were preparing breakfast while the radio on the kitchen counter played Glen Miller's 'Moonlight Serenade.' Madelene poured a cup of coffee for herself and sat down at the table.

"What is wrong with these biscuits?" Alice asked. "Madelene, these biscuits aren't rising. They should be in the oven by now. Did you remember the yeast?"

"Of course I—Oh, no. Alice, I'm so sorry," Madelene said as she rose from her chair. "I'll get started on another batch right away."

"No, that's all right, dear. We haven't got time. They can just have toasted bread, I guess." Alice glanced at Madelene. "Have you decided what you're going to do?"

The morning news program began on the radio as Madelene shook her head. "There just doesn't seem to be any way out of this."

"What have you come up with so far?"

"I don't know whether to tell Garvin. If I tell him, he'll want to come back and live here. But from what I hear, he's been down at the Woodside bar every night. He's barely keeping his job at the mill. What kind of father is that? On the other hand, if I don't tell him…well that's just not right either."

"Well, I hate to remind you, but he'll find out soon enough anyway."

Madelene sighed again. They stood for a moment in silence while the radio news continued. News of the war caught their attention: "In other news today, the Germans rampaged through Soviet territory and captured an estimated 500,000 prisoners. The number is unconfirmed at this point, but sources say it could go higher. The invasion that most thought might be over in a month has now been going on for nearly three months. For an on-the-spot report, we go to—"

Alice reached toward the radio and snapped it off. "We don't need to hear any of that now. Fools. What do they think they're doing? Do they think they can conquer the entire world?"

Madelene shook her head. The whole world had gone mad, even Trennen. As she sipped her coffee, someone knocked on the front door.

She walked to the foyer and opened the door. Garvin's mother stood before her. She pushed her dark blond hair away from her eyes and asked if they could talk. Madelene glanced over her shoulder and saw Alice looking at them from the kitchen. She motioned Garvin's mother to the porch and shut the door behind them.

"I hope you don't mind if we talk out here," Madelene said. "We were just getting ready for breakfast."

Garvin's mother wore a dark brown cotton dress that hung past her knees. What had once been a belt buckle was broken, its intact half stuck to the dress. Her dusty leather shoes looked like they had been well-used and discarded by a previous owner several years ago. The woman dropped to the stoop and clasped her chapped hands in her lap.

Madelene's food-spotted apron hung over her knees as she sat down next to Garvin's mother. Garvin's mother. Madelene realized she didn't even know the woman's name. What did she want? Had something happened to Garvin?

"I understand you threw my son out of the house," Garvin's mother began. She brushed a lock of hair from her forehead.

Uh-oh, this couldn't be good.

"I can't say as I blame you, though."

"What?"

"I was hopin'…that is, I thought he wouldn't turn out like his father. But the truth is, he's exactly like the man. He can't stay away from the bottle. Just like his father."

Madelene fidgeted with the corner of her apron. "Mrs. Quaid, I don't understand. If you knew, if you even suspected that Garvin was like his father, then why didn't you warn me?"

"I only approved of this marriage because I thought a baby would give him the sense of responsibility he needed. I thought he would be forced to grow up. You understand, of course, that my son doesn't keep me informed about his marriage. I barely know you. But I've heard about him from the neighbors. They say they see him at the Woodside drinkin' his pay from the mill. It's a wonder he can still keep his job. His father couldn't." Her cracked, dry fingers smoothed her wrinkled dress.

Why was she here? "Mrs. Quaid—"

"Maureen. You can call me Maureen. 'Mother' is kind of out of the question, isn't it? I've got ten kids of my own anyway. Why am I here, you're wonderin'. Well, I know this isn't good news for you, but bein' as my son isn't staying here anymore an' I can't afford it anyway, well…I guess I'm trying to tell you I can't afford to pay for your stay."

Madelene felt the bottom drop out of her stomach. Not pay? What would she do now? But she could see the woman's point. Ten kids had to be expensive, especially since Garvin's father didn't seem to be helping.

Maureen was staring at her. What was she supposed to say?

"I'm sorry," Maureen said. "I need the money. You're young; you can work. Now that the baby's gone, maybe you could go back to your own father." She stood up. "Good luck to you." She walked toward the picket gate.

Madelene was tempted to tell her about the new baby. But one look at Maureen's hunched shoulders and shuffling feet convinced her to keep quiet. Besides, she was right. As long as Garvin no longer lived here, why should his mother pay for a girl she barely knew? Now what would she do?

She sighed. She couldn't go back to her father, not with another baby coming. He would just say the same thing he'd been saying for over a year now. He would be right, too. She had humiliated him once, and another baby would only continue his embarrassment. There was only one thing left to do. She had to get a job.

She walked through the front doorway and saw Alice standing in the sitting room. "Alice, I'm afraid I've got more bad news. Garvin's mother can't pay for the rent anymore. I guess I need a job." Despite her best efforts not to panic or feel sorry for herself, she felt a lump in her throat. "Do you know of any?"

"Of course I do," Alice said with a grin. "I've got a job right here."

"Oh, Alice, you've been so good to me ever since I got here. But I can't take advantage of you anymore. I need a real job."

"I've got a real job."

"I mean one that pays money." Madelene smiled in spite of the situation.

"I'm not going to be able to run this place forever, you know." Alice ran her fingers through her salt-and-pepper hair. "In case you haven't noticed, I'm not a youngster anymore. You already know how to run the meals. Now I can teach you the rest of it. When you're ready and I'm ready, I'll retire and this can be your boardinghouse. How about it, dear?"

The idea intrigued her. But she still had to pay the rent. "Alice, I really like the idea. But it's time I started taking care of myself. I can get a job and learn the business in my off hours."

"Sounds wonderful, dear. Just don't overdo it now that the new baby is coming." She plopped down on the sofa and drew her brows together. "Let's see." She tapped her finger on her cheekbone. "I think I heard they need a waitress down at Lunn's. And by the looks of things, Dr. Dallan needs someone to run the clinic while he's out."

The stairs creaked as Mr. Roth descended to the sitting room. "Someone looking for a job?" he called to them from the staircase.

"Yes, Fred. Our young friend here needs employment. Have you heard of anything?"

Mr. Roth walked across the wooden floor to stand between them. He scratched his head for a moment and said, "You know, I think I heard my boss say we need someone to take orders at the mill. The last girl quit a few days ago."

Madelene smiled at them both. "Thank you. I'm sure something will turn up."

~ Nineteen ~

After breakfast, Madelene went to her room and stared at the clothes hanging in the wardrobe closet. What should she wear? What would she say? She didn't finish high school. She had no secretarial or waitressing skills. All she had ever done was keep her father's house and cook for him. And she had dusted the pews and washed the stained glass in the church. Just how did any of that relate to what she had to do now?

She finally decided on a white, v-necked blouse and a black dirndl skirt. She found her stockings in the back of her dresser drawer and her patent leather slingback pumps in the back of the closet. After she had dressed, she stared at herself in the mirror as she brushed her chocolate brown hair into a smooth sheen. The brown eyes staring back at her had lost something in the last year. Innocence, perhaps. Adam. The thought of his big smile and soft baby skin rushed back at her. She thought she might cry again.

She tossed the brush back onto the dresser and took a deep breath. She couldn't cry just yet. She had to get a job. She glanced out of the back windows, up past the gold and orange leaves, and into the bright autumn sky. *Lord, help me to find a job!*

When she went to see Dr. Dallan he admitted he needed secretarial help, but he couldn't afford to hire anyone. On her way out, she noticed a mother and son sitting in Dr. Dallan's waiting room. The mother soothed her boy while he cried. Madelene sighed and looked away. Maybe she couldn't have worked there with so many sick children and worried mothers. Perhaps the restaurant would be a better choice.

But Lunn's restaurant proved to be even worse. Dirty, grizzled old men sat in booths laughing at a young waitress as she apologized for dropping a glass of water. Dishes crusted with bits of dried egg were stacked on the tables. The manager bellowed at the girl and frightened her so much that she dropped an entire tray. Food and dishes crashed to the floor. He screamed at the girl again and she ran from the restaurant. Madelene hastily followed her. The mill was her only hope.

She had to hike about a mile out of town to get to the lumber mill. She passed the funeral parlor on her right. Pictures flashed through her mind: Adam lying in his tiny casket, people shaking their heads, black clothing. A young mother walked by pushing a dark blue baby carriage, its silver wheels flashing in the sunlight. Madelene glanced inside at the baby, a girl wearing a pink bonnet edged in white lace. She seemed about the age Adam would be now. The mother smiled at Madelene and hurried past.

Madelene stopped and turned her head to watch the woman. That could have been her. If only she hadn't been so careless…if she hadn't exposed Adam to…if…. Tears sprang to her eyes. She swallowed hard and placed her hands on her stomach. Maybe this time.

She walked by a beauty parlor on her right and felt the eyes of the town's biggest gossips staring at her as she passed. She held her head even higher and kept her eyes on the dusty road ahead. She crossed Washington street and walked past the high school. She remembered Ruth and the way the two of them had giggled, laughed, and teased. Those times seemed very far away.

The grade school sat next to the high school. The playground was filled with children at this time of day. She stopped for a moment, remembering the child who would never play there. She closed her eyes and bit her lip. No matter what she did, everything seemed to remind her of Adam. She sighed and headed toward the mill.

Mill Road wound through the forest when it left Trennen. Madelene passed only a few houses. She traveled alone on the road, her heels crunching on the brown leaves.

A truck rumbled up behind her and she stepped off the road. The '38 blue Ford truck passed as its driver beeped the horn. Wood chips bounced on the truck's flat bed, and several chips fell off, leaving a trail on the road. As she walked farther, she spotted another truck traveling toward Trennen with its bed stacked high with cut timber.

Soon, she heard shouts in the distance and the crack of falling trees. The unmistakable see-saw sound of men cutting trees echoed through the forest. To her right, she saw the mill in a clearing. Madelene stared at the rambling two-story building. Conveyors carried logs into the mill at one end, then rolled two-by-fours out at the other end. Men in denim worksuits hurried to the end of the conveyor line where more flat-bed trucks waited to be loaded. The shouts of the crew chiefs filled the air.

A separate shack with its two front windows cracked open sat in front of the main mill. A hand-painted "Open" sign hung on the door. She assumed this was the office. As she stepped onto the wooden porch, the sound of clacking typewriter keys confirmed her guess. She was about to reach for the metal knob when the door swung open.

A man about forty years old stood before her with his mouth hanging open. She gasped and stepped back.

"What are you doing here, missy?" The man placed his fists on his hips and stared at her. His large hands and curly brown hair, as well as his denim shirt and overalls, were sprinkled with sawdust. His voice sounded gruff, but his gray eyes widened a little, and his full mouth turned up at the corners.

For a moment, Madelene forgot what she meant to say. Then she blurted, "Mr. Roth said you might need someone to take orders?"

The man laughed, a deep laugh that began in his stomach and burst from his mouth. "Missy, I've been trying to get someone to take orders since I started this place. If you're willing to take orders, I'm ready to give them." He chuckled again.

Madelene drew her brows together. Surely she had been misunderstood. "I don't want a job in the forest. I meant that I heard you needed someone to answer the phone...."

"I knew what you meant," the man said as he shook his head. "I was joking, see."

Madelene dipped her head as she glanced up at him. She felt the flush begin in her cheeks when she realized he had indeed been joking and she had missed it.

The man stuck out his hand and said, "Steve Atwood, owner."

She shook his hand, afraid her small fingers would get lost.

"Don't worry, missy, I won't bite. But it would help if I knew your name so I wouldn't have to keep calling you 'missy.'" He tilted his head as he eyed her. "Unless that is your name?"

This time she smiled. "Madelene Quaid."

Mr. Atwood motioned her into the office. The small room was just big enough for three desks, one of which was empty except for a phone and some stained coffee cups. His auburn-haired secretary sat at the desk to the left of the door. She paused to look at Madelene, then resumed typing. The clacking ceased, though, when she sighed and reached for the white eraser at the right side of the typewriter.

"Remember, Brianna, more than three holes in the paper and it's Swiss cheese, not a letter," Mr. Atwood said to the girl.

"Yes, sir!" Brianna raised her hand to her forehead in a mock salute.

Madelene sat in the chair offered to her and looked back and forth between Brianna and her boss.

"Now, missy, er, I mean, Madelene, you're looking for a job, are you?" Mr. Atwood began the interview. "Well, you heard correctly; my last girl left a week ago to stay home and take care of her new baby. I told her she could set up her carriage in here, but she wanted to stay at home. Now what was your last name again, Madelene?" Mr. Atwood grabbed a sheet of paper from under a folder on his desk. He chose a pencil from a round holder and waited.

After she answered him, he looked up with a puzzled expression. "I have a Quaid working here. Well, working when he feels like it, that is. You're not any relation are you?"

"Yes, Mr. Atwood, I am." She glanced over at Brianna then back at Mr. Atwood. "In fact, there are a few things you should know."

Mr. Atwood was quick to interpret. "Brianna, why don't you take your lunch now. I'll see you in half an hour."

Brianna nodded. A lock of hair fell into her face as she stood up, and she pushed it away. She stepped to the door and stopped for a moment to look over Madelene from head to toe. She smiled and left, her thick-heeled pumps clopping down the porch steps.

"Now then, what's so mysterious? How are you related to Mr. Quaid?" Mr. Atwood dropped the pencil onto the paper. He leaned in, propped his elbows on the desk, and rested his chin in his upturned hands.

"I'm his wife."

"Oh? Well then, I guess I'm missing something here. Why would you need a job if your husband already works?"

"Mr. Atwood, maybe we should just talk about the position. I mean, there's no point to your hearing the whole story if I'm not right for the job, is there?" Madelene clasped and unclasped her hands in her lap. Her heart hammered in her chest. Was she right for the job?

Mr. Atwood sat back in his chair and slapped his hands on his thighs. "Well then. Can you read, Madelene?" He picked up the pencil again.

"Yes, of course." No one had ever asked her that before.

"Can you write?"

"Yes."

"Can you add and subtract?"

"Yes, I always got good grades in school."

"Do you know how to answer the phone?"

"Huh?"

"You know, it's that funny-looking contraption that rings when someone far away wants to talk to you." Mr. Atwood's eyes twinkled back at her.

In spite of her nervousness, Madelene smiled.

"Well then. I need someone and here you are. You seem intelligent enough. A bit too serious maybe, but we can work on that. So

I'd say that yes, Madelene, you can have the job. It pays 20 dollars a week, is that okay?"

Was it okay?! She would have her rent covered in one week and still have enough to spend on the food bill, clothes for the job, and baby clothes too. Madelene nodded.

"Good! The job is yours. Now why don't you tell me about your reservations?"

Madelene's hopes sunk. What if when he heard about her and Garvin, he didn't want to give her the job after all? What if he didn't want to take a chance on another girl who would soon have a baby?

"I assume your husband knows you came here for a job," Mr. Atwood broke into her thoughts.

"No, Mr. Atwood, he doesn't."

"Steve, please."

"No, uh, Steve, you see Garvin and I are, um, living apart. It's a long story, really. I'm sure you don't want to hear it."

"No, please go on. If you're going to work here and it will be a surprise to your husband, then perhaps I need to know the story so I'll know what to say to him when he finds out."

Madelene bit her lip. "I'm not sure what to tell you, but I guess you also need to know that I'm expecting." She tried to gauge his reaction. "I'm sure my landlady will watch my baby while I'm here. And I need this job, so I won't quit to stay home."

"And your husband? Why doesn't he know you are applying here?"

Madelene sighed. It was so hard to separate what Mr. Atwood needed to know from what was better kept private. Should she tell him about Garvin's abuse? Should she tell him about Garvin's drinking?

"Garvin and I are living apart, as I've said before. We couldn't get along, really, and I don't think things will get better between us. But, I don't believe in divorce either. Anyway, I decided I needed a job so I could keep my room and pay the food bill—and for the baby."

"Surely though, with the baby coming, he'll come back and try to make things right."

"It didn't work that way before." Madelene's voice dropped to a whisper.

"Before? You mean you already have a child? And he still won't make things right?" Steve's voice rose in pitch.

Madelene looked away. "We, uh, we lost our baby, Mr. Atwood. Garvin tried to be a good father, but when we lost Adam, Garvin just snapped. Things between us went downhill after that." She felt tears rising to her eyes and she blinked them back. She couldn't cry now, not in a job interview.

"I'm sorry. Look, Madelene, I can see you need this job, and as I said before, it's yours. If you ever need to bring the baby here, that's fine too.

"However, I cannot see any way to keep Garvin out of the office since the men pick up their paychecks here every Friday. Plus he's bound to see you coming to work or going home. If you take this job, I hope you'll tell him about it ahead of time so he doesn't get surprised and mess up his own work. He's trying my patience as it is." He rose, tossed the pencil onto the desk, and continued, "And who knows? Maybe your taking this job will help him realize he needs to provide for you and the baby."

Madelene shook her head. She looked into his broad face and saw a man she felt she could trust. "He doesn't know about the baby."

Mr. Atwood sighed and shook his head. "Look, I know this is none of my business. But this is his child, Madelene. He has a right to know. And that's one thing you can't keep hidden from him."

"I know, I know. I just can't seem to bring myself to tell him now. But I will. I've still got a couple of months." She paused and looked at the clock on the wall. Brianna's half-hour was up. "Do I have the job, Mr. Atwood?"

"Of course. Can you start tomorrow?" He held out his hand.

Madelene nodded and rose to shake it. As they left the office together, Madelene glanced up at him. She hadn't realized how tall he was. They stepped outside into the autumn sunshine as Brianna returned from lunch. She paused at the bottom of the steps and tilted her head to one side as she looked at Madelene again.

"Brianna!" Mr. Atwood called. "Meet my new order-taker, Madelene Quaid. Madelene, this is my secretary, Brianna Connor."

Brianna stretched out her hand, her long fingernails painted red.

Her wide mouth broke into a grin that showed gleaming white teeth. "Nice to meet you."

Madelene grasped Brianna's warm, moist hand and nodded.

"Good. Now, Brianna," Mr. Atwood boomed, "Madelene will sit at the vacant desk and she'll start tomorrow. So, I need you to get a pad of paper and some pencils, a rubber stamp and stamp pad, stapler—"

"Yes, your majesty."

Mr. Atwood grinned and shook his head. "Sometimes, girl...."

Madelene watched the exchange and wondered if she would fit in. She had not been brought up to interrupt or speak sarcastically. Yet, as both Steve and Brianna laughed, she had to smile too. None of this was done to hurt anyone. It was just an easygoing relationship, probably born out of working together for a number of years. "How long have you been working together?"

"Oh, what, about six months now, isn't it?" Brianna asked Steve.

"That sounds about right."

Madelene drew her brows together. "The way you talk to each other, I assumed you had worked together for a long time."

Steve laughed again. "Brianna is my sister."

"Oh! But she's so much—" Madelene stopped before she stuck her foot any farther into her mouth.

"Younger?" Steve finished her sentence for her. "That's okay, Madelene. It's no big secret. My father died when I was just a teenager. My mother remarried an Irishman named Connor."

"And I was the happy result," Brianna giggled.

"And I've been looking out for her ever since, although it hasn't been an easy job."

Madelene smiled at them. She wondered what would it have been like to have a big brother. A pick-up truck rumbled from around the side of the office and broke into her thoughts.

"Fred!" Steve called. "I'd like you to meet my new order girl."

"Already have," a familiar voice yelled back. Madelene turned and saw Mr. Roth waving from the driver's side. She waved back. Mr. Roth stuck his head out of the window and asked, "Need a ride home? I've got to make a delivery in town, so I'll be going that way."

Madelene glanced up at Steve. He waved and said, "See you tomorrow."

$\sim$ *Twenty* $\sim$

The next day, Madelene dressed for her job and worried about how Garvin would react when she told him about it. Steve said the men came in to the office for their paychecks on Fridays. Today was Tuesday.

She combed her hair, then smoothed it with her hands. She stuck her face close to the mirror and stared. Her hair never seemed to look any better no matter what she did with it. But, why did she care what she looked like? She shook her head. Then she grabbed her purse from the bed and skipped downstairs to meet Mr. Roth.

As they stopped in front of the main office, Madelene realized how lucky she was to have a ride. Many workers still traveled to their jobs on foot. Those who did have an automobile or truck, parked along the road leading up to the mill. Madelene thanked Mr. Roth and headed into the office. She took a deep breath, inhaling the smoky smell of sawdust. Men shouted greetings to each other as they strode to their line jobs or into the forest. Everyone seemed to be bustling and productive. *"Thank you, God, for giving me a job,"* she whispered.

She stopped at the foot of the office steps and straightened the wrinkles from her dress. She had just placed her foot on the first step when she heard his voice crackle through the air: "What are you doing here?"

Madelene gasped and felt her heart stop. She whirled around to see Garvin with his fists clenched and blue eyes flashing. Instead of three days, she had had three minutes. She felt her fingers turn to ice. "I—I, uh, well, Garvin, I guess you don't know, but your mother couldn't afford to pay the boardinghouse rent anymore. I—I needed a job." Her voice shrunk to a whisper.

"And you had to get one here? Why don't you just move home where your daddy can protect you? You aren't much of a wife." He stepped in close and stared at her. His hand flashed in front of her and she flinched. He ran his fingers through his black hair and dropped his hands to his sides. "What's the matter? Are you afraid of me? Afraid I might want to get close to you again? Huh?" His lips twisted into a snarl, and the odor of whiskey wafted from his mouth.

"Garvin, if you're referring to our last time together—"

"You mean the time you threw me out? The time your boardinghouse pals tossed me onto the porch? The time your old lady friend threatened to call the police? That time?" His eyes flashed. His hand flew up toward her face.

"Garvin, no!" She ducked her head.

"Hey, what's going on here?" A female voice yelled at them from behind Garvin and he backed away. Brianna ran toward them with her auburn hair flying behind her.

"This is none of your affair," Garvin growled.

"Look, mister, I don't like it when one of you brutes thinks he can do whatever he pleases to a woman. Back away!" Brianna stepped between them and held her arms around Madelene as a shield.

Several men stopped on the way to their jobs and stood in a small circle around the three of them. Then, Steve Atwood pushed his way through the crowd. "All right, everyone. Get on to your work."

As the workers dispersed, Steve nodded at Brianna. "Why don't you go into the office. I'll take it from here."

Brianna dropped her arms and glared at Garvin before stepping past Steve.

After the door closed behind her, Steve turned back to Madelene and Garvin. "All right. Now suppose one of you tells me what's going on here."

Garvin's eyes narrowed as he stared at Madelene. "Nothing, sir," he said through clenched teeth.

"Then I suggest you get to work, Mr. Quaid."

Garvin glared at Madelene again. Then he turned on his heel and stormed out of sight, dust clouding up behind him.

Madelene began to shake, her breathing erupting into uneven rasps. Her feet seemed frozen to the ground. The trees around her blurred into meaningless shapes.

"What happened between you?" Steve asked. "What has he done to you?" He laid his hands on her shoulders and guided her up the steps. Inside the office, Brianna stood holding a mug of steaming coffee.

Steve pulled a chair out for her and Madelene sunk into it, her knees buckling beneath her. She couldn't stop her hands from trembling as she grasped the coffee mug. Both Steve and Brianna stared at her.

She lowered the mug to the desk and held her head in her hands. Slowly, her breathing returned to normal. "Oh," she mumbled as Steve and Brianna continued to look on, "how foolish I must look to you. I can't even talk to my husband without needing someone to come to my defense. What's the matter with me?"

"From what I've just seen, that man scares you to death," Steve said. "Maybe you shouldn't work here."

"No!" Madelene's head jerked up. "I need this job, Mr. Atwood. Please. I'll try to stay away from him, I promise."

Steve shook his head and sighed. "Well, then I'll fire him. He's close to being fired anyway. He spends half his time picking fights with the other men on his crew. They can defend themselves, but you—"

"No, please don't fire him!" The consequences flashed like lightning through her brain. He'd blame her, get drunk, and come after her again, just like when Adam died.... She felt the hair rise on her arms.

"I don't understand you. The man frightens you, and yet you don't want him out of here? Especially since I'm willing to fire him."

"Easy, Steve," Brianna said. Her green eyes searched Madelene's face. "I think it's best to leave things as they are for the moment. Maybe Madelene can start her day a half hour later?"

Steve pressed his lips together in a thin line as he stared at the two women. "Well, perhaps we can try that for now."

The rest of the morning was filled with instructions for order taking and filling out forms. At lunchtime, Madelene and Brianna carried their sack lunches to the porch.

"This will probably be one of the last days we'll be able to eat out here," Brianna said. The October day had grown warm. The women settled on the steps and opened their paper bags packed with sandwiches and fruit. Brianna's manicured nails shone like bright jewels against the white bread.

Madelene glanced at her and said, "Brianna, I want to thank you for what you did this morning. I don't know what I would have done if...if...you know."

Brianna dropped her uneaten sandwich onto the paper bag and looked straight at Madelene. "He's hit you, hasn't he? Perhaps, many times?"

Madelene's eyes popped open. How did she know that? She dropped her head and nodded. "I was in the clinic once."

Brianna leaned back against the wooden porch column. "I thought so. You're afraid to stay married to him, and you're afraid to divorce him, right?"

Madelene nodded again, amazed. "How did you know?"

Brianna sighed. "I had a cousin who married a man like your husband. She was afraid of the same things, afraid to even move for fear he'd say it was in the wrong direction."

Madelene bit her lip, as Brianna leaned toward her.

"Listen to me, Madelene. Divorce him. Fight back as well as you can. You've got to learn to defend yourself."

Madelene's mouth dropped open and she drew her brows together. Divorce him? Fight? No one had ever said these things to her before. She took a deep breath and asked, "Brianna, what happened to your cousin?"

Brianna looked away. "She's dead."

"What?"

"The doctor, the police—they all said it was an accident, that she fell down the steps. But I know. Her clothes were torn, and there was blood on her mouth. Her eyes were blackened. His fists had to be taped up. Said he hit them with a hammer that same day. Otherwise, there wasn't a scratch on him. She never fought back."

"I'm so sorry." Madelene wasn't hungry anymore.

Brianna waved her off. "It was a long time ago. I try not to think about it."

"I'm sorry," Madelene said again. "But that won't happen to me. I've got this job now, and he's been thrown out of the boardinghouse. Those are good steps, aren't they?"

Brianna nodded.

"I'll think about what you said, Brianna. But there's something you don't know. I'm expecting a baby in May. I'm not sure it's right to think about divorce when there's a child involved."

"All the more reason. What good will you be to that child if you're hurt? If all that child ever sees is his father hitting his mother, well, what kind of example is that? He'll grow up thinking it's okay to treat women that way. Is that what you want?"

"I—I guess I never thought of it that way."

Just then, the office door opened and Steve poked his head out. "Lunch is over, ladies, and you haven't touched your food. Boy, oh boy, when two women get together…."

The women gathered their uneaten lunches and took the food to their desks.

"She's really remarkable," Madelene said to Alice later that evening. They were studying the ledger at the table in the sitting room. "She's spirited and bright and funny. And very pretty, too. I wonder why she doesn't have a boyfriend or a husband."

Alice sighed. "I don't know, dear. But if you don't stop going on about Brianna, we won't get through this." She pointed to the left-hand page of the ledger and began again, "Now in this column we write the residents' names. In the following columns we record the rent paid."

"I wonder about Steve, too. He never mentions a girlfriend or a wife. There's no wedding ring either. I know he had a wife who died when she was young, but he never talks about it beyond that."

"Madelene, it's not nice to gossip." Alice rose from her chair and turned on the radio which sat at the left side of the table. "Let's forget about the books tonight. Let's listen to the end of 'The Aldrich Family.'"

Madelene grinned at her friend.

"How about some hot cocoa?" Alice started toward the kitchen and Madelene trailed after her.

"Do you know what she said about Garvin?"

"No, but I'm sure I'll hear about it." Alice gathered the cocoa and the milk.

"She said I should divorce him. What do you think of that?"

"I don't think divorce is the answer. Especially now that a child is on the way."

"I told her that too. But she said it wouldn't be right for a child to watch his father hitting his mother. She said the child would grow up thinking that hitting was okay."

Alice poured the milk into the saucepan. "I never thought of it that way."

"See what I mean? I never would have thought of that." She leaned against the countertop and asked, "Do you suppose Garvin grew up like that?"

"Do you mean that Garvin's father may have—"

"That's exactly what I mean, yes. It would explain many things." Maureen's words 'just like his father' sprang into her mind. Maybe Maureen didn't mean the drinking.

"It would, indeed. But that doesn't excuse his actions." Alice stirred the cocoa in silence, then continued. "Have you decided when to tell him about the baby? In another few weeks he'll know without your telling him."

"I know. I just can't seem to find the right time or place. I only see him at work, and I can't tell him in front of the other workers. Mostly though, I'm afraid."

"Well, maybe he'll be happy about it. Maybe he'll look at this as a second chance."

The radio in the other room blared the warning sounds of a news bulletin. Alice motioned for Madelene to turn on the kitchen radio.

Madelene switched it on and she and Alice strained to listen as it warmed up. Another 600,000 Soviets had been taken prisoner by the German army. "The total number of Soviet prisoners is now over one million. Army experts are hoping the hard rains in that country will deter the Germans from moving any further toward Moscow. For reactions from the White House, we now go to my colleague in Washington."

"They're all a bunch of fools," Alice said. "Almost makes me wish I weren't German."

"It's so senseless," Madelene agreed. "Where will it end?"

They stood in silence, not even looking at each other. Soon the smell of burnt milk wafted up from the saucepan. Alice smelled it too, and she grimaced. Both women sighed and decided to forget about the hot cocoa after all.

⸺ *Twenty One* ⸺

On the day before Thanksgiving, Madelene and Brianna finished the day's duties before heading home for the holiday. Brianna had issued the paychecks earlier while Madelene joined Fred Roth on a delivery run. Not only did this get Madelene away from Garvin at pay time, but she turned out to be a good company representative when someone complained about an order.

Madelene now hunched over her desk and wrote up the last order of the day. She could hear Brianna's fingers clacking on the typewriter, and she smiled. The sounds of the office, including her own pencil scratching, were normal, calming. No shouting, no crying, no violence.

Then the door opened and Steve ambled into the office. Snowflakes flew in as he shut the door.

"You had to build this place so the door faced west, didn't you?" Brianna complained without looking up from the typewriter.

Madelene could almost hear the grin in his voice as Steve replied, "Just for you, honey." He stamped the snow off his boots and threw his coat onto the rack next to the door. He walked to his desk and sat down. Madelene caught him glancing at her while he shuffled papers on his desk.

"If you're going to pretend you're working, at least make it look better than that," Brianna said.

Steve stopped shuffling and straightened the papers into a stack. Madelene finished her order and placed it in her "out" basket. She saw Steve leaning back in his chair running his thick fingers through his dark curly hair. His nose was still red from the raw wind.

She smiled and placed her pencil in the desk drawer. When she looked up again, Steve was staring at her. "What's the matter?"

"Nothing."

Brianna's typing ceased and she stared at both of them.

"You were looking at me. What's wrong? Do I have a piece of food in my hair?" Madelene combed her fingers through her hair, just in case.

Steve chuckled. "No, nothing like that. You look wonderful as always." Suddenly his cheeks flushed and he looked down at a coffee stain on the desktop. "I was just wondering if you have plans for tomorrow. You shouldn't spend the holiday alone."

"Thank you, but I'm spending the day with Alice and her family." Madelene wondered why he looked away. It wasn't as if he had asked her for a date or anything. Or had he? She jerked her head up to look at him, but he was still studying the coffee stain.

"Well, that's good," Steve said as he traced the stain with his thick index finger. He stood up and declared, "Well ladies, I think we've worked hard enough for one day, don't you? Let's go home and come back on Friday." He crossed the office, grabbed his coat, and ducked outside.

Madelene looked over at Brianna. "What was that?"

Brianna just shrugged and smiled.

A couple of weeks later, Madelene sat in her rocking chair reading the Bible late on a Sunday afternoon. Every Sunday, Alice urged Madelene to join her at St. Andrew's, but Madelene could not bring herself to go. She gathered a dark green quilt around her and read by the dying winter sunshine sifting through the back windows.

That day, she read Psalm 140: "Deliver me, O Lord, from the evil man: preserve me from the violent man; Which imagine mischiefs in their heart; continually are they gathered together for war." The violent man. Could this be her prayer about Garvin?

She read further: "They have sharpened their tongues like a serpent; adders' poison is under their lips. Keep me, O Lord, from the hands of the wicked; preserve me from the violent man; who have purposed to overthrow my goings." Madelene lowered the book into her lap and looked out the side window at the sky. *Lord, preserve me from the violent man,* she prayed. Visions of Garvin's face screwed in anger flashed before her. She could almost hear him screaming at her.

No, wait. That was Alice! Madelene shot out of the chair, the Bible tumbling to the floor. "Alice?" Alice was still shouting.

Madelene ran to the door and yanked it open just as Mr. Rosemonde and Mr. Alden opened their doors. From the hallway, it was easier to hear what Alice was yelling.

"They've bombed us!"

They ran to the end of the hallway. Mr. Alden reached the steps to the attic first, followed by Madelene and Mr. Rosemonde. Alice stood in the middle of her room staring at the radio. They stood together and listened to the announcer's voice.

"And it appears that the Japanese flew over Pearl Harbor in Oahu, Hawaii, and attacked the U.S. naval base and a few army barracks. We do not have a full account of the number of Japanese planes involved, or the exact number of U.S. ships sunk. Nearby citizens reported seeing heavy smoke, and Japanese planes dropping torpedoes and dive-bombing this U.S. territory. Reports coming in also say several civilians were shot in the streets of Honolulu and in Wahiawa, a nearby town. We're trying to reach our correspondent in Honolulu right now."

The reporter's voice droned on. He did not give many details; perhaps there were not enough to give. Madelene looked at Alice, whose face had turned ghostly white. Her blue-gray eyes stared at no one. "Army barracks," Alice said.

Edwin: Alice said Edwin was stationed in the Army in Hawaii. She crossed the room and clasped Alice's ice-cold hand. "There, there, Alice. Let's sit down on the sofa for a moment." She tried to get

Alice to walk to the sofa, but she would not move from her spot in front of the radio.

Madelene looked over at Mr. Alden and Mr. Rosemonde, her eyes pleading with them to help. Mr. Alden took Alice's other hand. Together they helped her to the sofa and sat down next to her. Mr. Rosemonde stood across the room and muttered against the Japanese.

Alice turned to Madelene. "They said Army barracks, Madelene. Army…barracks…." Alice gasped and tears gathered in the corners of her eyes. "Edwin's there, did you know that? My Edwin is there."

"Shh, Alice. Shh. We don't know anything for certain yet. Perhaps it was a mistake. The announcer said that details were very sketchy."

"How dare they fly over here and kill our men on our own soil. How dare they!" Mr. Rosemonde shouted from across the room.

Alice winced.

"Be quiet, man!" Mr. Alden commanded.

They heard footsteps, and everyone but Alice turned to see Mr. and Mrs. Roth in the doorway. "You've heard," Fred said.

"We were in the kitchen with the radio on," Ida added.

The group fell silent and their attention turned once again to the radio. "It has now been confirmed," the announcer was saying, "that the U.S.S. Arizona has been sunk, and the U.S.S. Oklahoma has capsized. Repeating, the U.S.S. Arizona has been sunk, and the U.S.S. Oklahoma has been capsized. We'll keep you informed of additional details as we hear them."

Madelene had not let go of Alice's hand; its iciness penetrated her skin. Alice stared at nothing and repeated the words, "Army barracks." Mr. Alden rubbed her shoulders, but she shook him off.

"How dare they!" Mr. Rosemonde jammed his fists into his pockets.

"For Pete's sake, will you shut up?" Mr. Alden yelled.

"Well, it's how we all feel, isn't it?" Fred asked.

"Yes, but poor Alice doesn't need this right now. Her son is stationed there," Mr. Alden reminded everyone.

"Mr. Rosemonde, why don't you come downstairs with me and

I'll make us some tea?" Ida laid her hand on Mr. Rosemonde's arm.

"Tea?! They attack us and spill American blood, and all you women can think about is tea? What the…." Mr. Rosemonde's tirade broke off as Fred and Ida wrestled him out of the room.

"American blood," Alice repeated.

"Don't listen to him; he's just angry," Mr. Alden said.

Madelene smoothed Alice's hair where it had escaped from her bun. "We'll just sit here with you until we hear more. Okay, Alice?" Alice did not acknowledge her, but sat upright on the sofa, her gaze not wavering from the radio.

— Twenty Two —

The next day Madelene, Mr. Alden, and the Roths sat around the kitchen table drinking coffee and listening to the radio reports. No one had eaten much since yesterday, but no one was hungry, either. Still, Ida made sandwiches and insisted that Madelene eat at least one for the baby. Knowing that Ida was right, Madelene did her best to eat, but it tasted like sawdust in her mouth.

The news reports said that servicemen on leave were reporting to their bases, and recruiting offices were overflowing with volunteers. "If only I were younger," Mr. Alden declared as he ran his fingers through his graying hair. Madelene looked at him, then, and realized she did not know his age. "I'm nearly 50; too old for the Army," Mr. Alden grumbled when he caught her looking at him.

"Well, if we go to war, I think that's where I should be," Fred said. His wife gripped his arm; the gold band on her hand glowed in the light. "I'm young enough to fight." Fred rose from his chair, but Ida's hand still gripped his arm. He looked down at her and caressed the side of her face.

The warning sound of another news bulletin rang into the room. A voice announced an upcoming message from the President of the

United States. After a brief pause, President Roosevelt's voice came over the airwaves.

"Yesterday, December 7, 1941—a date which will live in infamy—the United States of America was suddenly and deliberately attacked by naval and air forces of the Empire of Japan. The United States was at peace with that nation, and, at the solicitation of Japan, was still in conversation with its government and its Emperor looking toward the maintenance of peace in the Pacific...."

"Peace in the Pacific? I guess that didn't work, did it?" Mr. Alden commented.

"Shh!" Madelene and Ida said together.

"The attack yesterday on the Hawaiian Islands has caused severe damage to American naval and military forces. Very many American lives have been lost. In addition, American ships have been reported torpedoed on the high seas between San Francisco and Honolulu.

"Yesterday the Japanese government also launched an attack against Malaya. Last night Japanese forces attacked Hong Kong. Last night Japanese forces attacked Guam. Last night Japanese forces attacked the Philippine Islands. Last night the Japanese attacked Wake Island. This morning the Japanese attacked Midway Island.

"Japan has, therefore, undertaken a surprise offensive extending throughout the Pacific area. The facts of yesterday speak for themselves. The people of the United States have already formed their opinions and well understand the implications to the very safety and life of their nation...."

"We're going to war," Ida said, her voice wavering.

"That's certain," Mr. Alden responded.

"I believe I interpret the will of Congress and the people when I assert that we will not only defend ourselves to the uttermost, but will make very certain that this form of treachery shall never endanger us again.

"Hostilities exist. There is no blinking at the fact that our people, our territory, and our interests are in grave danger. With confidence in our armed forces—with the unbounded determination of our people—we will gain the inevitable triumph—so help us God.

"I ask that the Congress declare that since the unprovoked and dastardly attack by Japan on Sunday, December 7, a state of war has existed between the United States and the Japanese Empire."

The President signed off, but the radio announcer continued with the news. The boarders looked at each other. The war that everyone had talked about in theory was now a reality.

"That's it then," Fred said. "Now I have to go. I'll head into town; surely someone knows where they're recruiting."

Ida turned in her chair and grabbed her husband's wrist. "Please," was all she said to him as she stared into his eyes.

Fred stroked Ida's hair and said, "Ida, honey, you know I've got to do this. What kind of American would I be; what kind of man would I be if I didn't go?"

Ida closed her eyes against the tears beginning to form and took her hand from her husband's wrist. Fred nodded to the rest of them and walked out of the kitchen.

Ida said nothing. She just stared at the crocheted doily in the center of the table. The others sat in silence while the President's words sank in. Madelene wondered what her father was thinking now. She wondered whether Garvin would volunteer. She thought of the men at the Woodside bar and wondered what kind of soldiers they would make. There always seemed to be so much fighting among them: Irish against German, rich against poor. Could they fight together for once, as Americans? She sighed and rose to warm the coffee.

Darkness overtook cold sunlight as the day faded. They had received no word from Alice's family. The cold sunlight returned on the following day. Again, no word. Darkness fell.

Madelene, Alice, and Mr. Alden sat on the sofa in Alice's room until dark on the fourth day. At 6:30, Ida stepped into the room holding a tray of sandwiches. "Um, I've brought you some food. I've also cleaned the kitchen and locked up for the evening, Madelene. Don't worry about breakfast in the morning, either. I'll take care of it." After Madelene thanked her, Ida left the sandwiches on the coffee table and tiptoed downstairs.

A little after 9:00, the sandwiches still lay on the tray, untouched. The three of them sat like statues in front of the radio. The station played songs when there was a lull in the news, but the "Chattanooga Choo Choo" only mocked the horror of what had happened.

The next news report said that over 500 men from the U.S.S. California and the U.S.S. Utah also had been killed. Alice had fallen asleep and slumped over onto Mr. Alden. In her sleep, she whimpered.

Madelene fell asleep listening to the endless reports of killings and attacks. Fire and blood swirled in the clouds of her dreams and Alice's face was there, her eye sockets showing only two black holes. "Army barracks," someone repeated over and over. She heard men screaming, then women. Then it was only one woman. Alice!

Madelene woke with a start. Her heart thudded in her chest as Alice screamed. Mr. Alden was trying to wake Alice by talking to her in soothing tones. But still Alice screamed. Madelene patted her hand and smoothed her hair. Alice stopped abruptly and woke up. "Edwin," she cried.

Footsteps thundered on the stairs and soon the rest of the boarders stood in Alice's room, their eyes wide with fear. "It's okay now," Madelene said. "She just had a nightmare." The group at the doorway sighed and filed back downstairs.

The pink light of dawn crept onto the horizon and Madelene glanced at the clock: 7 a.m. The radio still crackled with news reports. Madelene reached over to the end table and picked up a handkerchief so Alice could wipe her eyes.

It was Thursday; she should go back to work. Steve had called off work for Monday and Tuesday, and she had stayed home Wednesday as well. But, she knew she couldn't leave Alice. Not now. She rose from the sofa, her joints stiff and unyielding at first. She rubbed the kink in her neck.

Another news bulletin broke in: "This is to confirm that army fields Hickam and Wheeler were also attacked. The known dead are said to number in the hundreds, as most of the soldiers were resting in the barracks when the attack occurred. Communications with the Hawaiian island are difficult at best, and those trying to reach their loved ones can expect a long delay. In other related events...."

Alice broke into sobs; her shoulders hunched over and shook. Madelene rushed to the sofa and hugged her. "Alice, we don't know for sure about Edwin. He may have been off the base. Let's wait until we hear more, okay?" A lump began in her throat as she watched Alice shake her head. For a brief moment, she thought of Adam. She wondered how she would have felt if Adam had lived to be a soldier.

At 10 o'clock, the phone in Alice's room rang. She cringed and huddled into the sofa cushions. Mr. Alden took her hand. The phone rang again. Madelene walked to Alice's desk. The operator's voice crackled over static, but Madelene could understand the word "Hawaii." Madelene's heart stopped for a moment. The operator repeated her request and Madelene accepted the charges.

A woman's voice, near hysteria, cried, "Mother? It's me, Rachel." Madelene was confused for a moment, thinking it to be a wrong number. Then she remembered that Edwin's wife's name was Rachel. Madelene bit her lip and closed her eyes. Her hand shook as she told the woman to wait a moment. She held the phone out to Alice.

Mr. Alden helped Alice from the sofa and she took the receiver. Tears were already running down Alice's face. Mr. Alden and Madelene stepped back, but their eyes never left her.

Mr. Alden grabbed Madelene's hand as they listened to the woman crying at the other end of the call. Alice clutched the edge of the desk with her free hand and whimpered, "No, no."

Tears welled in Madelene's eyes. She tightened her grip on Mr. Alden's hand as they waited.

Through her tears, Alice managed to ask, "And Louis? Is he all right?"

They could not hear Rachel's voice anymore, but they saw Alice nod.

"Okay, dear. I'll—I'll tell the rest of them. I'll talk to you soon...." Alice paused as Rachel said something else. Alice answered, "I know, dear. I know. Good bye." Alice dropped the phone and sunk into the desk chair, dropping her head into her hands. Her hands muffled the sound of her gasps and sobs.

Madelene glanced at Mr. Alden, who was looking back at her. What should they do now? Together, they edged forward to stand next to Alice and lay their hands on her shoulders.

Finally, Madelene spoke. "I'm so very sorry, Alice." The words caught on the lump in her throat and she felt tears spill over onto her cheeks.

"Alice, honey, we're all here for you, every one of us. If there's anything we can do...." Mr. Alden's voice trailed off.

Alice nodded, sobs shaking her body.

"Would you like us to call your other children?" Madelene offered.

"No. I'll do it," Alice's muffled voice sounded from the desk. "Would you leave me alone now, please?"

"Of course, honey," Mr. Alden said. "We'll be right downstairs if you need anything."

The announcer's voice and the radio static grated into the silence of the room. Madelene switched the radio off before they left.

Trudging back to her own room, Madelene remembered the Psalm she had been reading. Now it seemed to mean something different. The "violent man" had now become a race of men: the Japanese. The reality was still sinking in like a cold fog. The United States had been attacked. Their own men had been killed; their own territory violated.

Madelene looked out at the cold, gray sky and shivered. Nothing seemed safe now. Whatever Christmas joy had been in the air had dissolved into fear and anger.

She sunk to her knees, clasped her hands together and prayed: *Oh, Lord, what now? The world is not the same place anymore. We're all so frightened. Another nation has risen up against us and killed our people. Oh, Lord, help those like my friend Alice who are mourning their loved ones. Help Edwin's wife and son. Please place your hand upon them and strengthen them in the coming days. Please put an end to all of this. Please bring us peace.*

Tears ran down her face again as she lowered her hands to her lap. She looked around the quiet room and decided she didn't want to be alone after all. She rose and wiped her face, then headed toward the kitchen.

⌐ *Twenty Three* ⌐

They returned to work, but no one could muster real motivation for his or her job. Madelene, Brianna, and Steve left the radio playing all day, and the workers filed in on their lunch breaks to listen. Germany and Italy had declared war on the United States.

Steve kept a running total of the men who had volunteered to fight. He told Brianna and Madelene that he wasn't sure he could keep running the mill without the men. Brianna suggested hiring women to load two-by-four's into the trucks, make deliveries, or perform any of the "lighter" jobs. Steve chuckled and said she was "all wet."

Alice's daughter, Minna, had arrived and was staying in Alice's rooms. Madelene and Ida prepared supper each night. Ida began the biscuits and the meat, and Madelene prepared the vegetables and set the table when she returned from work. Ida agreed to help in the kitchen for as long as Alice needed her. She said she needed something to keep her busy in the evenings now that Fred would be gone.

As Madelene placed the supper plates on the table, she heard a familiar swishing sound. She turned to see Alice in the doorway. Madelene rushed to wrap her arms around her friend. Then, she stepped back and saw Alice's red, puffy eyes. Alice's usually neat clothing was rumpled. "Thank you for all your help, my dear," she said. "And thank you, Ida, for helping Madelene with the meals. Madelene, let's sit down for a moment."

Alice sat next to her and grasped her hands. "My dear, I've got to say good bye. There's a memorial planned for Edwin, but it's in California where Rachel's family lives. Rachel will settle down in San Diego after that." Her voice faded away, but she tightened her grip on Madelene's hands. She took a deep breath and continued, "And, well, I've decided to stay with my daughter-in-law and help her with my grandson. I—I'm not sure how long I'll be there, but I know that's where I'm needed right now."

"But what about—"

"This place? Well, Madelene, dear, don't you know? I said I couldn't run this place forever. I just didn't know it would come this soon. You know what to do. And I'll leave instructions. You'll be fine."

"But I already have a job. Steve and Brianna need me, especially now that we're at war. They're shorthanded at the mill."

Alice sighed. "Well, I can't tell you what to do with your life, but you're more than qualified to run this place. I'll be completely out of it. You can keep the profits for yourself and your little one."

Ida crossed the room to stand next to them. She rested her hand on the back of Madelene's chair. "I'm sorry, but I couldn't help overhearing. Madelene, I could help you. Maybe I could cook the meals. We could split the cleaning."

Alice smiled. "There you go, dear. Just as I had a helper, so shall you. What do you say?"

Madelene looked from Alice's red eyes to Ida's soft hazel ones. "I'm not sure…. May I think about it?"

"I'm leaving the day after tomorrow," Alice said. "Minna is helping me pack."

Madelene took a deep breath and said, "Then I'll let you know tomorrow."

Madelene sat in her room later that night thinking about Alice's offer. Steve and Brianna needed her. If she went to the mill, Ida could cook the meals. Then she herself could work on the books and clean when she got home.

But what about when her pregnancy was further along? Would she be able to do all of that without tiring? What about after the baby was born? She couldn't haul it out to the mill every day.

Maybe she could still take orders for the mill from the phone at the boardinghouse. That way she wouldn't have to be away from the baby.

She already knew that she wanted to run the boardinghouse, if only for Alice's sake, and with Ida's help, perhaps that was possible. She would miss Steve and Brianna, their easy bantering and their smiles. Steve's grin and his sawdust-covered hair flashed in her mind for an instant and she smiled back at it. But, now she knew what she had to do.

When she broke the news the next morning, Steve wished her well. He said he could find another order-taker since many more women would need a job in the coming months.

Two days later, Madelene stayed home and said good bye to Alice.

Mr. Alden had loaded Alice's suitcases into Minna's car earlier that morning, so she was ready to go. Minna, Alice, Ida and Madelene stood in a small circle on the walk in front of the boardinghouse as small snowflakes floated around them. Ida took Alice's hand and hugged her as they said good bye.

Madelene couldn't believe Alice was leaving, but she knew Alice's family had to come first. When Ida released Alice, Madelene rushed forward. She wrapped her arms around Alice's broad shoulders.

"You'll be all right," Alice said into Madelene's hair.

Madelene felt tears rising again as she nodded. "You be careful out in California, okay?"

Alice stepped back and held Madelene's face in her warm, fleshy hands. "Now, you take care of yourself and that little one, do you hear?"

Madelene nodded again and wiped the tears from the corners of her eyes.

"I left Rachel's address on the desk in my room. Write to me and let me know how you are. And let me know about the baby. Listen to me: Be strong. Be strong for me, for your little one, and for everyone you can. And whatever you decide to do about your mister, don't ever let him hurt you again. Mr. Alden will be here if you need him." Alice kissed Madelene on both cheeks. "Take care, my dear friend."

"Mom, it's time to go now," Minna said.

Alice hugged Madelene again before crossing behind the car to get into the passenger's side. Minna started the car and Alice waved as they drove away.

Madelene and Ida watched the car until it rounded Pine Street and disappeared from view. "Good bye, Alice. God speed," Madelene whispered.

Later that afternoon, Ida decided to go to the market to buy supplies. Mr. Alden was out. Mr. Rosemonde had left an hour earlier to go to the drug store and "run errands," which meant he might stop by the Woodside bar.

Alone in the house for the first time, Madelene wandered through the kitchen, the sitting room, and Alice's vacant room. She couldn't believe she was running this place now. What if she wasn't ready?

She walked back downstairs, trailing her palm on the railing. In the sitting room, she sank onto an old, cloth-covered chair. Well, baby, she said to her unborn child, it will be quite a different world when you get here. I hope we straighten things out before you're old enough to realize what a mess we've created.

Then, she heard heavy footsteps on the porch. Someone pounded on the door and she jumped.

She got up and cracked open the door to see who was there. The door flew open and crashed into the wall, sending her stumbling backward into the room.

Madelene gasped. Garvin stood swaying before her. His shirt was torn, his hair was disheveled, and he wore whiskey like a cologne. Blood trickled from his lips as he stood there grinning at her. "I heard you were runnin' the place now. Isn't that swell?"

"Go away." Her heart skittered in her chest.

"How 'bout some money for your old man, seein' as how you got dough now?" He stumbled toward her and she backed away until she felt the stair railing between her shoulder blades.

"Get out, Garvin. I don't have any money for you."

"Then, how 'bout a room?" He leaned in; his breath turned her stomach.

She turned her face away. "Not for you. Now get out."

"Ooh, didn' we get some moxie in the last few months? Then how 'bout I share your room? We are married, after all."

"Only when it's convenient for you. The rest of the time you want to be a bachelor, drinking and spending time with your women."

"'Cause my wife doesn't want me!"

"You don't even remember that I was the one who wanted to be married to you? Well, you should have thought about that before you hurt me. Now you want me? Now you love me? Well that's too bad!"

His fist shot up in a flash, but he held it in front of her face. She cringed. "The only person I ever loved was my son and you killed him."

"I did not kill our son!" She tried to blink back her tears. "Don't you realize I miss him every day of my life? Don't you know I would give my life in a second if it meant that his would be restored?"

"So, now that you've killed my son and ruined my life, what do you go and do? Why, you get a job at the mill. What did you do that for? Did you taunt me behind my back to my friends, to my boss?"

"Garvin, please, just go."

For a moment, he dropped his hand and turned away from her. She edged toward the open door, but he whipped around and grabbed her hair.

"Garvin, please let me go. Please, I'll—"

"Shut up!" He swung his free hand at her face.

"Please, Garvin! I'm begging you. Let go. Please."

"I said shut up!" He released her hair, and she crumpled to the floor; blinding white dots swirled in front of her eyes. She heard his jagged breathing above her.

As her vision cleared, she could see him swaying. She rose to her feet, tasting blood on her lips.

"But it doesn't really matter now anyway," he said, his voice calm. "'Cause I'm goin' to war. Gonna kill me some foreigners. Hey, maybe I'll even kill one of your family. What do you think of that?"

As she stood before him, all she could remember was Alice's voice saying, 'Be strong for yourself and your little one.' But she hadn't. Tears spilled over onto her cheeks and her vision of Garvin swam before her. 'Don't ever let him hurt you again,' Alice had said. But here it was, a few hours later, and he had struck her again. And she was crying. But, no more. He would never make her cry again.

"Good bye, wife." Garvin stumbled out to the porch.

No more. She used her fists to rub the tears from her eyes. He would never make her cry again. No more! The words roared within her like hot flames: NO MORE. She raced to the door and screamed, "I hope you never come back! I hope you die, do you hear me? I hope you die!" She slammed the door and threw the bolt.

Twenty Four

After that, her words of hatred screamed through her brain for many months. She couldn't believe she had said them. She was frightened by her rage, for she had meant what she said. The only thing she could think to do was pray. So Madelene prayed every day for herself and her child. She prayed for her country and for the world. When she read in Matthew to pray for your enemies, she even prayed for the Japanese and the Germans.

But the days grew weary. News of death and destruction became normal. The God she wanted answers from did not seem to exist. Instead, her father's God was taking out His punishment on the unbelievers, and the rest of the world was caught in it. What was that verse? "...Your Father which is in heaven...he maketh the sun to rise on the evil and on the good, and sendeth rain on the just and on the unjust...."

At Christmas, Madelene, Ida, and Mr. Rosemonde ate a small dinner together. Mr. Alden visited his sister in nearby Lancaster, and Steve and Brianna celebrated with their own family. Madelene had picked up the phone to call her father, but she could not think of the right words. Perhaps, she never would.

Rubber rationing began two days after Christmas. Old and "idle" tires were needed for the war effort. To reduce tire use, gas rationing followed. Soon rationing became a way of life.

As the anniversary of Adam's birthday grew near, Madelene could not bring herself to get out of bed. She cried out to God that she was sorry for her sins. She wondered why God had to punish Adam for her evil. Some part of her brain knew that wasn't true, but her heart could not let go of the notion. Ida tiptoed around her and spoke softly to her as the days of February passed.

But despite the changes in the world, life did remain the same in some respects. Steve found many women who needed work and he was able to keep the lumberyard running. Restaurants served hot meals, movies played on, and babies still entered the world.

Spring bloomed and Caroline was born. During the last week of May, 1942, Madelene rocked her new baby in her arms. She hadn't settled on a name until after Caroline was born. Then, there she was: a sweet baby with reddish-blond hair and a tiny, delicate chin. Madelene felt as if her own mother had been reborn. So her mother's name, Caroline, was the only name for this baby.

She wrote to Alice, who sent her congratulations and reassured Madelene that Rachel and little Louis were getting along much better.

A few weeks later, Madelene turned her attention to a certain area in the back yard. The government wanted citizens to plant "victory" gardens to help conserve food. The more Americans could produce for their own use, the more America could afford to send to the troops. At least this was something she could do to help the war effort.

So during the second week in June, Madelene placed the baby in Ida's care. Then Madelene donned her first pair of denim pants. She twisted a blue cotton scarf into a long string and tied it around her head to keep her hair out of her face. Then she headed outside to stare at a four-by-twelve-foot patch of grass. Carrots, radishes, lettuce, cucumbers, she nodded at the patch as she divided it up in her head.

After a couple of hours, Madelene had marked the borders of the garden and begun to dig out the sod. As took a break to stretch her back, a man's voice called from the back of the house, "So now you're a gardener, too? Will your talents never end?" Madelene smiled as she recognized Steve's voice.

He walked toward her and she noticed his eyes twinkling from his already tanned face. He slowed as he neared her. His eyes linked with hers.

The smile faded from Madelene's face, and she asked, "What's wrong? What are you staring at? I know, I look terrible, I've been digging...." Her voice dropped off as she tried to smooth her hair into place.

Steve shook his head and flashed a smile. "It's nothing. So you're out here making mud pies on this fine Saturday afternoon?"

"It's a victory garden. Well, at least it's going to be. Would you like some lemonade? It's actually more lemon than ade, but it's not bad. I'll just go inside and get another glass." She started for the house, puzzled by his look and the small fluttering in her heart when she caught his stare.

Steve caught her arm. "No, thank you, Madelene. I just came to see how you and the baby were doing."

"She's fine, Steve. We're both fine. I want to thank you for stopping by during the winter and after Caroline was born. I really liked the little sun dress you bought for her." She glanced up at him and wondered why he took such an interest in her welfare. She didn't need that kind of looking after anymore, not like when Alice was here.

Then she caught him staring at her again. He wrapped his fingers around hers and she looked at him. "Is there something wrong?"

Steve shook his head as he took his hand away. "I'm sorry for having bothered you, but I was wondering if you had room for a new boarder. There's a man working for me who just got into town. He's 4-F. Flat feet, he says. But we're glad to have him. Anyway, yesterday I found out he's been sleeping in the mill at night. Can you imagine? I had no idea he had no home." Steve shook his head. "So I thought of you. You have an empty room, don't you?"

"Of course. Actually, I should have moved my things to Alice's room in the attic, since that's where the official 'office' is, but somehow I couldn't bring myself to do it." Madelene wiped the sweat off her forehead with the back of her hand and asked, "What's his name?"

"Oh, I'm sorry. His name is John Williams. May I bring him over later today?"

"Certainly." She looked down at her denims now smudged with dirt. "But you'd better wait until after supper. Or better yet, why don't you come over for supper and bring John with you?"

"Sounds great. What time?"

"Is six o'clock all right? What does he like to eat? We'll try to make him feel at home as soon as possible."

"Well his favorite meal is—I mean, actually, I don't really know what he likes to eat. I haven't had lunch or anything with him yet." A grin flashed across his face.

Madelene drew her brows together. What was he up to? "Well, we'll think of something. Fried chicken and potatoes perhaps?"

"I'm sure he'll love it. See you at six." Steve kissed her on the cheek. Then he walked out of the yard, whistling.

Stunned, Madelene touched her cheek where his lips had been. Her fingers curled on the spot that had grown suddenly warmer than the rest of her face. What in the world....

Caroline's cries broke through her thoughts, and she realized it was time to feed her. Dinner at six o'clock. She had to tell Ida.

"Now let me get this straight," Ida said as she rolled dough for biscuits. "First he said the man's name is John Williams. He started to tell you what John's favorite meal was, but then he changed his mind and said he had no idea?"

"Don't you think that's rather odd?" It was five o'clock. Madelene tied a white apron around her dress as she finished telling Ida about Steve's strange behavior.

"Yes, it does. But I guess you'll have to wait another hour to figure out what's going on."

Madelene poured water into a pot for boiling potatoes. "John Williams. It even sounds like a made-up name, doesn't it?"

"I suppose. But so does John Smith, and there are plenty of those around."

"I guess you're right."

"Mr. Atwood has been a good friend to you, hasn't he?"

"Yes, he has. He gave me a job when I needed one. He brought a gift for Caroline. He checks on my welfare...."

"And he's over here at least once a week. Pretty devoted, don't you think?"

Madelene crossed the kitchen and bent over the vegetable bin. She picked up two potatoes and started to pick up a third when she dropped all of them back into the bin. She straightened and faced Ida. "And what do you mean by that?"

"Just that it seems he spends a little too much time over here for just being a Good Samaritan."

"Why that's ridiculous. He's just a friend, he's—"

"Stuck on you, if you ask me," Ida said, a tiny smile playing at her lips.

Madelene blushed and grinned. "Do you think so?"

Ida nodded.

"So I suppose you're dying to know if I feel the same, aren't you?"

"Naturally."

"He is handsome, isn't he? And intelligent. And funny. And so caring and kind. Ida, I've tried to tell myself that I'm married, that he's too old for me—he's forty-one, did you know? I didn't mean to feel anything for him." She sighed. "My father would have a fit if he knew. What am I going to do?"

"I don't have any answers for you, Madelene. I really don't. But I agree with you about Mr. Atwood's qualities. And when I think about what your husband has done, I can't help but wonder what would have happened if you had met Mr. Atwood first. But all the 'ifs' in the world don't matter because they're not what is."

"I'm married, and that's that."

"But on the other hand, your husband has caused you nothing but grief and pain. What good has he done?"

Madelene bit her bottom lip and looked down at the floor. "Ida, when he left for the war, I told him I wanted him to die. And that would just solve all my problems wouldn't it?" Tears sprang to her eyes. "What kind of person am I that I would actually wish someone were dead?"

"One who had reached her breaking point," Ida patted Madelene's arm.

"Hey, what time is supper?" Mr. Rosemonde called from the doorway. Ida waved him away. "Women." He shuffled back to his room.

Madelene sighed. "Thanks, Ida. But there's nothing I can do until Garvin comes back from the war."

At six o'clock, Ida put the biscuits and fried chicken on the table. Madelene had just finished setting the last place when she heard a car horn. Her heart fluttered in anticipation as she walked to the front door.

She saw Steve hop out of his 1934 Nash car. He stopped for a moment to grin at her, then he crossed to the passenger side. Why wasn't 'John' getting out of the car himself? Unless Steve brought a woman over. And for a second, the thought depressed her.

But as Steve opened the passenger door, Madelene glimpsed a familiar head of auburn hair. "Brianna! What are you doing here?" Brianna smiled and waved, then bounded across the lawn to stand before her. "Are you John?" Madelene laughed. The women hugged each other.

Behind them, Steve grunted as he hoisted two overstuffed suit-cases, an oval-shaped cosmetic case, and two hat boxes out of the car. As he stepped onto the porch, the hat boxes slipped from his grasp and tumbled down. The lid popped off one of the boxes, and a black felt hat tumbled out and wobbled upside down on the porch. "Brianna, when I asked you to bring along 'only the essentials,' did you honestly think these stupid hats were essential?" Steve leaned down to scoop up the hat.

"Yes, I did. I cannot live without these hats. You should see all the ones I left behind."

Madelene giggled and Steve groaned.

"Please come in and meet everyone," Madelene said. She directed Steve to place the luggage in the foyer until after supper. "Brianna— or is it John?"

Brianna chuckled. "When I said I needed my own place, Steve thought maybe I could live here. But he didn't think he could ask you directly because you might think he was too forward or something like that. So he worked up this little scheme like there was a man who was new in town. Seemed pretty dumb to me, when he could have let me call and ask you myself."

The group walked into the kitchen, and Madelene stared at Steve. He suddenly found his feet very interesting and she noticed that his neck had turned red. She assumed his face was the same color. She wanted to ask what was going on, but instead she introduced them to the boarders who now were standing in the kitchen.

"I've heard so much about you both," Ida said.

"Oh?" Brianna asked, her left brow arched.

"Let's eat already," Mr. Rosemonde said.

As they sat down, Ida asked, "Brianna, how long have you and your brother lived in Trennen?"

"My family lives just outside of town, on Mill Road. Steve came here with our mother when she married my father. It's a little confusing, actually…." Brianna's long, slender hand twirled a fork in her mashed potatoes while she told them about the Connor and Atwood families.

Madelene glanced at Steve across the table from her. He did not add to Brianna's account. He certainly had been acting strangely. Suddenly he looked back at her and their eyes locked. Then he lowered his eyes to concentrate on his dinner.

Mr. Alden asked Steve about the future of the mill now that the war had erupted. Soon everyone was talking about the war and rationing and who had been killed. Alice probably would have stopped the unpleasant conversation, but Madelene scarcely paid attention. All she could think about was Steve's strange behavior.

It had started at Thanksgiving, just before Pearl Harbor. She remembered how he had stared at her while they worked. Then, he had visited and brought a gift for Caroline. Next he stopped by to see if she needed anything. Now this odd 'mysterious boarder' story. Brianna was right; she could have called about the room herself. Was Steve really just a concerned ex-employer?

She had done nothing to encourage him. Or discourage him. If she allowed herself to think about him, she realized she looked forward to Steve's visits, his stares, his smile. Boy, was she in trouble.

After supper, Mr. Alden left to run errands and Mr. Rosemonde retired to his room to listen to "The Green Hornet." Madelene, Ida, Brianna, and Steve remained in the kitchen. Madelene began to clear the dishes, but Ida said, "I'll do that."

"I'll help," Brianna said.

"But I should show you to your room and help you get settled," Madelene protested.

"That's okay. I'm sure Ida can help me," Brianna said with a wink in Ida's direction.

"Of course. Madelene, why don't you show Steve how you've staked out the victory garden?"

"Ida, it's after eight thirty. It's practically dark."

"Nonsense. There's some light left. You can take a lantern."

"Come on, come on," Steve said and linked his arm with Madelene's. "I think they don't want us around here anymore."

Madelene shrugged and let Steve lead her outside into the cool evening air. The screen door creaked behind them. As they strolled into the yard, she could hear the crickets chirping.

Madelene peered into the blue-gray shadows and pointed to a spot that was a darker gray than the rest of the yard. "I guess that's the dirt patch. I'm thinking of planting radishes on this end, maybe the carrots after that...." Her voice faded off as she realized that pointing to a dirt patch in the dark was becoming ridiculous. "Steve, what's going on here?"

"Would you like to sit down? How about this big tree stump over here?" Steve released her arm, and they sat down together.

Steve took a deep breath, then let it out slowly. "Madelene, I couldn't help myself."

"Do you mean this 'John Williams' thing? Why did you concoct such a story? Didn't you know I'd be happy to have Brianna here?"

"I know, I just didn't want to impose. I didn't want you to think I was using Brianna in some way to...to make it even more convenient for me to be here. Oh, I'm not making any sense at all." Steve dropped his head into his hands. "I'm sorry. I hope you're not angry with me for having lied to you."

"Of course not. It was just a little fib anyway." Madelene nudged his shoulder with her own.

"I just thought that maybe you'd notice how often I was coming over here and that you might resent it."

"Once a week, according to Ida's calculations." She heard Steve groan and she grinned. "But I certainly don't resent it."

A dog barked next door. Fireflies dotted the darkness.

"See, Madelene, the thing is, I—Oh, I can't do it."

"What?" Madelene's voice dropped to a half-whisper. Her heart fluttered in her chest.

"I can't."

"What is it, Steve? Please tell me."

He sighed and shook his head. "It's impossible. It's all so impossible."

Madelene searched his eyes in the growing darkness. She waited while the fireflies beamed around them. Could it be possible? Could he really feel something for her?

Suddenly he reached over and touched her hand. "Ever since I bumped into you outside my office, I haven't been able to think about anyone else. You seemed so innocent, so frail. But as I got to know you, I realized you are strong. You lived through your husband's abuse, yet you can still treat other men kindly. You don't just cook meals and collect rent, you care about your boarders' welfare. You dig a victory garden to help your country. You amaze me."

Madelene trembled while Steve's words chimed through her like a song.

Then he used his free hand to cup her chin. "And I left out the most important part. You're beautiful." She shook her head. "Yes, you are. Your eyes are like a fawn's, your hair is so soft—Oh I sound like an idiot." He took a deep breath. "You see…the truth is…I love you, Madelene."

She was sure he was waiting for her to push him away. But his words still rang in her ears. She felt warmth curl itself around her. His eyes drew her to him. They leaned toward each other, and their lips brushed in a soft kiss.

Suddenly his hands caressed her face as he embraced her. Her arms circled his broad shoulders.

Then he broke away from her. "I'm sorry. I had no right to do that."

Her heart pounded in her ears and all she could feel was the warmth on her lips. "What do you mean?"

"Just that. I have no right to kiss you or tell you that I love you. I should have kept it to myself."

"But I kissed you back." She felt the warmth spread from her lips to her face. Her body felt like melting ice. The truth had been hidden under that ice the whole time she had known him. "I didn't want to admit it, even to myself. But the truth is, I love you too."

"But you're married to another man."

"Yes, one who screams at me, beats me, then says maybe he'll kill my family in the war. A man who brags about all the women he has been with. A man who says there is no God. What kind of a marriage is that?" Her voice grew stronger.

"A marriage is when the two of you work together for your future. A marriage is when you watch out for each other when you're together and pray for each other's safety when you're not. A marriage is everything I don't have." Madelene finished and blinked back tears.

Steve wrapped his arms around her. He smoothed her hair and said, "I shouldn't have told you. I'm sorry. I never wanted to make you cry. I'm so sorry, Madelene."

The softness of his shirt caressed her face. She felt safe. It wasn't right, but it felt that way. She wiped her eyes. "It's okay. It's just that you made me realize what I could have had. I didn't realize how different things could be. He never writes me, you know. He probably doesn't even know the address.

"Now I don't know what to do with my life. I want to be with you. But with Caroline and the war, everything is so uncertain. I can't make any decisions now."

"Then I'm willing to wait until after the war." Steve took her hand in his, and they stared into the darkness. "Then there's that other thing."

"What's that?"

"I'm twenty years older than you."

"Twenty-one. And I don't care."

They sat together in the dark until Madelene grew cold. Then they strolled back to the house. Ida and Brianna had cleaned the kitchen and moved Brianna's things to her room. The kitchen and sitting room stood empty.

"I'd better go," Steve said. They walked to the front door where he held her hands in his and kissed her. "I can't believe how lucky I am," he whispered into her ear.

"I love you," Madelene said.

Steve left, and Madelene leaned back on the door. She smiled. He said he loved her. He thought she was beautiful.

His eyes danced before her; his voice rang in her head. All of her senses seemed to come alive and swirl like a kaleidoscope. She felt the softness of his shirt; she tasted the slight saltiness of his lips; she smelled the sawdust lingering in his hair. *Oh, God, thank you for sending him!*

She crossed to the kitchen, turned out the lights, and danced upstairs to bed.

～ Twenty Five ～

Early the next morning, Madelene woke to Caroline's cries. She dragged herself from the bed calling, "Coming, baby, coming."

She padded to the cradle and lifted Caroline. She held the baby to her chest and smoothed her daughter's strawberry-blond hair. As she fed her, she noticed Caroline looking at her with what Madelene knew to be total trust. She prayed that she would never fail her as she did Adam. Caroline stared back at her with her father's eyes of electric blue. Everyone told her that all babies' eyes were blue at first, then they changed to their true color. But, Madelene was sure the color wouldn't change.

When Caroline finished feeding, Madelene changed her diaper and dressed her in a light, cotton, sleeveless jumper. Then, she dressed herself and they walked down to the dark kitchen.

Madelene frowned. Where was Ida? She always got up early to start breakfast.

Since there was no one to leave Caroline with, she turned around and went back upstairs. She got to Ida's door and rapped on it. She found Ida sick in bed with a cold.

Ida was supposed to watch Caroline that day while Madelene

went to the market. Now Miss Caroline would have to go shopping, too.

Later that morning, Madelene was writing a list for the market when Brianna came downstairs. She wore a tailored, emerald green suit. "How are you and Steve getting along," she asked.

"Do we have enough salt?" Madelene mumbled as she searched the cupboard.

"Madelene."

"I heard you. No, we don't have enough salt and I wouldn't know how we're getting along since I haven't seen him all week."

"Yes, but I know he calls you."

Madelene placed her pencil on the counter and folded her list in half. "And he tells you...about us?"

"No, of course not. My brother is the perfect gentleman. But I know he stays late at the office and waits until I'm gone and the doors are locked before he calls you. I see him through the windows."

"Brianna! You're a little spy."

"Can I help it if he shoos me out at five o'clock and picks up the phone while he's doing it? Can I help it if there are windows in the office and I happen to pass by them on my way home?"

"You're still a spy."

"Am not." Brianna stuck her tongue out and laughed.

Madelene smiled and shook her head as she grabbed her purse from the counter. "Is there anything you need from the market?"

Brianna dug into her jacket pocket and pulled out some money. "Would you buy a war bond for me while you're out? I think you can buy them at the school."

"Sure. I only wish I had some extra money so I could buy one too. I feel so helpless sometimes when I think about how much everyone else is doing for the war."

"That's okay; you do what you can—like the garden." Brianna paused. "Listen, I've got to get to work. I'm meeting Mr. Alden outside. See you for supper."

After hearing Brianna's heels click across the floor as she left the kitchen, Madelene turned to check on Caroline, who gurgled in her cradle. For several moments she listened to Caroline's "happy sounds" drifting into the warm air like music.

"Hello, baby," Madelene cooed. "Are you ready to go to the market with Mommy?" She picked up Caroline and walked to the front door. While balancing the baby on her hip with one hand, she opened the door with the other and squinted in the bright sunshine. Then she walked down the steps to where Caroline's dark blue carriage sat at the edge of the walk. She laid the baby in the carriage and pulled the cap up to shade her face.

As she walked down Pine Street past the whitewashed homes, she thought of Steve. She could still feel his hands on her face and his kiss. She blushed just thinking of him. He was so wonderful.

Madelene turned right onto Old Creek Road and glanced at the police station on her left—Garvin's part time home. Oh, if only she had waited to meet Steve.

At Main Street she turned left. Her father was walking toward her in front of the market entrance. She stopped as he approached her.

He looked the same to her. What would she say to him?

His eyes never left her face. Her hands grew clammy as they clutched the metal bar of the carriage. She had never called him after Caroline was born.

Then he stood before her. "You're looking well," he said.

"Thank you."

His gaze shifted down to the carriage.

"This is Caroline." She lowered the carriage cap. "Your grand-daughter. She's a little over two months old."

"Caroline," he said as he peered into the carriage. "I can see how she got the name." His voice wavered.

Was he about to cry?

He straightened and closed his eyes. Then he opened them, looked past her, and asked, "And your husband?"

"He's in the war."

He nodded. "Are you getting along all right?"

"Yes, fine. I'm still at the boardinghouse, but now I run it." His eyebrows lifted, but he did not look at her. He peered into the carriage again.

"She's a pretty baby."

Could he finally want his family back? "Would you like to hold her?"

"No." He glanced to his right. "I've got to go. I'm visiting someone at the clinic." He walked past her.

Madelene turned the carriage and called after him.

Daniel stiffened and stopped, but he did not turn around.

"You're welcome for supper any time," she called out.

He shook his head and rounded the corner out of sight.

Madelene bit her lip and blinked back tears. Oh, Father. Why does everything have to be so cold between us? Why won't you love me?

～ *Twenty Six* ～

On the last Saturday of that September, Madelene lay in a metal, green and white lawn chair in the yard while she read her Bible. Caroline slept in the carriage parked next to the lawn chair. The rest of the boarders were out, so Madelene decided to take advantage of the rare quiet.

She had been so busy with Caroline and running the boarding-house that she hadn't found time to read her Bible. But that after-noon, as the wind rustled the leaves above her, she sat down and opened the book.

She had left off somewhere toward the end of the book of Ephesians. As she began the fifth chapter, she crossed her legs in front of her and began to read aloud. "But fornication, and all uncleanness, or covetnousness, let it not be once named among you, as becometh saints; Neither filthiness, nor foolish talking, nor jest-ing, which are not convenient: but rather giving of thanks. For this ye know, that no whoremonger, nor unclean person, no covetous man, who is an idolater, hath any inheritance in the kingdom of Christ and of God."

What did that mean? She laid the book face down on her lap. Her father had called her unclean. He mentioned 'fornication' when he spoke of her relationship with Garvin. If she was unclean, then she didn't inherit the kingdom of God. But wasn't there another verse somewhere that said everyone had sinned and fallen short of the glory of God? If that was true, then who went to heaven?

She shook her head and continued reading. A few verses later she read, "And have no fellowship with the unfruitful works of darkness, but rather reprove them." Was this what her Father was doing? Was she the 'unfruitful works of darkness'?

She read on, then stopped short at these words: "Wives, submit yourselves unto your own husbands, as unto the Lord. For the husband is the head of the wife, even as Christ is the head of the church: and he is the saviour of the body. Therefore as the church is subject unto Christ, so let the wives be to their own husbands in every thing."

What? Submit to your husband in everything? She shook her head. She thought of the married couples she knew. Did Ruth do this? Had her mother submitted to her father? What about Ida?

Madelene hadn't known Ida very well until after Alice left. Ida never said much while Fred was around. It seemed as if she was content to submit to Fred. Why?

The pages of the Bible rustled in the wind. She read on. "Husbands, love your wives, even as Christ also loved the church, and gave himself for it…So ought men to love their wives as their own bodies. He that loveth his wife loveth himself. For no man ever yet hated his own flesh; but nourisheth and cherisheth it, even as the Lord the church: For we are members of his body, of his flesh, and of his bones. For this cause shall a man leave his father and mother, and shall be joined unto his wife, and they two shall be one flesh."

So God gave husbands a commandment as well. Madelene thought of Ida and Fred again. Maybe Ida was content to let Fred be the head of the family because Fred truly loved her. Anyone could see it.

And then there was Garvin. Was she still obligated to submit to him even when he hit her? She remembered Alice's words as she prayed above her in the clinic: 'Surely when you said wives should be submissive to their husbands you didn't mean this.' But what if He did?

She closed the Bible, shut her eyes, and rubbed her temples. *Surely not, Lord.*

She stretched out and drifted to sleep with images wavering just behind her eyelids. She heard Garvin screaming, Alice crying, and bombs exploding in a war far away. Then she was standing at the market holding out her ration book, but no one would take it. "Unclean, unclean," they chanted. All the faces looked like her father. She cried to him to take the ration tickets: She had a baby to care for. "Fornicator," he said to her. She cried and pointed to Caroline in the carriage, but he turned his back and disappeared. Then Caroline started crying. She bent to pick her up, but the carriage began to roll. She ran after it. Wait, she called after the carriage. Stop!

Caroline's cries continued. Then, Madelene realized she was dreaming, yet the cries were real. She bolted upright and the Bible tumbled to the ground.

"Shh. Mommy's here, baby." Madelene reached into the carriage and picked up Caroline. She could feel dampness in the diaper and she scolded herself for having fallen asleep.

After she changed the diaper, she walked back outside. She held Caroline in her lap and watched the baby's red-gold hair wave in the breeze. A memory of her mother flashed through her mind. When Madelene was a child and she needed warmth and comfort, her mother sang to her. Madelene smoothed Caroline's hair and kissed the top of her head.

She remembered her mother singing "Abide With Me" and she tried to remember the words. She couldn't, so she just hummed it. Caroline played with Madelene's hair and Madelene smiled. She rocked Caroline in her arms and hummed until she drifted to sleep again.

Placing the baby back into the carriage, Madelene bent to pick up the Bible. She brushed some dirt and grass from the cover and tried to smooth the pages. One section was folded over and slightly damp. She tried to bend the pages against the fold to straighten them, but the book of Matthew was hopelessly mangled.

She stared at the pages. Words in all capital letters stood out: "Ye have heard that it was said by them of old time, Thou Shalt Not

Commit Adultery; but I say to you, That whosoever looketh on a woman to lust after her hath committed adultery with her already in his heart…. It hath been said, Whosoever Shall Put Away His Wife, Let Him Give Her a Letter of Divorcement; But I say to you, That whosoever shall put away his wife, saving for the cause of fornication, causeth her to commit adultery: and whosoever shall marry her that is divorced committeth adultery."

Oh, no. If she and Garvin got divorced, did that mean Steve would be an adulterer if he married her? Then she remembered the first verse she read, that even if a man looks lustfully at a married woman, he is an adulterer. Did that mean—

"Hey there, what are you doing?" Suddenly, Steve was behind her. She hadn't even heard the gate open. He bent down and kissed her on the cheek, but she gave him only a slight smile. The word of God rattled her.

"What's the matter?" Steve settled to the ground in front of her.

She took a deep breath and said, "I've been doing some reading and I'm worried. About us. About you."

"What about me? I'm fine."

"Not your physical health. Your spiritual health." Steve frowned at her, but she would not be put off. "Do you read the Bible, Steve? Do you know what it says in here?" She held the book out to him.

Steve stared at the Bible in her hand. "I don't read it as much as I should, I suppose. But, I know a lot about what it says, sure."

"Read this." She pointed to the passage she had just read. She watched his face as he read. His brows drew together and he shook his head.

"Okay, now I know what you're thinking, because I definitely look lustfully at you. But this was written over a thousand years ago. Don't you think things have changed since then? Don't you think God wants you to be happy?"

"Just because times have changed doesn't mean we can use a different Bible. Just because we all don't live as farmers and shepherds, just because we're a little more sophisticated with our airplanes, radios and cars doesn't mean that God's word doesn't apply anymore."

"Easy, Madelene. I just think that God would understand. He knows the kind of husband you have."

"But—"

"And I can't believe that what we have is wrong just because you're married. We love each other. And I for one have not been this happy in a long time."

Madelene could not look at him. "Did you read the part about if a man marries a divorced woman he also commits adultery? What if Garvin comes home, we get divorced, and then you marry me? Don't you see? In the eyes of God you'll be an adulterer. I can't live with that."

"Well, according to the other verse I'm already an adulterer. So what's the difference?" Steve pounded the ground at his side.

Madelene winced and he apologized. He knelt beside her chair and took her hands in his. "I love you, Madelene. I didn't set out to love you. I didn't purposefully become this 'adulterer' in the eyes of God. Is there any leniency in this God? Will He look kindly on those of us who—who just had bad timing? That's all it is, you know, bad timing. If I had met you earlier, then all of this would be moot. I think God wants us to be happy. And I'm happy with you."

She looked into his eyes and felt the warmth of his hands. She felt her objections melting. But a thin cord held her to the words in the Bible. She couldn't shake the feeling that they were doing something wrong. She turned her eyes away from him and said: "You just can't put pretty paper on our relationship, dress it up, and call it 'bad timing.' You can't twist it around and expect God to say, 'Okay, just this once.' You can't do it, Steve. It's adultery in the eyes of God, no matter what it looks like to us."

Steve dropped her hands and stood up. "What about the other parts of that book?"

Madelene looked up at him.

"The parts about love. The part about how we don't have to live under these laws anymore since Jesus already fulfilled them for us. I can't quote the book and verse, but I know it's there." He paced beside her as he spoke. "You're missing a big portion of this, Madelene. I swear to you, you're missing the biggest part."

"But you can't use one part and discard the rest. You can't take the Bible and mix and match its passages so they suit your life. You can't do that."

"I'm so sick of hearing what I can't do. You are not my judge, Madelene!"

Caroline wailed from her carriage and Madelene reached in to get her. She said over her shoulder, "Why don't you go home now."

Steve stormed from the back yard without another word.

"I don't know," she told Brianna later that evening, "Part of me wants to believe that God wants us to be happy. But, part of me also thinks that God wants us to be happy in the right way. Does that make any sense?" The rest of the boarders had long since gone to bed, and she and Brianna sipped coffee at the kitchen table. The house was quiet except for the clink of their cups and the chirping of the crickets.

Brianna wrapped her hands around the coffee cup and brought it to her face to inhale the aroma. She placed the cup back onto the saucer in front of her and sighed. "I love the smell of coffee, don't you?"

"Yes, it's very nice. But Brianna—"

"Just smelling it makes me happy. So does the smell and taste of a good red wine, don't you think?"

"Brianna, make your point."

"The Bible says drunkenness is evil, doesn't it? But it doesn't say not to drink wine. Jesus, Himself, drank wine at the wedding feast in Cana. We drink wine during communion. So, the Bible says adultery is also a sin, but it doesn't say you're not allowed to love anyone."

"That's different. When you're married, you're to remain faithful because you're one flesh. Loving someone else in that way only makes you an adulteress, regardless of whether you have a physical relationship. I can't have these feelings. I'm not allowed." Madelene bit her lip.

"For Pete's sake, Madelene, divorce the man! He's brought you nothing but pain, both emotional and physical. Why should you wait for a man like that, especially when you love someone like my brother? Why shouldn't you be happy for once? I don't understand you." Brianna leaned back in the chair and crossed her arms.

"It's in the Bible."

"What did you once tell me about Garvin? You said he bragged about the other women he was with. Now in all your reading, didn't you run across the passage about how you can divorce your spouse on the grounds of fornication? Well, what more proof do you need? Even the Bible says you can divorce him under that circumstance."

"I've read that. But I have no real proof that he had affairs with other women. What if he was only trying to hurt me by lying about it? What if he was faithful after all?"

Brianna reached across the table and grasped Madelene's hands. "In your heart, Madelene, do you really believe he was faithful to you?"

Madelene bit her lip again and could only shake her head.

She did not talk to Steve all day Sunday. She was afraid their relationship was sinking and she wasn't sure what she wanted anymore.

By late Monday morning, the everyday routine swept her up and she didn't have much time to think about her conversations with Steve and Brianna. Still, as she and Ida chopped vegetables for soup, Madelene's thoughts drifted. She could not bring herself to confide in Ida, so she let her go on about Fred's latest letter. In the back of her mind, she heard Ida recount Fred's opinions on C-rations and the slowness of the mail, but all the while, the words "adultery," "fornication," and "divorce him" swirled in her brain. What should she do? Her heart tossed back and forth between what was right and what made her happy. Why couldn't they be the same?

At one point, Steve called her to say she should read Romans 10:4, "For Christ is the end of the law for righteousness to everyone that believeth."

She knew he was telling her that they no longer had to fear disobedience to the old laws, since Christ died for mankind's sins. But, that would mean everything in the Old Testament was just a good story! She didn't know what to believe.

⌒ *Twenty Seven* ⌒

Madelene did not see Steve until the following Saturday. He arrived one evening while she and Ida were cleaning the supper dishes. They were discussing the proposed rationing of gasoline and nylon when they heard the front door open and close.

"Steve! I was afraid—that is, I thought maybe after last week I...."

He wrapped his big arms around her and kissed her. "I'm sorry I haven't called. It was a real mess at the mill this week. You wouldn't believe it. I meant to call you, but things got so busy." They walked into the kitchen and Steve nodded to Ida.

"Would you like some coffee, Steve?" Ida offered.

"No, thank you. I really need to speak to Madelene alone, if you don't mind."

Ida glanced at the countertop still piled with dirty dishes, then she looked back at Madelene.

"It's okay, Ida. I'll clean it later."

"And I'll help," Steve said.

Ida shrugged and untied her apron. She said good night and went upstairs.

Steve pulled out a chair at the kitchen table for Madelene. After they sat down, he took Madelene's hands in his and gazed at her.

"What is it, Steve? Has something happened?" Fear jabbed at her. What was he going to tell her?

"This is so hard to sort out; it's so difficult to figure out what to say. My week at work...it was terrible. Everything seemed to crash in on me at once. Two women quit. They were key people that I needed at critical stations. True, they were doing a job that men had done before, but they performed well. I don't know what I'm going to do. Some of the men heard that the steel mills in Allentown were really busy because of the war effort, so they quit to go up there. I've lost ten employees already." He sighed.

"Steve, that's terrible. You know, I could go back if you need me."

"No, your place is here with Caroline. Lord knows you're needed here. It's just...."

"What?"

"There's more. Some of the customers called this week. They canceled their orders because they weren't building anything. They're too busy working on other projects for the government." Steve sighed again and shook his head.

"Could you get a government contract? Surely they need lumber too."

He shook his head. "They need food. They need steel. They need grease for explosives. They need nylon for parachutes. They need money. But they don't really need lumber and they get what they do need from the big mills out in Oregon. They're not going to bother with some obscure mill in Pennsylvania."

Madelene squeezed Steve's hands a little tighter.

"And on top of all that, I was worried that you were angry with me. I thought after our 'discussion' last week that you might be pushing me away. Please say I'm wrong, Madelene. Please."

He thought she was angry with him? How awful that he had to worry about that while worrying about his business. Madelene wrapped her arms around him. "You are wrong, Steve Atwood. I love you and I want to help. Tell me what can I do."

He returned her embrace. Then he smoothed her hair with his left hand and said in her ear, "Just don't push me out of your life. Whatever happens between us, whatever happens in the world or this town, please don't make me stay away from you. I can't bear the thought of being without you."

"Oh, Steve." She kissed his cheek. He placed both of his hands alongside her face and kissed her lips. As she sank into his embrace, Madelene forgot where she was. She forgot all about the war and the rationing and that she already had a husband.

~ *Twenty Nine* ~

When summer ended, the howling winds and icy rain followed. The red and gold leaves blew off the trees as fast as they turned color on the branches. Before Madelene knew it, November had arrived. She had not heard from Garvin. But Ida received a letter from Fred every other week.

Gasoline rationing began that year, so none of the boarders planned to travel to their relatives' homes for the coming holiday. On a stormy Monday morning during the third week in November, Ida and Madelene discussed plans for Thanksgiving dinner.

"Could we get a turkey?" Ida asked.

"I'm not sure, but if we can't, maybe a ham would be okay."

"We could still have yams, but without the sugar they won't taste as good."

"And coffee is out." Coffee rationing had just begun, and Madelene missed her morning cup.

The two women stood facing each other in the kitchen: Madelene with her hands in her apron pockets, and Ida with her arms folded in front of her. "It's going to be a little dismal, isn't it?" Madelene asked.

Ida sighed and nodded. Then, the wind roared and they looked up at the kitchen window. Rain slammed against the window, freezing as it landed. "Another storm. Just what we need," Ida said.

"A cup of coffee would be good right now, wouldn't it?"

While the women discussed dinner, Caroline played with her cloth dolls and teddy bears in a wooden playpen in the corner of the kitchen. One of the mill workers had given it to Steve when the family no longer needed it. Madelene remembered how Steve had beamed when he brought it to the door and presented it to her and "Miss Caroline."

"I think it's time for Miss Caroline to eat," Madelene said as she headed toward the playpen.

"I'll mix her cereal for you." Ida sprang into action.

Madelene's hands cupped Caroline's bottom when she picked her up, and the diaper was wet. "Thanks Ida, that will give me time to change her. Come on, little one." She kissed Caroline's cheek.

As she headed toward the stairs, the phone rang. Madelene stopped for a moment, but Ida said she would answer it. Madelene continued up the stairs.

After she reached the attic room and opened the door, she heard steps pounding behind her. Puzzled, she turned to see Ida running through the hallway below. "Madelene!" Ida's face was flushed, and her hazel eyes were wide. She ran up the steps to stand before Madelene at the attic doorway.

"What is it? Is everything all right?"

"It's Fred!" Ida gulped for air. "He's coming home!" She threw her arms around Madelene and Caroline, and sniffed back tears. "He's coming home."

"Oh, Ida, that's wonderful! Is he all right? Why is he coming home now?"

Ida stepped back and wiped her eyes. "He was in a battle somewhere in Algeria, but he'll be okay. He was shot in the knee and I guess he's in a lot of pain right now. He'll probably have a limp for the rest of his life, but other than that he'll be okay. Oh, Madelene, he's coming home!" Ida brought her hands to her mouth and wept.

Madelene placed her free arm around Ida's shoulders. "I guess we were wrong about Thanksgiving being dismal, weren't we?"

Ida nodded through her tears. "I don't care if we only eat beans as long as Fred is home." Together they walked into the attic room to make new plans for Thanksgiving dinner.

———— ⌒ ∽ ————

"And I give thanks to you, oh Lord, that you brought my husband home for Thanksgiving. Thank you for being with him during bad weather and the hardships of battle. Thank you for sustaining him and seeing him safely home."

Ida squeezed Madelene's left hand during their Thanksgiving prayer. Madelene, Ida, Fred, Mr. Alden, and Mr. Rosemonde sat around the kitchen table with their hands joined in prayer. Caroline sat in her high chair between Madelene and Mr. Alden. A small turkey graced the middle of the table, its golden brown-skin gleaming in the candlelight, while the aromas of turkey and baked bread surrounded them.

The only people missing were Steve and Brianna, who had gone to spend the day with their mother. They promised to stop by later for baked apple dessert.

When it was her turn to give thanks, Madelene prayed, "Dear Lord, thank you for Caroline. Thank you for my good friends, Steve and Brianna, and for all those here today. Thank you for bringing Fred home safe and sound. And Lord, please watch over our friend, Alice, who cannot be with us this year."

It hardly seemed like a year since Alice had left. Madelene received an occasional letter, but the mail service was limited. She gazed around the table and was filled with a sense of belonging and of peace. She closed her eyes again and said a silent prayer: *Thank you for my new family.*

Christmas blew in with bitter cold, and a storm that sculpted snow like sand dunes around the porch. Madelene and Ida trimmed a small tree with popcorn and a few wooden ornaments that had belonged to Ida's mother.

Madelene knitted a new sweater, hat, and mittens for Caroline. She also stuffed a stocking full of small toys she had found at the market. Mr. Alden bought a doll for Caroline. Even Mr. Rosemonde bought a small teddy bear. Fred and Ida purchased a small, wooden rocking horse and tied a big red ribbon around its neck. Caroline squealed in delight as she opened her gifts.

Steve stopped by late Christmas evening after Caroline had gone to bed. His arms were loaded with gifts for everyone at the boardinghouse. The others opened their presents from Steve, while they drank mugs of hot cider together. Around 10 p.m. they went to their rooms, allowing Steve and Madelene some privacy. Steve smiled at Madelene and took her hand.

They snuggled together on the small sofa. She felt his warmth beside her as she breathed in the scent of the evergreen.

"I got you a present," they said together, then laughed.

She retrieved a medium-sized box, tied with green ribbon, from under the tree. At the same time, Steve reached around the side of the sofa and pulled out a huge box wrapped in red poinsettia paper.

Madelene gasped. "The big one is for me? I thought surely it was something for Caroline." She handed him her gift and said, "You first."

Steve opened the box and smiled. "Another creation by the famous Madelene?" He placed a French accent on her name and grinned.

She giggled. "Try it on, so I'll know whether I made it the right size."

Steve pulled out a hand-knitted, forest-green cap with a matching scarf. "This is wonderful," he said. He wrapped the scarf around his neck and pulled the cap over his head. "It fits, too. Thank you, sweetheart. How long have you been working on this?"

"Since August. I noticed you never wear anything on your head when you go out, even on cold days like this. I didn't want you to get sick."

"Ah, always thinking of me." Steve kissed her. "Now you."

Madelene grinned and tore the paper. A hat box? She opened the box and reached in. Softness brushed her fingers. She pulled out a deep-blue, felt hat with a matching satin ribbon tied into a bow on the side. "Oh, Steve, it's so beautiful!" She ran her hands back and forth over the material.

"I figured a real lady should have a real lady's hat. I wanted to get you more, but things being as they are…." His voice trailed off as he studied her. "Do you like it?"

"It's the most beautiful thing anyone has ever given me," she said as she stroked the felt.

"But you don't seem…I mean, what's wrong?"

Madelene gave him a small smile. "When I got into trouble with Garvin and had to leave my father's house…. Well, I spent that first Christmas feeling so lonely. Alice barely knew me. She gave me knitting supplies for Christmas. And by last Christmas, Alice was gone. Ida and I were just getting to know each other. Mr. Alden gave me a small Christmas cake he'd purchased from the market. That was all I got. I just figured my life would always be that way, that I'd never fit in anywhere. And now, here's this beautiful hat and you are apologizing that it couldn't be more. You've given me so much. I belong somewhere. I belong with you." She reached for him then, and they clung to each other.

~ *Twenty Nine* ~

The new year of 1943 brought hope that the war would soon be over. Surely they couldn't go on fighting for another year. After all, the other nations had been fighting the war long before the United States entered it.

But hope paled during the winter weather that kept getting worse. Snow piled up around them. Sometimes Mr. Alden could not get his car out of its space on the street. Blackouts continued in an effort to keep the town safe from potential air strikes.

As winter plodded on, February brought another round of rationing. This time it was canned meats and fish. The rationing hurt many in Trennen because fresh meat became scarce in the winter and they relied on canned meat for their suppers. But, they made the best of it because it helped the war effort.

One day during the first week in March, Madelene heard a car pull up outside as she cleared lunch plates in the kitchen. Normally, her afternoons were quiet since everyone was working or "running errands," as Mr. Rosemonde called it.

Puzzled, she opened the front door and smiled when she spotted the Chevrolet truck from the mill. She swung the door wide when Steve got out. "What are you doing here?"

Her smile disappeared like a wisp of fog when she saw Steve's downcast eyes and slumped shoulders. He trudged toward her with his hands in his coat pockets. His hair, normally peppered with saw-dust, was clean.

"Steve? What's wrong?"

He sighed as he reached for her and wrapped his arms around her. "It's gone."

"What's gone?"

"The mill. My work. It's gone." Steve's head rested on her shoulders.

"What do you mean, it's gone? What happened?" Feeling him shiver, she added, "Let's go inside. It's still too cold out here."

After they walked indoors, he plopped onto the sofa. He slumped forward and dropped his head into his hands. Then he sighed again.

Madelene sat next to him and rubbed his back. She could think of nothing else to do while she watched him melt in front of her.

"Do you remember a few months ago when I said the orders weren't coming in like they used to?"

Madelene nodded, but the question didn't really require a response.

"I got only one order last month, none this month. We were sitting around staring at each other. I dreaded the moment I had to face the workers. You should have seen them, Madelene, especially the women. They knew it was coming, but they still cried when I told them. I felt like crying with them. They depend on their jobs to feed their children while their husbands fight overseas. One of them begged me—grabbed my hands in hers and begged me—to keep the mill open. Her husband was killed last November and she's the breadwinner now. I had to turn away." He hung his head still lower.

"And I didn't even mention the men. Some threw boards against the walls. Some walked out without a word. I gave them their last check and waited until they left. Then I just walked around staring at the conveyors, the saws, and the dust on the floor. After I locked up the mill, I went back to my office and all I could imagine was Brianna laughing at her typewriter and you scratching orders at the other desk. My life was there, Madelene. I took an abandoned mill and rebuilt it with my own money. I hired everyone there. I bought most of the equipment. It's not fair!" Steve bolted from the sofa and began pacing.

"Steve, I'm so sorry. What will you do? Is there anything I can do?"

"Nothing. No one can do anything. My business is gone; my life is ruined. I don't know how to do anything else. What will I do, become a waiter? Can you see me doing that? How will I pay for my house? How can I help my mother when I don't have any money? What am I going to do?" He stopped pacing and turned to face her. His wide eyes flashed before her. He held out his arms as if to say, 'Look at me. What will happen now?'

Madelene couldn't bear it any longer and she rushed into his arms. "I'm so sorry," she repeated as she laid her head against his chest. His arms closed around her and they stood together for several minutes. Then, she took his hand and led him back to the sofa.

"First, you can sell the equipment," she said. "That will be good for a few dollars at least, right?"

"Who can afford to buy it?"

"Someone can. Besides, even if you have to reduce the price, you'll still get some money to live on. Second, we'll try to find another job for you. Not a waiter, though, since you seem to have such disdain for it." He smiled slightly at that, and she smiled back. "Something manly," she added and earned another small smile from him.

"And most important of all, that mill was not your life. Yes, it was a business you started. It was a place you went every day and made money, sure. But it was not your life. Your life is your mother, Brianna, and your friends. That's what is most important, not some place you go to earn money."

"You forgot yourself," Steve said as he embraced her. "You're my life, too."

Mr. Alden came home late that night. He had left his car at the Woodside and stumbled home on foot. Madelene had never seen him drunk before. He mumbled some of the same concerns about his life, but Madelene could not talk to him for long. He passed out on the sofa in the middle of a sentence. She shook her head and called for someone to help.

Fred and Ida had been standing in the kitchen and heard most of it. They helped Madelene remove Mr. Alden's shoes and coat. Fred picked up his feet, and Madelene adjusted his head until he lay on the sofa. Ida fetched a blanket and covered him. They shook their heads. It seemed as if an old friend had died.

A few days later, Mr. Alden left for Allentown when he heard about a job opening there. As he and Madelene stood on the front porch, a cold wind whipped around them. Madelene shivered even though she wore a coat. Mr. Alden grasped her shoulders and said, "You know, Madelene, I never had children. But if I had, I would have liked to have had a daughter just like you." He smiled at her reddening cheeks.

"Thank you, Mr. Alden."

"Marshall, please. A year ago I would have worried about leaving you, but not now. You've grown into a strong, capable young woman. Take care of yourself and that beautiful daughter of yours. I'll write when I can." He squeezed her arms and kissed her cheek.

"Good bye, Marshall. Be good to yourself." Madelene hugged him.

He smiled again and patted her cheek. Then he picked up his suitcase and said goodbye again. He waved as he drove away.

Madelene sighed. Mr. Alden had been a good friend to just about everyone he met. Now he was gone, another casualty of the mill. At least Steve had gotten another job. He was a deliveryman for the drug store on White Street. It wasn't like the mill, but at least he got a paycheck.

As Madelene stepped back inside and took off her coat, the phone rang.

She rushed into the kitchen to answer it. Steve's voice croaked a quick hello from the other end of the line. Something was wrong. "What is it, Steve? Aren't you at work?"

"They called me in to take a phone call." She heard his voice break. "My mother had a heart attack. She's—she's dead." Steve's voice broke off.

"Oh!" Madelene's free hand flew to her mouth and her stomach sunk within her. "Oh, Steve, I can't believe it."

"I—I don't know what to do. Go to the funeral parlor, I guess. Make arrangements—" His voice broke again, and Madelene could hear him crying. Her heart felt like it was breaking. She knew what it was like not to have a mother anymore.

After she hung up with Steve, she asked Ida to watch Caroline. Caroline was a bundle of energy now that she was walking, so Madelene promised not to be gone for long.

She walked to the drugstore, taking care to use Washington Street instead of Main Street so she wouldn't have to walk by her father's house.

But when she arrived at the drug store, they told her Steve had already taken the truck to the funeral parlor. She paused in front of the drug store as she realized she would have to pass by her father's house after all. She turned left and headed toward Main Street. When she got to the corner, she stopped for a moment and stared at the house.

How odd that a place she once lived in could seem so foreign to her. The paint was peeling off the front porch. The screen door was crooked. Dead stalks stood where her garden used to be. Then she thought she saw her father's face in the window staring straight at her. She looked away and hurried down Main Street to the funeral parlor.

As she walked inside, memories of Adam's funeral rushed into her mind. She saw his tiny body lying there with his black hair stark against the white blankets. She heard Ruth crying and Alice's soothing voice. Her knees weakened. She felt herself trembling and thought she might faint.

Then she saw Steve and Brianna rounding the corner. She held out her arms for both of them as she tried to push away her own grief. She had to be the one with the soothing voice now. The three of them hugged and cried together in the quiet hallway.

～ Thirty ～

Madelene remained at Steve's side throughout the next several weeks. At first, she must have heard a hundred stories of what his mother did when he was little. She couldn't help but wonder what it would have been like to remember hundreds of things about her own mother.

Over time, however, Steve became more and more withdrawn. She figured it was his way of getting past his grief.

One evening in late April, they sat together on the tree stump in the back yard. She had been telling him about how Caroline had played that day, pretending to be a mother to her baby doll. She chuckled, but then she noticed Steve staring out across the lawn. "What is it, Steve? You haven't heard a word I've said."

"Huh? Oh, I'm sorry, Madelene. I guess I've just got a lot on my mind lately." He ran his hands through his hair, tilted his head back, and sighed.

"Do you want to talk about her?"

"Mother? No, not really. I guess you've heard all the stories anyway."

"Is something else bothering you?"

"It's nothing, really. I'll get over it." Steve looked away from her and stared at the beginning of that year's garden.

"Tell me. Whatever it is, I want to know."

"It's stupid. It's just that—I miss the mill. This job is okay. It keeps food on my table. But it's not the mill. I miss the sound of the saws and the smell of the woods on a warm spring day." He chuckled. "I even miss not having to brush sawdust out of my hair at the end of the day. See, I told you it was stupid."

"No, it's not." She took his hand in hers. "You built up that mill from nothing but a shell. It was part of you. Just give it more time. You've only had this job for what—a month or so? You had the mill for years. You can't expect to love this job right away."

"That's just it, Madelene, I don't love this job. And I loved the mill right from the start. I remember building that office. I remember staying up late at night wondering if I could pay the three men who were working for me. I remember pricing cords of wood. I remember my first customer. It was so hard, but I loved every minute. Delivering medication to Dr. Dallan is probably more righteous, but I don't really like driving around all day. This job just isn't for me."

Madelene sighed and patted his back. "Well, no one says you can't look for another job."

"I think I'm better suited to the mill. Any mill."

"There, um, there aren't any more mills here. Not even in Lancaster." Madelene bit her lip, fearing what he would say next.

"Well, I, um, I called around and got the names and addresses of some of the big mills in Oregon. I'm thinking about going out there. It would be a chance for me to get back to doing what I love. Even if all they need is someone to saw trees, that would be better than driving a truck all day." He turned to face her, and his eyes locked onto hers.

She jerked her hand away from his and folded her arms in front of her. "Fred drove truck for you. Fred drives the school bus now. What's wrong with driving all day?" How could he leave? How could he?

"Madelene, it's just that—"

"I get it, all right? You love the mill. You've probably got sawdust in your veins. But your life is here. How could you even think about

160

leaving Brianna or me? Make this job work, Steve. If not this one, then get another, but get one here." Madelene started to cry.

"You don't understand, Madelene."

"I understand. You're thinking more of yourself than your family or me."

"If you'd let me finish…I want you to come with me."

Madelene stared open-mouthed at him.

"Come with me, Madelene. Pack your things so you and Caroline can come with me. We'll have a great life together. I hear the west is beautiful. Maybe we could live near the ocean. Wouldn't that be exciting?"

"Leave here?" Was he proposing? "I can't go with you, Steve. I'm still married. What if he comes home?"

"Yes, what if he does? He'll probably beat you again. He might, God forbid, abuse Caroline too. Have you ever thought of that? Some time in the army isn't going to change him. Wouldn't it be better if you weren't even here when he gets home? You wouldn't ever have to face him again. We could be together without having to worry who's around the corner. Come with me, Madelene."

She shook her head. "I want to know if he's dead or alive. And if he's alive, then maybe I'll think about getting away from him. But, legally. Then we can be married." Madelene paused for a moment before asking in a small voice, "You still want to marry me, don't you?"

"Oh, of course I do. I've never changed my mind about that. I love you so much, Madelene. But, if it means getting you away from that man, then I'm willing to live with you without a legal marriage. I'm afraid of what will happen if he comes back and I'm not here to protect you."

"What are you saying? There are so many things wrong with what you just said, Steve. I can't believe you really heard yourself. First of all, living together without a legal marriage is a sin, especially since I'm already married. Haven't you heard anything in church? Second, I don't need anyone to protect me anymore. I'm not the little girl who came to you asking for a job a year and a half ago. And third, the real reason you want me to come with you is for yourself. Admit that, at least."

Steve shook his head, but he was grinning. He held up his hands in surrender and said, "Okay, I guess I am selfish when it comes to you. No court would hold that against me."

"Will you reconsider moving, just for now? Wait until he comes back. I'll think about divorcing him then, and we can be together after that. Just please stay here with me."

"Now who's being selfish?" They smiled at each other. "Okay. I'll stay until he comes home. And I'll make sure he doesn't harm you."

"I said—"

"I know what you said. I'll be around anyway, for my own peace of mind." He reached for her and they held on to each other as the warm evening enveloped them.

Before Madelene knew it, Caroline turned one year old. Madelene held a small party, complete with pointy party hats and a very small cake she was able to make by saving her sugar rations. Only Fred and Ida, and Steve and Brianna attended, but there was enough laughter for 20 people.

Caroline sat on the floor to open gifts, her chubby legs sticking out like two thick branches of a tree. She tore open her presents, her blue eyes dancing as she unwrapped each new treasure.

Madelene laughed as Caroline played in the cake and rubbed it all over her face. The whole group laughed when Steve strapped one of the tiny party hats on his big head. They were still laughing when Caroline got up from the floor and ran to Steve, squashing wrapping paper and bows in her path. "What is it, honey?" Steve asked. "Do you like my funny hat?"

Caroline giggled and said, "Da-da."

The entire room fell silent as all eyes turned to Madelene. They looked away as the smile faded from Steve's face. "No, honey, I'm not...you see...." He looked up at Madelene.

"I'll see about cleaning up," Ida said. "Fred, will you help me in the kitchen?" The two of them exited the room.

"I, um, I'll just be in there too." Brianna pointed after Ida and Fred.

Madelene watched them go, then she turned to Caroline with

outstretched arms. "Come sit here beside Mommy for a minute, Caroline. I've got something to tell you."

Caroline grinned at Steve again before bounding over to sit on the sofa.

Madelene stroked her daughter's red-gold hair and began, "I know you like Steve very much. We all do." She flashed him a quick grin. "But Steve is just a good friend. Your daddy is away at war." Caroline played with a toy bracelet on her arm and fidgeted.

At war. What did a one-year old know of war? With any luck, she would never know of it. Madelene took a deep breath and tried again. "Your daddy had to go away for a while. I know you've never met him, but he'll be home someday. I'm sure he'll be so glad to know you, and he'll love you as much as I do. As much as Steve does. But Steve is only our friend, okay? Do you understand?"

Caroline looked into her mother's eyes and nodded.

"Then give me a kiss."

Caroline leaned forward and touched her wet lips to Madelene's. She grinned and hopped off the sofa. She ran to Steve, threw her arms around him and smiled. "Da-da," she repeated.

Steve looked at her over Caroline's head. Now what?

Later, Steve pulled Madelene into the kitchen. They walked to the far end of the room near the back door.

"What is it?" Madelene asked.

He sighed and bowed his head. "I wasn't going to tell you this until later, but in light of what happened in there, I guess I'd better tell you now." He took a deep breath. "I want you to know that I did not call these people. They called me."

"What people?" Her heart felt like it had just stopped.

"There's a lumber mill in Oregon. Their manager died a few weeks ago and they need someone now. Their orders are coming in faster than they can keep up with them."

"How did they get your name?"

"Like I said, I didn't call them. One of my customers knew the old manager. When he heard they needed someone, he remembered me. They called me a couple of days after that. I didn't know how to tell you."

"Tell me what? That you're leaving? How long have you known about this other job anyway?" Her heart was beating again, but it thudded against her rib cage.

"I found out about a week ago."

"What?"

"I'm sorry to have waited this long. I wasn't sure what to do, you see. I thought I'd figure something out that would benefit both of us. I don't know. I didn't know what to do, and I didn't know how to tell you."

"You're going, aren't you?"

"Madelene, you know how unhappy I've been with my job. And this job is practically what I was doing before, except that I won't own the place. I've been so torn about this. You know the only reason I've stayed is because of you." He took her hands in his.

She wrenched her hands away. "So I've held you back, is that it? Was it so wrong for me to want you to stay here? Go ahead then, if this is what you want. Heaven knows I wouldn't want to keep you from your precious trees!" She turned her back to him, feeling tears welling in her eyes.

"Madelene, please—" Steve grabbed her shoulders, but she shook him off. "Don't you see? Caroline made my mind up for me tonight. When she called me Daddy, I knew I should go. We can't go on like this. She already thinks I'm her father. God knows I wish I were. But I'm not and she's too young to know the difference."

Madelene bit her lip as tears coursed down her cheeks. Deep down, she knew he was right. Having Caroline think of Steve as her father just wasn't right. And how could they stop that if he was the man she always saw her mother with? Then when Garvin came home, wouldn't that just confuse her more?

"Don't you see, Madelene? My being here is just not good for Caroline." He eased up behind her and wrapped his arms around her shoulders.

She sniffed back tears. "Don't go."

He caressed her shoulders and murmured, "I love you. Don't you realize how hard this has been? It's a choice I didn't want to make."

"Then don't make it."

"I'll call when I can. I'll write as often as I can. And when you decide about Garvin, call me. I'll come and get you."

She nodded. Why did she ever get mixed up with Garvin? Why? And if she didn't have Caroline to think of now, things might be easier. For one fleeting moment, she resented Caroline. But, no, somehow she'd get through this. She had to do what was best for Caroline and if that wasn't what was best for her, then so be it. She sighed and turned to face Steve. "When are you leaving?"

"Friday." He took her face in his hands and kissed her. "I don't want to go."

"I know." Then despite the quivering in her heart and the voice that wanted to shout at him to stay, she added, "It will be better for Caroline this way and it will be good for your career. I shouldn't have made you stay in the first place. I'm sorry for that. I just wish—well, you know what I wish."

On Friday afternoon, a taxicab from Lancaster pulled up to the boardinghouse. Steve got out, told the driver to wait, then headed for the porch. Madelene bit her lip and felt tears rising as she watched him from the window. He rushed in, and seeing no one else in the sitting room, he folded his arms around Madelene and kissed her.

"Come with me," he whispered in her ear.

Tears rolled down her cheeks as she shook her head no. "Caroline—Caroline has the right...." She couldn't say the rest.

He closed his eyes and nodded. "I know."

They held each other tightly with seemingly nothing more to say. Yet, they had everything to say. Stay here, she wanted to plead. Don't leave me.

"Is Caroline here? I thought I might say good bye."

Madelene shook her head. "Ida took her out for the afternoon."

Steve sighed. "I can't bear this, Madelene. Please, please come with me."

Madelene looked up into his eyes and felt as if she could see right through to his heart. She bit her lip and shook her head. "I can't." Tears flowed again, but this time she wiped them away. "As soon as I hear anything from Garvin, I'll let you know. If he's—dead, I'll pack my things as soon as I hear. I swear it. If he comes home, I'll

165

have to see how it goes. Maybe the war will change him."

"For Caroline's sake, I hope you're right. But I don't think anything can change a man like that."

"But you didn't see him with Adam." Madelene remembered the Garvin who held their son. "He tried to change for our son. Maybe when he sees Caroline, he'll try again for her."

Steve took her chin in his hands and tilted her head until he looked into her eyes. "Madelene, listen to me. I hope he becomes the husband and father he should have been in the first place. But if he doesn't, then please don't stay with him. Call me and I'll come back to get you."

"Oh, Steve."

"I mean it, Madelene. Don't ever let him hurt you again. If he hurts you, I swear I'll kill him." Tears welled in the corners of his eyes.

"Steve, don't ever say that. You're not capable of it."

"When it comes to your safety, yours and Caroline's, I wouldn't think twice."

"All right, enough. You know I wouldn't let anyone hurt Caroline. Besides, Ida and Fred will be here. Brianna is here. Mr. Rosemonde is in and out. I've got another couple coming to look at Mr. Alden's room. Please don't worry."

"I'll always worry," he said, taking her into his arms again. He kissed her, his left hand caressing the side of her face. "Madelene. I love you."

"I love you too," she whispered.

A few moments later, he said, "It's getting late. I have to get to the train station by five."

Madelene nodded.

"I don't want to leave you. Ever."

Madelene laid her hand on his shoulder. She wanted to cry out: Stay with me! Instead, she said, "Go. It's for the best."

He touched his lips to hers. "How can I leave? You're all that matters to me."

The driver honked the taxi's horn.

"Go," she said. "I'll be all right, I promise."

"Say good bye to Caroline for me."

"I will."

They kissed again, neither one bothering to wipe away their tears. The taxi driver honked the horn once more. "I love you," they said to each other in unison. Then he broke away from her and walked to the cab.

As the cab pulled away, Steve turned around in his seat and waved from the back window. Madelene held her hand up, watching the cab turn the corner onto Old Creek Road and disappear from her sight.

She closed her eyes against her tears, still feeling his hands on her face. What had she done? Oh Steve, come back! She sunk to the porch and sat on the first step. She hung her head and sobbed.

~ Thirty One ~

A few weeks later, Madelene sat on her porch steps and read Steve's first letter. He loved his job. He loved the beautiful woods in Oregon. He had rented a small house outside of Portland, complete with a room for her and Caroline. She smiled and then sighed; somehow she knew she would never go there. Life was too uncertain, both at home and overseas.

Before she knew it, almost two years had passed with no word from Garvin. Allied forces had increased their air bombing attacks against Germany. Mussolini had been stripped of his power, but Hitler marched on. Would he ever be stopped?

It was the beginning of 1945 and Madelene was tired. "I can hardly bring myself to open the newspaper or switch on the radio anymore," she told Ida. "But, if I don't try to keep up with this awful war, then I'll never know when it ends. If it ends."

Both women sighed. "What are you going to do with the victory garden?" Ida asked.

"Oh, Ida, have you seen the weeds in it? I'm afraid I didn't take very good care of it last summer. I don't seem to have the energy to start it up again."

"I know what you mean. And you've been quite busy with Caroline. Does she ever stop asking questions?"

Madelene grinned. "Only when she sleeps. Although, I think I heard her ask why the sky was blue during one of her naps. Every now and then, I wish Steve, or Garvin, or someone was around to be a father to her. She needs that."

"What about a grandfather?"

"My father? Ida, I've just about given up on him. It's been what now, five years? How can anyone cut someone out of their lives like that, especially someone they're supposed to love? I saw him in town at the market the other day. The lines on his face are deeper than the last time I saw him. He looked so much like he wanted to hug Caroline, but he just looked the other way."

"Did you tell Caroline who he was?"

"No. There was no sense in getting her hopes up about having a grandpa when he doesn't want that role for himself." She sighed. "I told her later that he was an old friend of mine. An old friend, can you believe it?"

"Madelene, I know in my heart that one day he'll change. He'll want to be a part of your life again. I'm not sure when, or even why I know, but I do know it." Silence followed for a few minutes. "Do you still hear from Steve?"

Madelene nodded. "We still write about our plans for the future. I'm just not sure we really have a future together. I'm not sure of anything anymore." Madelene remembered Steve's strong jaw and sawdust-covered hair, and she smiled in spite of her mood. After reading each letter, she would refold it and place it in the box with her blue felt hat. It was almost as if she kept her small world, hers and Steve's, in that box. She hid the box on the floor in the back of the wardrobe closet in her bedroom.

After putting Steve's latest letter away, Madelene stared around her attic room. She realized they would not hold her and Caroline, and Caroline's toys, much longer. She had been able to save money over the last several years, and since her neighbor had placed her house up for rent, Madelene had decided to rent it.

She and Caroline moved into the house in March of 1945. Madelene took a few things from the attic rooms of the boardinghouse, including Alice's desk. Then she rented the boardinghouse attic rooms to a young widow.

The new house was a one-and-a-half story bungalow. She showed it to Ida and Fred a few days after she moved in. Steps to the left of the front door led to her bedroom and a bathroom. Just past the steps, off the left corner of the livingroom, was a small downstairs bedroom that was Caroline's.

"I'm glad you rented the house furnished. It would have been rough trying to find a sofa, or even an endtable, without driving to Lancaster," Fred said. A dark brown sofa and a gold velour chair filled the living room opposite the stairs. A walnut end table accompanied the chair, and a free-standing lamp illuminated the sofa.

"There's not exactly a big department store in Trennen, is there?" Madelene agreed. "What do you think about placing Alice's desk next to the wall by the steps, over here?"

"That's fine," Fred said.

"Madelene, I love this library table. It's oak, isn't it?" Ida said. The four-foot wide table lined the wall opposite the front door. The table rose from two sturdy columns that sat on a pedestal. Madelene had perched the photograph of her mother on it, next to a small lamp.

They walked through the living room, to the right, and then through an arched doorway to the kitchen, which was laid out like the boardinghouse kitchen, but the opposite direction: the cupboards, sink, and cookstove were on the left wall. An ice box was in the far right corner and a sturdy pine table, with four accompanying chairs, sat in the open area near the doorway.

"Very nice," Fred said.

"Madelene, these curtains are lovely. You made these yourself?" Ida stood at the window and fingered the red and white material. The sun was shining through them, and rosy beams softened the stark black-and-white-checked linoleum at their feet.

"Yes, believe it or not. I finally convinced myself I could do more than just knit."

"Well, your home is very cozy. I really like it," Ida said.

They left soon after for a potluck at the church. Madelene wished them a happy day, then turned to unpacking more boxes.

Caroline napped in her room and Madelene hummed softly as she unwrapped each item. Except for Steve's absence, her life was nearly perfect.

~ Thirty Two ~

About a week after Caroline's third birthday, Madelene hung laundry on the clothesline while Caroline played in the back yard.

VE Day had brought an end to the war in Germany and, at last, days of hope were dawning. The war with Japan continued, but it felt like the end was near. Madelene didn't know where Garvin had been fighting, so she wasn't sure when he would come home. If he came home.

That particular day warmed to near summer-like conditions. Caroline yelled to her to "watch this!" Madelene dabbed sweat from her brow and smiled.

She had just grabbed the last dress in the laundry basket when she heard Ida calling from the front gate. Madelene told Caroline to stay in the yard.

Ida's dark hair escaped the bun on her head and blew into her wide eyes. "What is it, Ida? What's wrong? Is it Fred?"

"No, Madelene. Listen to me." Ida grasped Madelene's hands. "You had better come to the boardinghouse. Immediately."

"Ida, what is it? I can't leave Caroline, you know that."

Ida shook her head. "I'll watch Caroline." She took a deep breath and said, "Your husband is home."

"What?" Madelene felt as if the wind had been knocked out of her.

"He came to the boardinghouse looking for you. He didn't know you had moved."

"But...is he hurt?"

"He's been injured, yes, but he seems fine. And he's impatient to see you. You'd better get over there."

Madelene felt as if she might faint. "Would you?" she asked, glancing back at Caroline.

"Of course. I'll stay as long as you need me."

Madelene's legs wobbled as she walked to the boardinghouse. A thousand thoughts coursed through her. He was home. What would he be like? Had he changed? What would she do? He hadn't bothered to write the entire time he was gone, why did he need her now? What about Caroline? She didn't know the answers. She didn't know anything at all.

Her heart raced in her chest as she climbed the steps to the front door of the boardinghouse. Her hands shook as she turned the knob and walked inside.

Garvin sat on the sofa staring straight at the door. She gasped. A big white bandage covered his left eye, and his left arm rested in a sling. He stood up to meet her and flashed a crooked smile that revealed two missing teeth. But his black hair was combed, and his face was clean. His dark pants and double-breasted plaid shirt were pressed. A small olive green duffel bag lay on the floor next to him. His good eye sparkled when he saw her. "Madelene! I've missed you."

She stood motionless; her hands hung limp at her sides. "Garvin. I—I don't know what to say. When I didn't hear from you, I didn't know what to think." She reached out a leaden arm to point toward his head. "How's your eye? Will you be all right?"

Garvin did not answer. He gestured toward the sofa and asked her to sit down. But she crossed the room and sat in the chair next to the sofa instead.

"Fair enough," he said, as he lowered himself onto the sofa. "You look even more beautiful than when I left. How have you been?"

Madelene was surprised that she did not smell liquor, but aftershave, and that he asked about her first. How odd. "I'm fine now, but it was rough for a while. I run this boardinghouse now."

"And you live next door. I'm impressed." He stared at her. She could feel her face grow warm and her breath short. "You've changed. You seem more...grown up, I guess."

She bit her lip, then asked again, "What happened, Garvin? How did you get injured?"

"It's a long story."

"Tell me."

"Well, my company was going to seize a bridgehead near the Rhine River. My buddy Chuck and I were edging toward the bridge when, the next thing I know, there's this flash of light and a huge explosion. Took out half the tree next to me, along with Chuck. My left side was burned, and some shrapnel flew into my eye. I didn't even realize my eye was gone 'til the medics got there. I just thought the flash had blinded me. I don't know what they did with Chuck. I guess they shipped his body home."

"Garvin, that's terrible!"

"Well, I'm kind of surprised nothing happened to me before that. I wasn't exactly the model soldier." He shook his head and continued, "Luckily, the burns weren't bad. After they healed, I was discharged. I've been in the States for the last four or five weeks."

"Four or five...weeks? I don't understand. Why didn't you come home?"

He shook his head again. "I called my mother when I got to New York. She told me my brother Felan had been killed. She sounded as if she blamed me for it somehow. My father was there, shouting into the phone something about whether I had killed enough foreigners for him and Felan. He was drunk again, of course. I hung up. I knew I couldn't face them."

His words about killing some of her family flew into her head. Now, it might be a matter of fact. She gripped the arms of the chair as he continued.

"Of course, I thought about you, but I was sure you didn't want to see me. Especially after the way we left things. You remember." He looked at her then, his gaze searching hers.

She nodded and looked away.

"So, I stayed in New York for a while trying to figure out what to do. It was frustrating having nowhere to go. I drifted from one city block to another and everyone I met knew I'd been in the war. They bought me drinks and offered me jobs. I even accepted one as a waiter in a nightclub: all the drinks you want for free. Then one night, some uppity New York creep stiffs me for a tip. I'd had a few drinks and I'd had a terrible day. So I confronted him, told him if he was short on cash, maybe I'd settle for some time with his girlfriend in payment, you know?"

Madelene winced, certain she knew where the story was heading.

"Next thing I knew, wham! He jumped across the table and went for my throat. So we duked it out and I landed sideways on a chair. I heard something in my arm crack and that was it. I never did get a tip." He looked down at his left hand hanging from the sling, then he looked back at her.

"So, I wandered around for another week just thinking about everything. The thing was, the only time I got in trouble during the war was when we had a little R-and-R and I'd had a few. Then I was back in the States and got a busted arm all because I'd been drinking again and had a smart mouth. Then, I thought about some of our problems, yours and mine, and I realized that if I didn't drink, like when we had Adam, I did all right for myself."

"You still drank then."

"Only on weekends. The rest of the time I did pretty good." He sighed and said, "So I thought about you again, Madelene: your eyes, your shiny hair, your creamy skin. I tried to forget about you, but somehow you wouldn't leave me. I got home, saw lots of women, but you know what? Not one of them could match up to you. They were all so brassy and loud, with their bright red lipsticks and heavy perfumes. Some of them looked down their noses at me when I walked by. None were like you.

"Then I noticed that I was comparing every woman I met to you. And that's when I realized it." He was looking straight at her and searching her eyes.

"What?" she whispered.

"That as hard as I tried to fight it…it seems I love you after all."

"Oh, Garvin."

"It's always been you, Madelene. Always. I came home to make it up to you. If you'll have me, that is." He stood up and walked to her chair. He reached down to cup her chin in his right hand.

Her skin tingled under the roughness of his fingers and she remembered that same hand rolled into a fist as it crashed into her chin. She remembered the drunkenness, the promises. In the same whirlwind of thoughts she saw Steve's face in front of her. 'I'll wait for you. As soon as you find out one way or another,' he had said. Now she knew and she still didn't know what to do. She thought about Caroline. It was because of Caroline that she and Steve were apart at all. *Oh Lord, I don't know what to do.*

His hand grew warm beneath her chin as he caressed it, his thumb moving gently across her skin. "Will you still have me Madelene? We're still married."

She shrank from his fingers; her breathing was shallow. "I—I'm going to need a little more time, Garvin. I wasn't prepared for this."

He dropped his hand. "Fine. I understand." He looked around the room. "Is there somewhere we could go to talk privately?" He glanced at the stairway.

"This is fine; no one is here."

"Someone might come in. We're in the common area after all. What about that woman who let me in, Roth is it? Won't she be back soon?"

"No, she won't. Ida is very sensitive to everyone's feelings. She'll know we need to talk." Madelene looked down at her hands now folded in her lap. The Bible said to submit to your husband. Surely with the way Garvin is now, God would want them to try again. Especially for Caroline's sake. She took a deep breath and said, "There's an empty room upstairs."

He took her hand, and together they climbed the steps. They walked down the hall past Ida and Fred's room to Mr. Rosemonde's old room. Poor Mr. Rosemonde had passed away a month ago and she had just finished cleaning and repainting for a new renter.

"I remember this place like it was yesterday," he said as he gazed around the hallway.

Madelene nodded as she opened the door and motioned him inside. There was no furniture now, only a ladder propped up against the far wall, and heavy, yellowed curtains hanging over the windows.

As soon as she closed the door, Garvin spoke. "Madelene, I've missed you so much. I don't understand how I could have been such a fool. You've got to know I'm going to change. I'm going to be the kind of husband you never had. I owe you that much. Please, Madelene, give me another chance."

She leaned back against the door, her heart pounding like a loose shutter in a strong wind. "I don't know, Garvin. I want to believe you, I do. But you promised before."

"I know, I know. But I never realized why I was like that. It was the booze. And I'm not going to drink anymore, I swear it."

"It's been so long. So much has happened, Garvin, so much you don't realize." She should tell him about Caroline now.

"It doesn't matter. Nothing matters as long as you say you'll give me another chance. I'll change, I will. Madelene, please." He walked toward her.

"But Garvin, you don't understand." She could feel tears welling up as she thought about what she had to tell him.

"What can I do to make it up to you? I swear I'll do it. Anything," he whispered as he edged toward her.

"You won't drink anymore?"

He took her hand and shook his head no. He leaned in, placing a soft kiss on her lips.

"You'll get a job?"

He nodded and kissed her again. "Yes, Madelene."

"It will be different between us? You won't, you know…." Her breath quickened as he caressed her face and ran his fingers through her hair.

"I'll never do that again, I promise," he whispered. "It will be different. Yes, Madelene, yes."

Wives submit to your husbands; she heard the words again. She felt part of her melt as his hand moved down to caress her neck and shoulders.

"Say yes, Madelene."

Wives submit to your husbands. "Yes."

177

"Oh, Madelene, I love you," he said as he buried his face in her hair.

And then it was like it had been between them before she got pregnant with Adam. Except that it was different too. She was stronger now and he had said that he loved her.

"Show me your house," he said afterward.

She had been about to place her hand on the doorknob, but she drew it back as if burned. "Garvin, there's something important I've got to tell you."

He looked at her, his head tilted.

"I meant it when I said a lot had changed. There's more than one reason why I seem so different to you. Before you left for the war—"

The front door slammed and interrupted her speech. "Mommy!" Madelene's heart nearly stopped. She heard Ida trying to take Caroline back outside, but Caroline would have none of it. "Mommy, come here. I've got something to show you! I made a house in the sand! Mommy, where are you?"

"I didn't know anyone here had kids," Garvin said.

If it hadn't been for the panic in her heart, Madelene might have laughed.

"Mommeeee!" Caroline's voice squealed. Then Madelene heard her daughter's tiny feet on the stairs. Not now.

"So what did you want to tell me?"

Madelene bit her lip. "I wanted to tell you this slowly, Garvin, but it must be now. When you went to war, I was pregnant with your child. You have a three-year-old daughter named Caroline. And she's coming up the stairs right now."

"I what?!" Garvin's good eye widened. He stumbled backward and said, "How? We rarely…."

"Mommy! Where are you? Mommy?" Caroline's cries grew louder.

"But we did. One time in August, before I decided not to see you anymore. And Caroline was the result."

Ida's voice was right behind the door. "Shh! Caroline, your mommy will see you when she's finished with her errand. Come downstairs now."

"I want my mommy now!"

Garvin shot to the door, and Madelene jumped out of his way. He flung open the door and stared down at Caroline.

Caroline shrank back against Ida as she stared at the man in front of her. Then she saw her mother behind the strange man. "Mommy?"

The fear on her child's face broke her heart. She stepped in front of Garvin and stooped to place her arms around Caroline. "It's okay, honey. It's okay. Do you remember how you always ask about your daddy?"

Caroline nodded, but her eyes never left the man in front of her.

"Well, this is him. This man is your daddy. He's come home from the war just like I told you he would. Isn't that wonderful?" She glanced up at Garvin, willing him to say something to his daughter. But his frown deepened as he studied Caroline. She realized he was staring at her hair.

"Madelene, this child doesn't even look like me."

"Of course she does. Look at the shape of her face. Look at her eyes! Those are your eyes, Garvin."

"Well, who gave her that hair? It's not mine or yours."

"My mother had hair exactly like this. That's why I named her Caroline."

"For my gramma," Caroline added. Then she stepped away from Madelene and stood in front of Garvin. "Do you want to see my sand house, Daddy?"

"I'm not your daddy," Garvin said and looked away.

"Garvin!"

He pushed past the three of them and stormed down the stairs. Madelene flew after him. She heard Caroline trying to follow, but Ida was able to restrain her.

She caught up to him on the sidewalk. "What's the matter, Garvin? Why won't you believe me when I tell you she's your daughter?"

He whirled around to face her. His good eye was flashing. His face was flushed. "The only thing I believe is that you are some kind of tart. The minute your husband goes to war, you hook up with the first guy who looks at you. Who is he?"

"How can you say that?"

"The guy, the real father of that girl. Who is he?"

"Garvin, how can I make you understand? Caroline is your daughter. I was never with anyone but you, I swear it."

"Oh yeah? Well I've been gone over three and a half years, and this child looks older than that."

"For Pete's sake, Garvin, I was pregnant with your child before you left, I already told you that. Didn't you hear me? She was born five months after you left. She just turned three last week. Her eyes are exactly the same color as yours, and your eyes are not your every-day blue. Surely, you must notice that."

"All I notice," he began, his fist clenching in front of her, "is that her hair is not mine or yours. All I can come up with is that you are the biggest tramp I know. At least the women in New York knew what they were. They didn't go around pretending to be pious wives and mothers. Now, who is he?" His breathing turned raspy.

Madelene shrank from him. "Garvin, control yourself. You said it would be different now. You didn't lay any conditions on it. You didn't say things would be different if there were no children. You said you loved me. Well, listen with your heart when I tell you I was with no one else while you were gone. Count the months if you have to, Garvin. The child is yours."

"Get out of my way." He ran away from her down the street.

"Garvin, come back! How can I make you see…." Her voice faded into the wind as she watched him round the corner at Old Creek Road and disappear.

"Mommy?" Caroline ran from the porch and stood behind her. "Where did Daddy go?"

Madelene sighed. "Well, honey, I guess your daddy had to go into town awhile. He'll be back later." She patted Caroline's shoulders, then she took her hand to lead her home. She took a deep breath and said, "Now let's see that sand castle."

⟶ *Thirty Three* ⟵

Madelene was slicing carrots for supper later that evening when the phone rang. She placed the knife on the counter and answered the phone. It was Fred.

"Madelene, I don't want to alarm you, but I saw your husband in town. It looked like he had been in a fight, and he was heading this way. Do you want to come over here awhile?"

"No, Fred, thank you. But, could Caroline have supper with you and the other boarders tonight? I think he and I have some more talking to do."

"Sure, Madelene, if you think you'll be all right."

"I'll be fine, Fred, thanks. You don't have to protect me anymore."

She dropped the receiver into its cradle, her mind racing. If he had been fighting, then he must be drunk. She rushed into Caroline's room and gathered Caroline into her arms. Her hands shook as she carried Caroline next door.

When she stepped outside of the boardinghouse, she could see Garvin stumbling down the street.

She ran back to her house, slammed the door and locked it behind her. Her heart thudded in her chest.

"Madelene!" Garvin yelled from the sidewalk.

She stepped away from the door. "Calm down, Garvin, or I won't see you." She hoped she sounded more confident than she felt.

"Madelene, open this door!" He kicked at the door, but the lock held. The handle wrenched back and forth, then she heard his fists pounding on the door.

"If you don't calm down, I won't talk to you."

"Let me in! I didn't find him, but I swear you'll tell me who it was before I'm finished. Let me in!" He kicked the door again.

Madelene backed away until she stood in the arched doorway to the kitchen. She started to feel safe until she realized she forgot to lock the back door. As ran to the door, she heard him running toward the back of the house. She fumbled with the lock. He banged on the house when he rounded the corner. "Madelene, let me in now!"

She clicked the lock into place just as he reached the steps, but the upper half of the door was nothing but a window. Before she could step away, his red face exploded before her. His good eye was wild, and the bandage hung from the other revealing a jagged purple scar where his eye used to be.

She screamed and lurched away from the door, "Back away, Garvin, or I'll call the police."

He stepped back from the door, and she breathed a quick sigh.

Suddenly glass shattered around her, and a rock flew across the room nearly striking her in the chest. She screamed again and searched for something with which to defend herself. She saw his hand reaching in to unlock the door, then she glanced back at the counter. The knife was still there. She ran to the counter and grabbed it just as Garvin burst into the room.

He stormed toward her, but he stopped short when he saw the knife. The color drained from his face, but still he smiled. "You have changed, haven't you, wife? The old Madelen' would run an' hide or run to the neighbors. Well look at you now. Ready to fight violence with violence, are you? What does your Bible say about that? How does it go: 'an eye for an eye?'" He took one step forward while staring at her. "But as you can see, someone already beat you to it. Hey, maybe one of the Goddards took your revenge for you. But bein' with another man while I was gone was pretty good revenge, I'd say." He stepped forward until he stood in front of her.

She raised the knife. "Stay away."

"Or what? D'you really have it in you? Do you, Madelene?" In a flash his arm flew up, and he grabbed the hand that held the knife. "Pretty good for a one-armed man, isn't it?" He smiled at her then, his breath flooding her with the smell of whiskey. He twisted her wrist, and the knife clanged to the floor.

"You're hurting me."

"Well you hurt me too!"

"How could I possibly have hurt you?"

"Don't you see? After all I've been through—the war, the blood. Crumbled shells where buildings used to be. I come through all that and realize the only thing that means anything to me is you. I come home. I tell you I love you. But you already loved someone else. See, that hurt, Madelene." He let go of her wrist and leaned on the counter next to her.

She rubbed her wrist and eyed the knife now lying on the floor.

"I knew you couldn't do it," he said.

"Do what?"

"Kill me. I knew you couldn't do it. You love me too, don't you? I mean, today meant something upstairs in that room, didn't it?" The anger was gone from his face. "Look, maybe we should start over. Maybe you only did it once and the guy is gone anyway. Just tell me the truth, Madelene. Was that how it was? That's all I want to hear." He wiped the sweat from his face with the back of his hand.

But she knew he didn't want to hear the truth. He had already heard it and didn't believe it. Should she tell him what he wanted? Would that ease his mind? No. She would make him see the truth somehow.

She bit her lip. "Garvin, I cannot tell you something untrue just because you want to believe that's the way it was. Don't you remember that night several months after Adam died? You came upstairs and you were sober. You swore you would never hurt me again. But after you left, I realized you'd promised that before and beat me just the same. So I told Alice not to let you up. That was the day Caroline was conceived, Garvin. I have not been with anyone in that way since then, I swear it."

"Three years, Madelene. It's been three years since then. And you never—"

"Never."

"But surely—"

"Garvin, I said never. You must believe that."

Garvin sighed. "Her hair, Madelene. The child's hair is red or blonde or whatever. It's not black or brown like ours."

"Oh for Pete's sake, Garvin! Does every one of your brothers and sisters look exactly like your mother or father? Sometimes traits from an entire family show up in a child. Surely you've noticed that."

"I never really thought about it."

"Well, think about it now." She picked up the knife and ran it under the faucet. "I'm making supper. You can stay if you want."

"No thanks, I'm not hungry. I'll just lie down if that's okay."

"The sofa will do for tonight."

He shuffled toward the living room, but turned around again to face her. "I'm sorry, Madelen'. Tomorrow I'll quit drinkin' forever. I'll try to get to know your girl. Maybe you could tell me about her first three years. I'll do whatever you want."

"She's your girl too."

"Mmm." He turned away and she heard him collapse on the sofa. Before she finished cutting the carrots, he was snoring. Would he really stop drinking? What if he came after her again? Or Caroline? Her fingers tightened around the knife. No, she had to believe he would try. For Caroline's sake, she had to believe it.

~ *Thirty Four* ~

At seven the next morning, Madelene headed downstairs to make breakfast for the three of them. She stopped short when she saw him. Garvin wore a clean white shirt and dress trousers; his hair was combed and his face was washed. He looked at her, then down at the floor.

"I'm sorry about last night," he said.

"Garvin, I—"

"No, let me apologize. It was the booze again. I just needed to think, I guess, so I ended up at the bar. But no more, I swear." He held his hands out at his sides with his palms turned up. "See? I'm ready to look for a job. Heard of any?"

Madelene smiled in spite of herself. "No, not really. But come into the kitchen, and I'll make some breakfast."

"Maybe you could come with me."

"No, I have to get to the boardinghouse and help Ida prepare lunch. I'm lucky she prepares breakfast by herself so I can be here with Caroline. You'll do fine; I'm sure you'll find something."

Garvin wandered to the back door and traced his finger around the jagged hole in the glass. "When I get home I'll see about fixing this. You know, I don't even remember most of last night."

She turned her back to him and stared out of the window above the sink. How could he not remember? His words, his face, and his yelling still whirled in her brain.

"I do remember glass breaking though. And I seem to remember that I broke it, although I'm not sure why. Later you tried to convince me the girl is mine. Right? I remember that. Then I must have fallen asleep. Sorry." He shuffled to the table and thumped down on a chair. "Do you have any coffee?"

She poured him a cup and set it on the table. "I need sugar," he said.

"We drink it without sugar now because of the sugar rationing." She grabbed an iron skillet from the lower cupboard and continued, "Rubber, canned meat, even coffee was rationed. It's been difficult, but at least we help the troops."

Garvin snorted. "A lot of good it does." He searched his pockets.

"What do you mean? Didn't you get enough sugar or meat?"

"Enough? What's enough?" He patted his breast pocket once more and swore. He dropped his hands onto the table.

"What are you looking for?"

"Cigarettes. Do you have any?"

"You smoke too? No, I don't have any."

He got up and pushed his chair under the table. "Yes, I smoke too. Not as bad a vice as drinking though, is it?" He walked up behind her and kissed her neck.

She fought the impulse to shy away from his touch.

"I guess I'll get an early start and pick up some cigarettes along the way."

Then they heard a door click open. "Daddy! Daddy!" Caroline ran into the kitchen, her red-gold hair bouncing around her bright cheeks. She clutched a teddy bear in one hand and ran until she reached Garvin and clutched his legs.

Garvin looked down at Caroline and back at Madelene. His eyes pleaded with her for something to say, but she did not help him.

"Will you take me on the swings today, Daddy?" Caroline's muffled voice sounded from Garvin's pant leg.

Garvin pried her small hands away from his legs. "No, I have to go out today." He stepped away, but she ran behind him.

"Where are you going?" Caroline asked.

"Just out. To look for a job." Garvin took longer strides to the front door, but Caroline still followed him. Madelene walked to the kitchen doorway to watch.

"Can I go too?" Caroline asked.

"No."

"Will you take me on the swings later?"

Garvin opened the front door and stepped onto the porch.

"Daddy?" Caroline toddled to the threshold.

"Go back inside. I've got to go."

"Let me go too."

"I said no." Garvin raised his voice, then turned and ran from the house.

"Daddy?" Caroline started for the steps, but Madelene darted toward her and picked her up. Caroline flung her arms around her mother's neck and said, "Daddy yelled at me." Tears filled her eyes.

Madelene had to bite her lip to keep from crying herself. The least he could have done was to give her a small hug and a 'maybe later' response. What was the matter with him? She took Caroline back inside and helped her dress.

Later, in the boardinghouse kitchen, Madelene recounted the scene to Ida as they cleaned. Caroline played in the back yard with her dolls.

"Did he really yell at her? That's terrible."

"Well, he wasn't really yelling. But he was very short with her. You should have seen him, Ida, prying her little hands away. He barely looked at her, and all Caroline wanted was a little bit of her father's time."

"Poor thing."

Madelene rubbed baking soda on the countertop to clean it. "But, at least he's going out to find a job." She stopped scrubbing. "What if he doesn't get it?"

"Oh, he'll get a job, I don't think you have to worry about that."

"That's not what I meant. I was still thinking about him and Caroline. What if he doesn't learn how to love her? What if, after losing Adam and being in the war…what if he can't be a father?"

"I don't understand."

"I mean, what if losing Adam took all the fatherly instincts out of him? Not to mention that I don't think he feels she's his daughter anyway. Are we struggling hopelessly? Are we trying to create a family when it's beyond our capabilities?"

"Give it some time, Madelene. He just got back yesterday."

"No, Ida, he didn't. He's been back for five weeks. Is that a man who is ready to become a husband and father again?"

"But he was in the war, Madelene. Maybe he couldn't face civilian life again. Fred said it happens to some men."

"Fred came right home, didn't he?"

"But Fred is not Garvin."

"Lucky for you, Ida. You and Fred have a wonderful marriage. I just wish...." She turned back to her scrubbing with a sigh.

They were quiet for a few moments. Then Ida asked, "Do you hear any more from Steve?"

Madelene stopped cold. "No, not lately. He hasn't been writing much." It bothered her more than she let on to anyone. Now she had to write the letter she hoped she'd never have to write. How could she tell him?

They worked in silence for a few more minutes before Ida said, "Did you hear about the Fourth of July dance? It's at the school. Maybe you and Garvin and Caroline could join Fred and me. I think Brianna is going too."

"I don't know...." The thought of the three of them going out as a family should have thrilled her, but all she could think about was how she had wanted to go out with Steve and couldn't. It would have started the tongues wagging throughout Trennen. She hadn't gone to a social event in years.

"Come on. It's time you had some fun. Fred wants to do the Lindy. I told him I think he's crazy, especially on his bum leg, but he insists." Ida chuckled. "I'm hoping the band plays 'As Time Goes By.' That's more my style, I think. Will you go?"

Madelene smiled when she thought of Fred doing the Lindy. "I'll ask Garvin."

But Garvin trudged home that evening and slumped onto the sofa. She could tell it hadn't gone well, so she decided not to ask him.

Another week went by, but Garvin still hadn't found a job. She let him rest while she made dinner. Caroline stayed at the boarding-house and ate with Ida and Fred.

As she peeled potatoes, she heard him mumbling from the living room. She called out for him to speak up.

"I said I can't believe there's nothing out there. The only job they had was for a janitor at the school. But since it's almost summer, the job doesn't start for a couple of months. Besides, who wants to empty wastebaskets for a living?"

"You do, if that's the only job around." Madelene tried to hold back the words, but they came out anyway. She grimaced.

"There's another job I'm looking at tomorrow. Someone told me they needed a gardener at the cemetery. Good thing my arm is almost healed up." He paused. "Too bad the mill closed down. That was a decent job."

At Garvin's mention of the mill, Madelene froze. What would her life had been like if Steve were still here and was Garvin's boss as well? How could they have borne it? Perhaps it was best to change the subject.

"Ida tells me there's a Fourth of July dance. She asked if we wanted to go with them. What do you think?" That was pretty far away from the subject of the mill.

She heard Garvin get up and shuffle to the kitchen. "Yeah, I heard about that while I was in town today. You know I can't dance."

"It was just an idea."

"That doesn't mean I don't want to go," Garvin said as he moved in close beside her. "We should go out together, get to know each other again."

"You really want to go?" Madelene turned to face him and saw him smiling. He looked even more handsome when he was smiling, despite the simple black patch he now wore over his left eye.

"Sure. Just you and me, the way it used to be." He leaned in and kissed her cheek.

"I thought.... I mean, I had hoped we could take Caroline. She'd love the music and the dancing. There's supposed to be games for the kids too."

His smile vanished. "Don't you think we ought to be alone together? We've been apart for three years."

Madelene sighed. "And you have a daughter who doesn't know who you are. Shouldn't you spend some time with her?"

"Madelene, I just got back. Do you know what it's like to come home and find there's a whole other person who belongs to you, but you never knew she existed? I didn't have the luxury of getting to know her like you did. Give me some time. That's all I'm asking."

She supposed it would be difficult. "Okay. You and I will go. It's just that everyone is going, and I don't know who will watch Caroline."

"Oh. I didn't think about that."

"Maybe we shouldn't go."

"No, no, that's all right. We'll all go."

"Really?" Madelene reached out and hugged him. "Thanks, Garvin."

He grinned back at her. "That hug was worth it. What's for dinner?"

~ Thirty Five ~

Garvin got the gardener's job at the cemetery and he started the following weekend. The first few days on the job involved weeding and trimming trees.

Over the next several days, Madelene watched him with Caroline. Although he didn't snap at Caroline too often, he still walked away from her or managed to be in a different room when she wanted his attention. Madelene wasn't sure how to bring them closer.

On the following Saturday, Garvin went to work as usual, but by evening he had not returned. Madelene prayed he had not stopped at the bar on the way home.

She served dinner to Caroline, who was busy chatting about her day. Life was a never-ending adventure for a three-year old and Madelene never tired of hearing about it. She wished Garvin could feel the same. A nagging thought kept coming back to her: If Adam were still alive, then Garvin would be different. She remembered the way he had stared at Adam, and his words: "my son." If only Caroline had been a boy. Madelene pushed the thought away. There was no point in thinking about it.

Caroline "helped" her wash the dishes, then Madelene put her to bed. Later, Madelene sat on the sofa using only one light for reading. She was in the middle of the book of Hebrews when she heard Garvin's steps on the porch. She marked her place and laid the Bible on the sofa next to her.

Fearing the worst, she rose to meet him. He did not come in; but she heard a thump instead. She walked to the door and cracked it open.

Garvin sat on the porch with his feet on the steps. His head leaned against the post attached to the porch railing. She approached him, ready to run if he became violent. He must have heard her, because he started to speak. "I can't go back there, Madelene. I can't."

She sat down next to him on the porch. She couldn't smell any alcohol.

He shook his head and did not look at her. "I'm sorry I didn't come home for supper. I just kind of walked around a while thinking. I quit my job, Madelene. I had to."

"What happened?"

"It was the cemetery." Suddenly he looked up at her. The moonlight cast shadows over his face. "What was I thinking? Why did I take the job? How could I have forgotten him? I forgot my son." He crumpled before her.

A chill raced through her. She had been so happy that he had found a job, that she hadn't thought of where he would be working.

"I forgot about him, Madelene. Until suddenly I'm running the mower right over his grave. I'm standing right on his grave. My son lay beneath me and I didn't even—" He broke off with a sob and began to shake. "Don't make me go back there."

Oh, my Lord. Tears sprang to her eyes as she reached out and touched his shoulder. He leaned his head against her hand, the tears coursing down his cheeks. "I want my son back."

She had no words to comfort him. They sat together on the steps for several minutes. She heard him sniff back tears. "I wanted a drink so badly tonight. I walked past the Woodside, then I turned around and walked back. I stood there, watching them laughing. I wanted to laugh again, too. I wanted to drink until I couldn't remember anymore."

"Why didn't you?"

"I don't know. Guess I thought of my promise to you. But, I wanted a drink. I still do. What am I going to do?"

She shook her head. "You know, I think there's an Alcoholics Anonymous meeting at the school library. Maybe you could go."

"I'm not an alcoholic, Madelene. For God's sake, you know I can stop drinking whenever I want. Haven't I proven that to you since I've been back? I haven't had a drink in weeks. I didn't even have one tonight when God knows I could have used it. Don't say that to me again." Garvin pulled away from her.

"I just thought—"

"Well, don't."

She sighed as she rose and walked to the door. "Are you coming in?"

"Not just yet."

She closed the door behind her, turned out the light and went to bed.

～ *Thirty Six* ～

On Monday, Garvin looked for another job, but he came home rejected. He lay down on the sofa and didn't even get up for supper. After supper, Caroline's small feet slapped the floor as she toddled to her father.

"Daddy, guess what?"

Garvin did not respond, so Caroline persisted. "Daddy, guess what? Guess." She tugged on his shirt.

"Go away." Garvin wrenched his arm from her.

Caroline turned and ran into the kitchen, flinging herself at Madelene.

"Garvin, she's just a little girl. Can't you make an effort? What's the matter with you?" She hugged Caroline and dabbed at her tears. "Come on, sweetie. You can help mommy do the dishes, okay?"

As they brought the dishes to the sink, she heard Garvin get up. The door slammed shut behind him.

It was nearly midnight when he returned. She had fallen asleep on the sofa, but she woke up when she heard him stumble onto the porch. "Madlen? Madlen, come watch me!" She heard a loud thump. With a sick feeling deep in her stomach, she opened the door. He lay sprawled on the porch. He was trying to get up and swearing all the while at his own clumsiness. She figured if he was too drunk to stand up, then he was too drunk to hit her. She walked out and stuck her hands under his armpits to help him up. He staggered a few steps next to her, then he slumped against the wall.

"You couldn't hold out, could you?"

"Nope."

"Now will you admit you have a problem with alcohol?"

"Yeah, there's a problem, there is. Not enough of it." He stumbled sideways and fell onto her.

She staggered under his weight and tried to drag him inside. Somehow, he found his feet again and swayed into the house. "Garvin, will you go to Alcoholics Anonymous or not?" She grunted as she struggled to hold him upright.

"I'm not an alc'holic!" Garvin turned and she saw his fist coming straight toward her. She stepped sideways and he crashed to the floor. He started to get up, but he passed out with his mouth hanging open.

"You're sick, Garvin. You disgust me." Her heart pounded as she stepped over him. She slammed the front door and stamped upstairs.

Garvin apologized the next day and again left to find a job. But he didn't come home for supper, so she and Caroline ate alone. Around eight o'clock, they sat on the sofa and read a story. Suddenly they heard Garvin yelling unintelligible words from the porch. "Caroline, would you go and stay in your room a while?"

"Can I see Daddy?"

"No, honey, not tonight. Go to your room now."

Suddenly, the door flung open and Garvin marched into the living room. He stared at Madelene, the black patch slipping from his eye socket. He waved his bloodied right fist in the air.

"Daddy!" Caroline hopped off the sofa and ran to Garvin with her arms open wide.

"Caroline, no—"

"Get away from me!" Garvin roared at Caroline as his right hand streaked toward her face.

"No!" Madelene screamed. She raced to Caroline, scooping her child into her arms just before Garvin's hand made contact. Caroline wailed, and Madelene suddenly felt heat rise like a wall of flame within her. She raised her shaking fist to Garvin's face and, through clenched teeth, she said, "Don't you ever raise a hand to this child again."

"Or what?" Garvin dropped his hand and grinned.

"Don't ever do it again." She whirled away from him and raced to the kitchen, exiting through the back door. Her heart thudded as she ran. She heard him yelling as glass crashed against the walls of the house.

She pounded on the front door of the boardinghouse and Ida soon opened it. Caroline still cried as Madelene gasped. "Call the police, Ida. He's out of control this time."

Half an hour later, they watched through the front window as the police led Garvin away in handcuffs. Then Madelene soothed Caroline to sleep upstairs in Ida and Fred's room. Afterward, she joined Ida, Fred, and Brianna in the sitting room.

"He was going to strike Caroline," she told them as she twisted the hem of her dress in her shaking hands. "Before, it was just me he took his anger out on. I never thought he would.... Never...." She felt her body shaking, and she tried to will it back to normal.

"I don't believe it," Brianna said.

"I thought I could always protect her, you know? But tonight, he was only inches away.... If he, if he had—Oh, I can't bear it." She buried her face in her hands and cried.

"But you did protect her. You did the right thing tonight, Madelene." Ida said.

Fred sprang from his chair and paced the room. "So help me, if he ever hurts that girl, I swear I'll take care of him myself."

"You'll have to take a turn after me," Brianna said.

"That's enough," Ida said. "There's too much talk of violence here. I won't have it."

Fred walked over to his wife and laid a hand on her shoulder. "You're right, dear. I'll be quiet now."

Madelene gave a small smile to Ida and said, "You sound just like Alice."

"Well, she's a good woman," Ida said. She patted Madelene's arm. "Now let's see about getting some sheets and a pillow for you."

"Oh, no, Ida. I'm not staying here."

"Of course you are," Brianna said.

"No, I'll just collect Caroline and go home. He's at the police station for the rest of the night. I'll be fine."

Fred insisted on walking with them back to the house. When she opened the door, she gasped. Her books had been tossed and flipped open; some of the pages had been ripped out. The end table and the gold chair were tipped over. Her mother's picture frame lay twisted on the floor, the glass broken. She glanced into the kitchen and saw eggbeaters, spoons, knives, and shattered glass littering the floor. "It's ruined."

"You're not staying here tonight," Fred said.

Madelene could only stare at the destruction and agree.

It took her most of the next day to clean up the mess. Luckily, most of the damage was confined to the living room and kitchen. But, broken glass still covered the floor, so Ida agreed to watch Caroline for a while.

Madelene finished putting away the last of the unbroken kitchen appliances around three o'clock that afternoon. Then she stood and stared at the pile of broken glass and appliances that she had stacked in the corner of the kitchen. She shook her head and wondered whether she would ever be able to replace it all.

After she hauled the mess to the shed, she put a roast in the oven before going next door to retrieve Caroline.

When she appeared on the boardinghouse doorstep, however, she could hear Caroline's voice and that of another child. Both children laughed and squealed as they played. Ida introduced Fred's sister and their four-year-old niece, Emma, who had come to spend the day.

"I just dropped by to take Caroline off your hands," Madelene said.

"Well, as you can see, she's been no trouble at all. She and Emma have been getting along quite famously."

"I'm glad, especially after last night, but dinner will be ready soon and Caroline needs to come home and wash up." Madelene stepped toward the children and bent to kiss Caroline's head. "Ready to go home, sweetie?"

"Mommy," Caroline pleaded. "I don't wanna go home. I wanna stay here and play with Emma some more. Please, Mommy?"

"No, honey, maybe next time Emma's here you can spend the day at Aunt Ida's. Besides, I made your favorite biscuits. We can put strawberries on them for dessert."

"But Mommy...."

"No 'buts,' Caroline. Help Emma put the toys away now."

Caroline hung her head and asked, "Will Daddy be there? I don't wanna eat with him."

Madelene bit her lip as she stared at her daughter's bowed head. "No, honey, not tonight. It's just the two of us." She looked up and caught Ida watching her. She could see the pain she felt reflected in Ida's eyes. In one flash of a hand, Garvin had ruined a child's love. What kind of father did that?

Ida cleared her throat. "You know, we've still got plenty of food. Why don't the two of you join us for supper?"

"Yea!" Caroline and Emma yelled together.

Caroline had made a new friend and what did she have to look forward to at home? Another night of wondering whether her father would come home drunk? They couldn't go on this way much longer. She sighed and said, "Thank you for the offer, Ida, but I've got to be alone for a while. Caroline can stay, if it's all right."

The girls yelled again and raced into the kitchen. Madelene smiled after them and turned to leave.

"Are you sure you won't change your mind?"

"I'd like to stay, Ida, but I need to sort some things out. Thanks again. I'll pick her up around eight."

As she trudged back home, she could think of only one thing: Something had to change and fast. She could not have another scene like the one last night. She would not place Caroline in danger.

A short time later, she sat down to dinner. She turned the water glass in her hand as she thought about her options. Either Garvin had to change, or she and Caroline had to leave. She wondered if she could still persuade Garvin to go to the AA meetings. She sighed. How many times had he promised to change? Would he ever?

Then Brianna's voice cut through her thoughts and presented another option. Divorce him, she had said.

Come with me, Steve had urged.

If you ever need anything, Ruth had said once.

You made your bed, Daniel had claimed.

And now, if what she suspected was correct, she had another problem. What should she do? She pushed the potatoes around on her plate and stared at the small slice of roast. The Bible spoke against divorce. In God's eyes, it wasn't right. But she was beginning to be very afraid.

Lord Jesus, help me. What am I to do? I'm not sure about anything anymore. I know you say I cannot divorce my husband. But Lord, what about Caroline? What if he hurts her? What can I do?

She ate her cold meal and devised a plan.

— Thirty Seven —

As she finished washing the supper dishes, she heard him on the porch. "Madelen'? Come here, you—Ow!" He stumbled on the steps and cursed.

Her heart skipped a beat and her hands froze. She stepped into the kitchen archway so she could see the front door. She had left it unlocked because she wanted to face him when she confronted him with her plan. She left the back door unlocked, too, in case she needed to escape.

"Madelene!" Garvin flung the door open and slammed it behind him. "I heard 'em talkin' about you today." He saw her watching him, and he stumbled toward her.

"Who was talking about me?" Her heart pounded and she stepped backward into the kitchen.

"Some of the boys at the Woodside. First they tell me I should be home with my wife. Then they tell me 'bout how pretty you are, an' if I didn't get home, then maybe they would take care of you themselves."

"That's disgusting."

"Yeah, well, I took care of 'em for sayin' that. Then, they tell me 'bout someone who did take care of you while I was gone. Said he

200

was some tall guy from the mill. Said they saw him over here with you quite a bit, they did."

"Garvin, that's ridiculous. I already told you—"

"I know what you told me." He edged toward her, wavering as he stepped across the kitchen floor.

She inched backward until she bumped against the counter. She stepped sideways toward the back door as she tried to calm him. "Garvin, listen to me. It doesn't matter what a bunch of drunks say. Listen to what I've told you. Now we've got to get beyond this—"

"Who was he?" Garvin asked as he advanced toward her.

"Garvin, please listen. You need help. You need to go to Alcoholics Anonymous." She inched farther to her left so she could grab the handle on the back door.

"Who was he, you tramp?"

"Garvin, if you ever want a life with me, then you'd better listen now." Her breath quickened as she told him the plan: "Go to AA now, or I'll take Caroline and leave you."

Garvin continued as if he hadn't heard her. "Who is he? Are you still seeing him? Do the two of you laugh at me behind my back? Am I your joke? Who is he?" Garvin grabbed her hair and twisted it.

Tears sprang to her eyes and her heart felt like it would skitter out of her chest. But, Caroline's tear-stained face flashed through her mind and she felt her strength return. "Did you hear me, Garvin? Either you go to AA or I'll pack up and leave you. I'll take Caroline with me, I mean it."

His good eye bored into her. He leaned in until she could smell the whiskey. Then he yanked her hair, snapping her head back. "Do you think I care about that brat? Send her away! I'm not raising another man's kid. Now who was he?"

She winced, feeling tears slide down the side of her face and roll onto her neck. Her head ached and she felt her knees buckling. "There was no one," she strained to whisper. "Ever."

"Liar!" Garvin let go of her hair. As she slid to the floor, he screamed, "You lie!" He kicked her in the upper abdomen; the blow sent waves of pain through her body.

She clasped her hands over her abdomen and cried out, "Garvin, don't! I'm pregnant! Please, don't…." Her tears spilled onto the floor.

She curled her legs up over her abdomen and whimpered, "Please, Garvin, no."

He stopped. She heard him stumble backward, then sink into one of the chairs by the table.

She struggled to a sitting position and leaned back against the wall. Her body throbbed and her face felt like it was on fire. She wiped the tears away and watched him.

He stared at her, blinking his eye as if to clear the alcoholic fog. "Was it that time I returned? You know, up in that room?"

She nodded. "Did you hear what I said?"

"AA. Yes, I heard." He paused. "There was no one else?"

"No, Garvin. Never."

He ran his hand through his hair and said, "Maybe this one will be a boy. Just like me."

She hoped not.

"Okay, Madelene. You win. I'll go to the meetings. For you and my boy."

She stood up and steadied herself on the counter. She noticed that he had not mentioned Caroline.

— Thirty Eight —

For the next week and a half, Garvin attended two AA meetings and again hunted for a job. She watched him struggle and she saw him waver. She saw him looking up the road toward town. She worried every time he left the house. So, on the evening of July 3, Madelene wrote a letter to Ruth.

Dearest Ruth,

I know you have enough on your mind, what with worrying about George and caring for your son, but I may desperately need your help. Garvin has returned home and the war has not changed him. He cannot get beyond his drinking. He has beaten me again and even raised his hand to our daughter. If it were just me, I probably would have left long ago. But, now I have Caroline and I thought maybe we could make a home for our daughter. The worst part is I'm expecting again.

Garvin is attending Alcoholics Anonymous meetings. We feel that if he can stay sober, our marriage might have a chance. But Ruth, I'm so afraid he won't be able to do it. He has promised to change a hundred times before. So in the interest of protecting my child, I may need to leave here one day. It will probably be a hurried

*decision. I need to have somewhere to go, preferably out of town.
Will you help? I'll be waiting for your answer.*
        Your friend,
        Madelene

She sealed the letter and tucked it into her purse. She knew she couldn't mail it until the day after the holiday. She remembered Ruth's laughter and her concern, right up through Adam's funeral. Even though they hadn't seen each other in years, she hoped their friendship still stood strong.

The Fourth of July dawned bright and hot. Madelene and Garvin woke to Caroline's bouncing on the bed and urging, "Mommy, Daddy! Get up! We have to go to the dance! Can we go now? Can we, Mommy?"

Garvin grumbled and turned over, pulling the sheet over his head. Madelene smiled at Caroline's eagerness. "We have to wait until this evening, sweetie."

Caroline thumped down on the bed and stuck out her bottom lip. "That's too far away. What're we gonna do 'til then?"

Madelene hugged her daughter and reassured her they would have plenty to do. The two of them rose and left Garvin to sleep a little longer.

After a breakfast of scrambled eggs, milk, and toast, Caroline played in the yard while Madelene cleaned the house. Garvin rose late and ate cereal by himself while he watched Madelene work.

"What are you going to do today?" she asked.

"I don't know. Maybe I'll go to town. Do we need anything?" Garvin drummed his right hand on the table. Even though Dr. Dallan had removed the cast on Garvin's left arm, he still favored it. Fortunately, he was right-handed.

"No, we don't need anything. What are you going to do in town?"

Garvin slammed his hand on the table and Madelene flinched. "Madelene, what are you thinking? Do you think just because I'm going into town that I'm going to stop and have a drink? You know I haven't had a drink in over a week. I've gone to the AA meeting. I got another job. What more do you want? Haven't I proven myself to you? Do you think you have to check on me every minute?"

"Garvin, I didn't mean, that is…."

"If you must know, I'm going to the hardware store to buy some glue. I'm going to try and fix some of the things I've broken around here. I saw them in the shed the other day." He pulled a cigarette package and some matches from his shirt pocket.

"I'm sorry." Madelene wished he wouldn't smoke in the house, but she didn't feel she could say so now.

By lunchtime, Garvin had not returned. She and Caroline ate without him. Caroline pushed the food around her plate. "What's the matter, sweetie? Aren't you hungry?"

Caroline shook her head and stared at her plate. Madelene reached over and placed her hand on Caroline's forehead. "You're a little warm. Maybe you should take your nap now."

"No, Mommy. I want to go to the dance."

"You can still take a nap. I'll wake you up in plenty of time to go, okay?" Madelene wrapped her arms around her daughter. "Why don't you come to your room with me now. Mommy will put a fan by your bed so you can sleep. I bet when you wake up you'll be all better."

Caroline still shook her head, but she did not resist when Madelene led her to her room.

During Caroline's nap, Ida called to say that she and Fred and Brianna would be leaving for the dance around seven and they would stop to pick them up.

By supper, Garvin still had not returned. It was a long time to find some glue. Surely the hardware store had closed long ago. She tried to convince herself that he was visiting his family or watching them set up for the dance, but she knew where he really was.

Her fingers shook as she chopped cucumbers and carrots for a salad. While she worked, she listened for him and wondered what degree of drunkenness he would have reached by the time he returned.

The day turned steamy, which didn't help Caroline feel any better. She and Caroline sat down to eat their salads, but Caroline refused to eat, claiming that her belly hurt. "Okay, sweetie. You can play in the living room if you like."

"I wanna go to the dance."

"Sweetie, I'm afraid you're not feeling well enough to go. Mommy will stay home with you. Later, Aunt Ida will tell you all about it. Maybe she'll bring you some cotton candy when she comes back."

Caroline stuck out her bottom lip again, and tears popped up in her pretty blue eyes. "No! I wanna go too."

Madelene smoothed Caroline's hair saying, "Sweetie, you're too sick to go. Maybe when the dance starts, you and I can go outside and listen to the music."

Caroline burst into tears and ran into her bedroom, slamming the door behind her. Madelene sighed and finished her salad in silence.

The boardinghouse group stopped by at seven, as promised. But Madelene told them about Caroline and said they should go ahead without them.

"Is Garvin staying home too?" Fred asked, peering around Madelene and into the house.

Ida pulled on his sleeve and scowled at him. "Well, we'll try to bring something back for all of you. We're really sorry you're going to miss it."

"Maybe I could stay here and sit with you," Brianna said.

Madelene looked into Brianna's eyes and saw her concern. Brianna knew Garvin was not there and she could probably guess where he was.

But, Madelene did not want to bother her friends anymore. "Of course not. Go to the dance and have fun. Win a game for me." She tried to smile, but she barely managed to pull up the corners of her mouth.

After the group left, Madelene cleared the table and piled the dishes next to the sink. Then she checked on Caroline. She read a story to her until Caroline fell asleep around eight o'clock. Caroline's slight fever seemed to have broken and her face had lost some of its flush. Madelene smoothed her daughter's hair, then she left the room and closed the door behind her.

She settled onto the sofa and tried to read a book, but the words didn't make any sense. She walked to the front window and peered into the front yard and up the street. The neighborhood was deserted.

Her mind began to race. She knew where he was. Her hands started to shake. Her breathing quickened. She should get away, now, before he came back. She should grab Caroline and go. But where? She wasn't going to mail her letter to Ruth until tomorrow. Maybe she could go to her father? No, he had made it clear he didn't want her anymore. He wouldn't believe her anyway. She bit her lip.

Maybe she could take Caroline next door for the evening. Surely the doors wouldn't be locked. Madelene walked into Caroline's room again and saw her sleeping. Did she really want to move Caroline now when sleep was probably the best thing for her? Besides, what if he wasn't drinking?

She closed the door to Caroline's room and tiptoed back to the living room. There she paced, thoughts and doubts swirling in her mind. Shouldn't she at least give Garvin some leeway? He had berated her only that morning: 'Haven't I proven myself to you? Do you think you have to check on me every minute?' Could he really change from who he had been that morning into the frightening person he had often been, just in the space of a few hours?

You know he's drinking, the other voice in her head argued with her, that's why he didn't come home today. That's why he didn't call you. Run! Pack some things, take Caroline and go. You know what he's like when he's drunk. You know it!

Madelene paced and clenched and unclenched her fists. The boardinghouse. It was the only place to go. She would lock the doors there and wait until Ida and Fred got home. Her heart pounded and her fingers shook, but she knew she had made the right decision.

In the growing darkness she filled a suitcase, throwing underwear and blouses into it without folding them. Then she dragged it into the living room. She grabbed her mother's frameless picture from the library table and dropped it into the case. Then she hurried into Caroline's room.

Without turning on a light, she fumbled through the dresser and pulled out panties, jumpers, and sunsuits. Her hands touched

Caroline's mirror and brush on top of the dresser, and she grabbed those, too. With her arms loaded, she rushed into the living room and dumped Caroline's things into the suitcase.

She was about to wake Caroline when she realized she had left her Bible upstairs. She ran up to the nightstand and scooped up the Bible, its smooth leather cover reassuring her for the moment. Then she hurried back downstairs.

Madelene dropped the Bible into the suitcase and snapped it shut. She heaved it onto its feet, then she turned to go to Caroline's room.

Hard footsteps thundered on the porch, stopping her cold. She whirled around to see the front door fly open, nearly exploding from its hinges. Garvin marched in and walked straight toward her.

She tried to move backward, but her feet froze. Garvin's good eye flashed in his red face. He snarled at her with contorted lips. His right arm flew forward and he grabbed her hair and dragged her toward him.

"So there was no one else, huh? Is that what you told me?" Garvin swayed before her. The smell of whiskey surrounded him once again, but it was not as heavy as it had been. Maybe she could reason with him.

"How many times do I have to tell you? There was no one. Why won't you believe me?"

"Liar!" His left hand clutched at her throat.

"Garvin...Caroline," she choked out the words.

"That brat is none of my concern, and you know it. Calls me daddy." He spat on the floor and tightened his grip. "Why do you let her call me daddy? Especially when she belongs to Steve."

Madelene's eyes widened; she felt her heart stop.

"That's right, isn't it? Steve Atwood? Didn't think I'd find out, did you? So you and my boss, huh? Don't deny it, Madelene, I can see it in your eyes. The minute I go off to war you and my boss get together. You make me sick!" Garvin released her throat and her hair and shoved her, sending her crashing into the library table.

Madelene heard a crack as her head struck the table. She crumpled to the floor as stars floated around her. Garvin was moving. She heard him yelling from their bedroom upstairs. She pulled herself to her feet, but the room swayed. She clutched the table to steady herself, and she heard him throwing things against the walls and onto the floor. What was he looking for?

It didn't matter. She didn't have time to find out. She glanced at the suitcase and knew she wouldn't have time to carry both it and Caroline away from the house. She took a deep breath and started to walk toward Caroline's room.

Garvin shrieked. She stopped sharply, but started again towards Caroline's room.

Then, she heard him running down the stairs. She stopped. If she took Caroline now, he would come after both of them. She ran to the kitchen, trying to put as much distance between herself and Caroline as she could. She reached the doorway to the kitchen, but he was too quick. Garvin wheeled her around and slammed her head into the archway.

"You slut!" Garvin shoved Steve's letters in her face.

The letters! How could she have forgotten about the letters? "Garvin, please. I can explain. Please let me explain. Please…." She begged him as she backed into the kitchen.

He stalked her, matching her step for step. "Where are you going, Madelene? Huh? Where is your precious Steve now? Are you going to him? Is that what the suitcase was for?"

Her heart beat so hard she could feel the blood rushing through her head. She inched back toward the sink. The countertop turned clammy in her hands. "No, Garvin. It's over. And I never lied to you about being with him, I swear. Please, Garvin, listen to me!"

His good eye widened, and the black patch on his other eye twitched. "Everything you told me was a lie! Wasn't it? I suppose Adam wasn't even mine, was he?"

"How can you say that? How can you twist everything around? Why don't you believe me?" Her right arm reached behind her and she felt the knife she had used earlier for chopping vegetables.

"You're mine!" Garvin screamed. He knocked her to the floor. The knife sliced her hand before it clattered to the floor next to her right hip.

She felt warm blood running down her face. Her head throbbed, but still she tried to rise.

She saw his fist flying at her again. She shielded her face with her hands. That's when they both heard a small voice from the doorway.

"Mommy?"

Madelene's entire body stiffened. "Caroline, please—"

"Get out of here!" Garvin roared. In two steps, he towered over Caroline. He scooped up her small body and threw her against the kitchen wall like a rag doll.

"No!" Madelene screamed and reached for the knife at her side.

"You little.... Can't you see your mother and I are trying to talk?" Garvin's leg wound back to kick their child.

"NO!" Madelene shrieked. She flew at him with the knife raised in warning. When she screamed, he turned to face her. She meant to stop in front of him, but she stumbled forward. Surprise flooded his face as the knife sunk into his heart.

He laughed as he slumped against the wall. "I didn't think you had the moxie." He slid to the floor. Then he closed his eyes and stopped breathing.

~ Thirty Nine ~

She stumbled backward and stared at her trembling hands turned up before her. Her skin grew cold and clammy as she stared at Garvin lying next to Caroline. His blood pooled on the checkered floor and rolled toward Caroline's feet.

Her mind stopped working. She stood in the center of the kitchen and stared. Her body shook, and she gasped for air. Tears flooded her eyes. Caroline! She extended her trembling hands toward Caroline, stooped down, and picked her up. She cradled Caroline in her arms and brought her ear to her child's face and listened. She was still breathing.

Madelene turned her back on Garvin and carried her to the sink. With her free hand, she turned on the faucet and poured cool water across Caroline's forehead. But, the blood from her hand mingled with the water and turned pink on Caroline's skin. She jerked her hand back as if it had been burned. Caroline murmured into Madelene's breast.

She carried her back to bed, then she stumbled into the kitchen. She could not look at Garvin. Help! She whirled around. Every area of the room seemed distorted. She didn't know what she was looking for. Her eyes raked over the curtains she had been so proud of.

Now, they mocked her and everything she thought a wonderful home should be. She couldn't stop shaking.

She grabbed the phone receiver and held it to her head. Ida. Fred. Brianna. They were at the dance. No one to help! The numbers on the phone swam in her tears. No one to call! She dropped the receiver onto the countertop, its loud "clunk" resounding through the room.

She turned and glanced back at Garvin, but he did not move. Through her tears, his image blurred into a mass of dark clothing and red blood. She clenched and unclenched her fists to try to stop them from shaking. She turned back to the counter and picked up the phone again. There was one person left.

Her fingers trembled as she dialed the number. She tried to calm her ragged breathing as the phone rang at the other end of the line. It rang several times before he finally picked up the phone. The words tumbled out: "Father? Oh, please, help me! I've killed him! I've killed him!"

Within minutes, Madelene heard her father's car creak to a stop in front of the house. She ran to the front door and flung it open just as he was walking up the steps.

Daniel stopped short when he saw his daughter. Madelene had not even thought about dressing her wounds, and her face throbbed where Garvin had hit her. Her lip felt raw and blood trickled from her hand. Her clothes clung to her in wrinkles. "Oh, Madelene. What have I done?"

"Help me!"

Her father rushed toward her and wrapped his arms around her. "I'm sorry. I'm so sorry," he repeated into her ear while she cried. "I never thought it would come to this."

Madelene sobbed into his shoulder as he held her. She cried for what she had done. She cried because her father was the one who was holding her. She cried for her daughter and her unborn child. Finally her tears broke off into gasps.

"Is the girl all right?"

Madelene backed away from him, closed her eyes and nodded. "He—he threw her against the wall. Then he started to kick her and

I…." Her words drifted away as fresh tears rolled down her face. "I didn't know who else to call."

"Are you able to take her to the clinic by yourself?"

"Yes, but the doctor is probably at the dance with everyone else."

"I'll find him. You'll carry her to the clinic where you can wait for him." Her father's eyes left hers for a moment as he looked over the house. "Where is he?"

Madelene looked down at her shoes and pointed a shaking finger behind her. "In the kitchen."

He nodded. "After I get the doctor, I'll come back and take care of him."

"Father, he's dead. You can't take care of him."

"Honey, you don't understand. I'll take care of his body." Daniel cleared his throat and said, "Now go get your girl. We can't waste time."

Madelene started for the door, but then turned and asked, "What are you going to do?"

"Never mind. Get your girl."

Madelene bit her lip and did what he told her.

She waited at the clinic until 10 o'clock. The doctor finally arrived and appeared shocked at the sight of Caroline. He carried her to the metal examining table and eased her onto it. After examining her for several minutes, he reassured Madelene that it was only a concussion. She did not have any broken bones.

Then he turned away to reach for a blanket. "How did this happen?"

Madelene bit her lip, but decided to tell him most of the truth. "My husband. He had been drinking. When he came home, we argued. He, uh, um, he hit me. Caroline woke up and found us fighting. He threw her…against the wall." She sniffed back fresh tears, and reached down to caress Caroline's matted hair.

"He did what? To an innocent child? I assume you called the authorities at once?"

"No. There wasn't time."

"Well, I'll call them. It's my duty to see that this doesn't happen again. Especially to a defenseless child." He walked to the medicine cabinet that lined the far wall. "As soon as I'm finished putting stitches in that cut on your hand, I'll do just that."

"No."

Dr. Dallan whirled around and stared at her.

"I mean, that's not necessary." Her mind raced. What she could tell him? "He's gone. He came to his senses after he realized what he did to his daughter. He ran off."

"The police should still be called. They can find him and throw him in jail until he dries out."

"No, that's all right. I'll call the police myself if he ever comes near me or Caroline again."

The doctor shook his head and turned back to the medicine table.

And so the lies began.

— Forty —

The doctor wanted to keep Caroline overnight, so Madelene stayed at the clinic. Dr. Dallan went upstairs to his apartment with instructions to fetch him if Caroline became any worse.

Madelene couldn't sleep, so she sat next to Caroline's bed and watched her. Her father arrived at the clinic around midnight. He pulled up a chair next to her and whispered in her ear: "I've taken care of it."

"What…what did you do?"

"I buried him in the woods two miles away, a mile or so from the abandoned mill. No one will find him there." He looked at the floor, then back at her. Dark circles rimmed his eyes. His face seemed to have aged ten years that night.

"Father, what am I going to say? Dr. Dallan wanted to call the police, but I told him Garvin ran off. What am I doing? Lying is wrong. And why did you do it? Why didn't you report me?"

He covered her hands with his own. "Because I feel responsible for all of it. How can I report you when…if I…if I had been a better father, more understanding…." Tears pooled in his eyes and he released her hands to brush them away.

"Father, don't do this. The two of us are all right now, aren't we?

Whatever happened before doesn't matter."

He shook his head. "I never should have pushed you on that boy. I should have accepted what you had done and tried to make the best of it. I heard rumors that the boy was violent, but I dismissed them. I heard you were in the clinic, but I didn't come to see you. I visited every other member of my congregation, but I didn't visit my own daughter. What kind of father am I?

"I sat alone in that house for five years. Every part of me knew I had made a mistake, but I was too stubborn to go back on my word. My word. What good is it when it's spoken in anger? I puttered around that house and stared out the window looking for you. Many times I thought about walking to the boardinghouse just for a glimpse of you, but I could not.

"When your boy died, my heart ached for you. I know what it's like to lose someone you love. I was there, you know. I watched some other minister preside over the funeral of my grandson because I was too stubborn to swallow my pride. I watched the anguish in your eyes, and I did nothing.

"So I'm going to make everything up to you. I did not love you as a father should, and because of that I will take full responsibility. For everything. This is my problem now."

"But Father, I did it. It's my fault."

"Hush! Don't ever say that again, not to me or to anyone else. You did what you had to do to protect your daughter. I may not have been much of a father, but I dare say I would have done the same."

Madelene threw her arms around him. "I've missed you, Father."

His voice broke as he said, "Come back home and live with me, you and your daughter. You can't stay in that house any longer."

"The house!" Madelene broke off from him. "It was a mess. The blood! Surely someone will—"

"Shh. I said I've taken care of it. After I took him to my car, I went back to the house and cleaned the blood off the floor. I swept up the broken things, and I buried them with him. No one will know."

"Oh, Father, I can't let you do this. You've always prided yourself on your honesty, your faithfulness, your character. You can't do this."

He closed his eyes and pressed his lips together. "My honesty, my character, my pride—I am your father, my concern should have been your feelings, your life, not mine. And, even if I wasn't going to act as your father, the least I could have done was to have been your minister. Even a good minister would have gone to his parishioner in her time of need. I did everything wrong, Madelene. My dearest Madelene." He shook his head as tears welled in his eyes.

"So, hush now." He blinked back the tears. "It's done. All you have to do is tell everyone what you told the doctor. And since your friends were gone, you called me for help. We made amends and you decided to move back home."

What was she hearing? She bit her lip and shook her head. "It's not right, Father. I did it in defense of my child. Surely, the police will understand."

"They might. But there would be a trial, maybe a long one, and Caroline needs you. Madelene, I want you to have the life you should have had in the first place. I want to give you this chance to start over. Please let me do this for you." His brown eyes searched her face.

She released her breath in a long sigh. "You know, Father, I wanted to marry him from the first. Your 'pushing' me was what I wanted all along. I thought I could change him, but I was wrong, and I jeopardized Caroline's life for it."

"Stop chastising yourself. It was only your youth that caused you to misjudge him. I should have been the one to protect you, then. I'm so sorry, Madelene. You'll never know how sorry." He stroked her hair. "Now, will you and Caroline come to live with me? The house has been so empty, so dull. I need to hear the laughter of children. I want to know my granddaughter."

Her father loved her after all. After all her mistakes, after all those years, he loved her after all. *Oh, Lord, my father loves me.* Tears rose to her eyes once more. "Oh, Father, I've missed you so much. You know I'll live with you." She wrapped her arms around him.

"I love you, Madelene." He stayed with her until morning.

— Forty One —

A car horn interrupted her memories. Madelene turned her attention toward the road in front of the house, which goldenrod now lined like lace. Caroline's new Ford Taurus rolled into the driveway, its wheels crunching the gravel and sending puffs of dirt into the hot, dry air. Helen waved from inside the car. Caroline parked in front of the house. Both doors opened and her daughters climbed from the car.

Caroline's red-gold hair had faded to light blond over the years. As the sun shone on Caroline's head, Madelene could see white streaks shining in her oldest daughter's hair. When did that sweet child get gray hair? Madelene rose and steadied herself with one wrinkled hand on the porch rail.

Helen smiled at her mother as she bounded up the steps. "Hi, Mom! Can you believe it? I just found out I'm going to be a grandmother!" Helen smiled again as she walked to Madelene and placed a quick peck on her mother's cheek. Helen was short like Madelene, but she had black hair like her father's. It was cut short, now, and permed to curl around her angular face. Her fine skin showed signs of wrinkles at the corners of her dark brown eyes. Except for her hair and her temperament, Helen was her mother's daughter.

"I heard. That's wonderful, dear!" Madelene reached for Helen, and they hugged each other.

"It is wonderful, indeed," Caroline called from the bottom of the steps. "But, I swear that's all this woman talked about the entire time we drove here. She forgets I have four grandchildren myself."

Caroline was a tall woman with broad shoulders and long legs. She wore a beige linen skirt with a white cotton blouse and soft suede pumps. She smoothed the hair from her face and held her palms out in front of her. "Sweat! I'm sweating already. Mother, I don't know how you can stand it in the sun. Don't you know it's over ninety degrees out here? Let me make you some lemonade at least." She kissed her mother and walked into the house.

"It's already made. All you have to do is pour it," Madelene called after her. She motioned Helen to a chair, and she sat down.

Helen crossed her bare legs in front of her and dangled a white leather sandal from her big toe. She was dressed in white shorts with a turquoise-and-white striped tee shirt. For jewelry, she wore only a chunky white necklace and her wedding ring. They could hear Caroline's bracelets jingling as she poured the lemonade.

Helen placed her hand on Madelene's arm and asked, "So, Mom, are you all right? Why did you call us today? You know we're still coming up next weekend, don't you?"

"I know that. I'm not totally daft, yet. Let's wait until Caroline joins us before I go any further." She looked at her youngest daughter and wondered how she would take this. She never knew her father, so maybe it wouldn't matter. No, he was still her father.

"Reading the good book again?" Helen gestured toward the table where Madelene had laid her Bible.

"You should try it sometime."

"I go to church."

"Yeah, at Christmas and Easter," Caroline said from the doorway. She pushed open the screen door with her shoulder and carried a tray with a pitcher of lemonade and three-glasses.

"Just grab a chair and sit down," Helen said, grinning.

Caroline sat down next to her mother. "What did you need to see us for, Mother? We got here as soon as we could."

How much did she remember? Caroline was only three or four when it happened. Madelene had never wanted to bring it up again. But sometimes when they got in an argument, Caroline would look at her a certain way, and Madelene would wonder. Did she know? It was time to find out.

"Mother?" Caroline prompted. She and Helen looked at each other, then back at Madelene.

"I'm sorry, girls. I was just thinking." Where to begin?

"You know, if it's about your care, we're going to discuss that next weekend when Tom and Bill can join us," Caroline said.

"No, no, that's not it. I know we'll discuss that next week. I know that. I'm not totally out of my mind yet, Caroline. It's just that I don't know...." She faded off, wondering again how to say it. *Lord, give me the strength to tell them.*

"What is it, Mom? What don't you know? Tell us, maybe we can help," said Helen as she patted Madelene's arm.

"I had some time to think before you came," Madelene began. "Well, actually, I've had your entire lifetimes to think." She saw the puzzled look in their eyes. "You know you had a brother who died before either of you were born."

"Adam," Caroline said. "Yes, we know."

"And I told you your father died shortly after he got home from the war."

"In an auto accident, yes, we know. But Mother, what's the point of bringing this up now? We remember what you told us."

Madelene looked out at the goldenrod and closed her eyes. She bit her lip and drew in her breath. "I just wanted to talk to you before my mind was too far gone. You both have a right to know the truth."

"What?" Helen and Caroline asked together.

"The truth about what?" Helen asked, her voice rising.

Madelene kept her face turned away from them. *Lord, give me strength.* "About your father." She sighed. "Girls, I've got something to tell you."

— Forty Two —

Madelene left nothing out. The words tumbled from her lips as if someone had opened a dam. Fifty years of secrets flooded the air around them as her daughters stared.

When she finished her story, she sighed. "No one ever found him. They turned the mill area into a wildlife reserve, or a park, or something. No one ever questioned his disappearance. Brianna might have looked at me strangely from time to time, but she never said a word. Your grandfather and I never told another soul." Madelene turned away and stared at the goldenrod through her tears.

Neither Caroline nor Helen said anything. Trees rustled in the wind and birds chirped, but somehow the sounds only amplified the silence.

Suddenly Helen shot out of her chair and it clattered backward onto the porch. "I don't believe this. I just don't believe this. How could you lie to us all these years, Mom? You and Grandpa both. You never said a word except that Dad died in a car wreck when he got home from the war. You both lied! How could you?" Helen charged into the house, slamming the screen door behind her.

"Helen, wait!" Caroline called.

"Let her go," Madelene said. "It's no less than I expected." She sniffed and picked up a wilted handkerchief from the table next to her. She wiped her eyes. "What about you? Why aren't you running off to disown me? It's only what I deserve."

"Mother, you say I was only three when this happened?" Caroline stared out toward the road as she spoke.

"Yes, that's right."

"Then, why do I remember him?"

"You do? How could you? You were so young."

"Well, it's not so much a picture of him as it is floating images. You know, him lying on the couch or smoking a cigarette. He didn't talk much, did he? I don't remember his voice." Caroline laced her fingers through her hair and lifted it off her neck.

"No, I guess he didn't talk to you much. He always thought you were someone else's child."

"Was I?"

"Caroline!"

"Sorry. Of course not." Caroline dropped her hair and reached for the lemonade beside her. "While you were telling us, other images flashed through my head. I thought they were only nightmares at the time. Are they remembrances?"

"What things?"

"I remember him yelling. I remember us running to another house to get away. I remember something about his face. Did he have only one eye?"

Madelene nodded as fresh tears threatened to spill over the rims of her eyes.

"That eye was staring at me. And I remember flying over something, the floor, maybe. I used to think it was all a dream. No one can fly by herself without a plane, right?"

"Oh, my Lord," Madelene choked. Tears ran down her face while she coughed.

"Mother? Are you okay?" Caroline knelt before her mother. She patted Madelene's back.

Madelene's coughing ceased, and she waved Caroline away. "I'm okay. Oh, Caroline, I didn't think you remembered any of that. I prayed you would forget."

"So they weren't just nightmares after all. Oh, Mother, I'm sorry for all you had to go through. If only I had been older…."

Madelene searched her older daughter's beautiful blue eyes. Caroline was apologizing to her? "My dearest Caroline. You have nothing to be sorry for. I'm the one seeking your forgiveness."

"But you had no one but Grandpa. And after he died, well, you were left alone with your secret. You could have told us sooner, you know. We would have understood." Caroline kissed her mother's soft cheek.

"Oh, Caroline. Since I decided to tell you, I've been so frightened. It says right in the commandments: 'Thou shalt not murder.' The Bible says: 'A man tormented by murder will be a fugitive 'til death; let no one support him.' And again it says: If your brother has something against you, you've got to leave your offering at the altar and make things right with him before standing at the altar again. It says to seek first your brother's forgiveness. That's why I had to do this now, before my mind is gone and I can't remember the truth."

"Mother, stop! You have nothing to be forgiven for. You did nothing but protect us and take care of us your entire life."

"But I killed your father! Let me face at it last: I committed murder. I lied about it for years and I let your grandfather lie for me too. You don't know what that meant, for him to lie to the entire town. But, he did it for me. Do you know what he said to me just before he died? He quoted from Galatians: 'Christ has become of no effect unto you, whosoever of you are justified by the law, ye are fallen from grace.' He said that's what happened all those years ago; he preached only about adhering to the law. Then he quoted, 'For sin shall not have dominion over you: for ye are not under the law, but under grace.' I know he was talking about Christ dying for me and saving me from the consequences of my sins. I know that up here." She pointed to her head. "But, I have never felt it here." She placed her hand over her heart.

"Mother, please don't torture yourself anymore. You don't need our forgiveness because Grandpa was right: God has already forgiven you. But, if it means that you can finally feel God's forgiveness, then I do forgive you. You must believe that."

"What about Helen?" Madelene nodded toward the front door. "She can't forgive me. Everything I told her was a lie."

"Just a minute." Caroline walked into the house, stamping her feet on the creaking porch floor.

Madelene rose from her chair and leaned against the porch railing. She heard her daughters' voices coming from the open windows, mumbling at first, then growing louder until Madelene could hear every word.

"You selfish woman!" Caroline shouted at her sister. "Don't you know what Mother has gone through for the last fifty years? Fifty years of carrying around that secret! Fifty years of wondering whether God will forgive her for what she has done. And all you can do is storm in here and cry like a baby about how you were lied to."

"He was my father and she killed him!"

"You wouldn't have wanted to know him! He beat her and he almost killed me! He never talked to me like a real father, as Grandpa did. He was nothing to us."

"He was my father. I had a right to know him."

"Weren't you listening? He was not a man you wanted to know. Now Mother is sitting down there begging for our forgiveness. Can you imagine keeping that horrible secret inside you? It's killing her, Helen. The least you can do is come back outside and listen to her."

"How could she do it?" Helen was crying.

"What would you have done if it had been you? Would you have told Julie and Mark about Tom if he had been a terrible person? Would you have destroyed their beliefs about the decency of the world, about what a family should be? I wouldn't. Please, come downstairs."

Madelene leaned against the post that was attached to the porch overhang. Caroline, my dearest Caroline. May God always smile on you.

A few moments later, Caroline and Helen emerged from the house. Both women were crying. Madelene searched Helen's dark brown eyes for the forgiveness she needed. Helen closed her eyes, hung her head and sniffed back tears.

They stood on the porch and Caroline studied her mother and

her sister. Finally, she cleared her throat and said, "Helen, I know you don't go to church much, but you must remember the verse: 'Judge not lest you be judged?'"

Helen raised her head, but she refused to look at Madelene.

Madelene couldn't bear it. "Helen, I'm sorry I never told you the truth about how your father died. I thought it was best to keep the whole thing quiet."

"You thought it was best? For whom? For yourself, obviously. So you went on pretending that some car accident took my father's life while you went on with yours. How could you?"

Madelene flinched at Helen's tirade, but she said nothing in her defense. She had no defense.

"You let Caroline and me grow up to believe that our father was a good man. You let us live a lie, too, one that you invented to cover up for yourself. Is that all you cared about, Mom? Saving your own skin? I—I feel like my whole image of you has exploded! I thought you were a loving, caring person who always put others' needs above her own, but now I find out you're nothing but a liar!" Helen cried and smudged the tears from the corners of her eyes.

"Stop it, Helen," Caroline commanded.

Madelene touched her shaking hand to her temple and finally spoke. "Helen, I've wrestled with this secret for forever. I fully intended to carry this to my grave, I mean that. But now, with the Alzheimer's, well, I just had to tell you…." Her voice faded off as she realized how empty her words sounded, even to her.

"What does the Alzheimer's have to do with it?"

"Because when I'm really far gone, then I'll start rambling. Life will be tough enough for you both when I can't recognize you any- more. I didn't want you to hear me babble the words 'murder' and 'blood' and mutter your father's name, and not have you understand any of it. I just thought I needed to tell you now, before I forgot." Tears spilled from her eyes and rolled down her face. She walked toward Helen. "Believe me, I never wanted you to hate me for it."

Helen still would not look at her. She lowered her head again. "I just can't believe you did it. You killed him and you never told a soul except Grandpa. How could you live with yourself?"

Madelene's stomach lurched. "Don't you see? I couldn't live with myself! I read over and over about God's love and I never felt it was meant for me. But finally, I read a verse that spoke to me. It said I should seek the forgiveness of those I've wronged. Then, I knew I had to tell you before I was too far gone. Please, Helen, search your heart. Forgive me, please. I kept a terrible truth from both of you. For that, you'll never know how sorry I am. But, I did it out of love. At least believe that." Madelene reached out with her trembling fingers and touched Helen's bowed head.

Helen inched her head up to stare at her. Madelene wasn't sure what she read in those eyes that were so much like her own. All she knew at that moment was that she had to hold her daughter's gaze no matter what happened next.

Then, like well-needed rain on dusty ground, Helen's tears washed the hardness from her eyes. She threw her arms around her mother and sobbed. "Oh, Mom, I'm so sorry! I could never hate you. It's just—I didn't know what to think, that's all. I didn't know what to do. It's hard to find out that your father was a—a monster. I just didn't know what to do." She squeezed Madelene tighter.

"Please forgive me," Madelene pleaded as she rested her head against Helen's shoulder.

"I do, Mom, I do. Please, please don't do this to yourself anymore. I love you, and you must believe that God forgives you too. He forgave you from the moment you said you were sorry."

Caroline hugged both women. The three of them clung to one other and cried as they stood in the middle of Daniel's porch.

Madelene could almost hear her father speak to her then, as the warm breeze caressed her hair. She heard his last words to her as clearly as if he were standing there with them: "For it is by grace you have been saved, through faith, and this not from yourselves, it is the gift of God."

Addendum
A Note to My Readers

Poor Madelene! She was mistaken about God's grace and forgiveness for so many years. But you don't have to be. God's grace is simply this: that His son, Jesus Christ, left His heavenly throne and became a human being, who lived on earth and died the horrible death that you and I deserve. And then He ROSE FROM THE DEAD to return to heaven.

You see, the laws of the Old Testament are very strict. They say you must be perfect in order to enter heaven. But God knew we couldn't do it on our own, so he sent his son, Jesus Christ, to live the perfect life and be the perfect person.

And then, in total unfairness to His son but in perfect love for us, He allowed Jesus to be put to death for our sins. Remember that Jesus lived his entire life without sinning. But Jesus was absolutely willing to take all our sin on himself, and to die our death and take our punishment for us.

How wonderful is this Jesus! Because of His sacrifice, you no longer have to fear death. That's right. You no longer have to fear death, and what happens after that, because Jesus already died and took your punishment for you. When you die, you will be raised to heaven to meet Jesus face to face.

And do you know what the beautiful part is? There is no "trick" to our going to heaven. There is no waiting line, no paperwork, no specific number of prayers to be said, or good deeds to be done. The only thing you must do is accept the gift that Jesus is handing to you right now. All you have to do is believe in your heart that Jesus did this wonderful thing for you. For you, personally. It was as if he turned his head while he was being nailed to a tree and stared through the centuries to look directly into your eyes. It's as if he looked into your soul and said, "I'm doing this for you. Believe in me."

Bibliography
Bible Verses Used in This Book

This section lists the Bible verses quoted within the book. It is not intended to be a Bible study, but if you are interested in reading further about sin and forgiveness, these verses may be a good place to start. Believe me, these verses are only a very small part of the words God has concerning this subject!

Old Testament
Exodus 20:13
Psalms 140:1-4
Proverbs 28:17
Isaiah 65:12, 14

New Testament
Matthew 5:23-32, 45
Luke 6:37
Romans 6:14
Romans 10:4
Galatians 5:4
Ephesians 2:8
Ephesians 5:3-5, 22-31
1 Corinthians 6:15, 18-19

Ordering
Information

If you would like to order one or more books to share with family, friends, or someone who is struggling with spousal abuse or understanding God's forgiveness, please use this form.

NOTE: A portion of the proceeds of this book will be donated to the Sparrow's Nest, a shelter that not only helps homeless women get on their feet, but also helps them to know the Lord.

Please fill out the form below or call ACW Press at 1-800-931-BOOK (2665).

Name: _____

Company or Organization: _____

Address: _____

City: _____ State: _____ Zip:_____

Price: $14.99

Sales Tax: Please add 6.25% for books shipped within Ohio.

Shipping: Please include $4.00 shipping for the first book, and $1.00 for each additional book.

Payment: By check, money order, cashier's check, or use your Visa or MasterCard.

Mail Order Form To:
P.O. Box 284, Curtice, OH 43412